DL JUNG

RAVEN'S SHADOW

THE WARBIRD BOOK 2

Xinlishi Press

The characters, organizations, events, and places in this book are a work of fiction and are a product of the author's imagination. Where historical people, organizations, events, and places are used, they are done so in a fictional context. With the exception of public figures, any resemblance to actual persons, living or dead, is entirely coincidental.

Cover illustration and design by Daria Tikhomolova (based on a design by Kit Foster)

Xinlishi Press
300 Coxwell Ave.
PO Box 22591
Toronto, Ontario, Canada
M4L 3B6

FIRST EDITION

ISBN 978-1-7751371-5-3 (mobi)
ISBN 978-1-7751371-7-7 (epub)
ISBN 978-1-7751371-6-0 (pdf)
ISBN 978-1-7751371-8-4 (print)

To Annabel

A NOTE ON RUSSIAN NAMES

Russian speakers use many different names to address the same person, depending on the situation. A Russian's full name consists of a first name, a patronymic, and a surname. The patronymic is derived from the first name of that person's father. Calling a person by their first name and patronymic usually denotes a level of respect or formality. In more casual situations, a diminutive form of the first name might be used. Very close friends, family or children might also be addressed by a "pet" form of the first name.

Take, for example, this novel's main character: Aelita Petrovna Makarova. Her father is Pyotr Makarov (note female surnames usually add an -a suffix.) Aelita's flight students generally call her Aelita Petrovna (derived from Pyotr.) Most friends just call her by the diminutive Aelya (I've chosen this particular spelling for ease of recognition.) Finally, her family refer to her as Aelitochka.

GLOSSARY OF SELECTED TERMS

There are many different systems for converting Russian Cyrillic spelling to Roman letters for those who read English. I've tried to use spellings of names most familiar or easy to pronounce for those readers, rather than any one system.

Aelita: science fiction novel by Alexey Tolstoy published in 1923; part of a trend for stories about Mars, its silent movie adaptation in 1924 became a box office hit in the Soviet Union; the story is about two intrepid Soviet explorers travelling to Mars, where they meet Aelita, daughter of the Martian ruler, and start a revolution

babushka: Russian for "grandmother"

Communist Party of the Soviet Union: In the single party system of the Soviet Union, the Communist Party controlled the government and all its operations. Among its policies were strict government control over the economy and property owned collectively by the people or the State.

dacha: a country house

Focke-Wulf Fw 190: versatile German fighter, known for its powerful engine and firepower; it was given the nickname "heavy" by some Soviet pilots

frontovik: slang term for Soviet foot soldiers who fought at the front

Great Terror: period of purges in the Soviet Union from 1936 to 1938 that resulted in mass arrests, deportations and hundreds of thousands of deaths

Hauptmann: rank in the German army, equivalent to a captain

Heinkel He 111: German medium bomber; frequently used against troop formations, installations or industrial targets; with two engines and a crew of five, it had a reputation for being able to sustain a lot of damage

Henschel Hs 129: German ground attack plane equipped with two engines and an anti-tank cannon under the cockpit; it was heavily armoured and designed for low-level attacks

Hero of the Soviet Union: a gold star medal; the Soviet Union's highest honour; during the war, fighter pilots were given this award after ten kills; they could be awarded the same medal additional times after scoring thirty kills and fifty kills

JG54: *Jagdgeschwader* 54 was a Luftwaffe fighter unit that boasted many top aces; they were nicknamed *Grünherz* (Green Hearts) for the insignia painted on their fighter fuselages

Junkers Ju 88: German medium bomber with a crew of four; two powerful engines gave it high speed that made it useful for many different roles

kolkhoz: short for *kollektivnoye khozyaystvo*; Soviet collective farm, where farmers collectively managed and worked land owned by the State, provided their agricultural output to the government and were paid for their labour

Komsomol: short for *Kommunisticheskiy soyuz molodyozhi* (Communist Youth League;) Soviet youth organization for both genders, aged 14-28; intended to promote Communist ideals and act as feeder for public service and the military; Komsomol groups frequently held activities for camping, sports, and other recreation; they also trained in paramilitary activities like shooting and flying in order to prepare young people for national defence

Kupala Night: summer solstice celebration for Kupala, an ancient fertility goddess of Eastern European origin

Lavochkin La-5: Soviet single-seat fighter with heavier armament and a more powerful engine than the Yak-1

Lisunov Li-2: Soviet transport plane which was a licensed version of the Douglas DC-3 design; it had two engines and could carry about 20 passengers

Luftwaffe: the air force of Nazi Germany

makhra: Russian slang for a foot soldier, similar to "grunt" or "GI" in America

Messer (Messerschmitt Bf 109): the main German single-seat fighter throughout the war

NKVD: *Narodnyi Komissariat Vnutrennikh Del* (People's Commissariat for Internal Affairs); this Soviet organization was a combination spy agency and national police force; responsible for the political repression that maintained control over the country for the ruling Communist Party; it would eventually become the KGB; their uniforms were known for their blue-topped caps

Order of Lenin: Soviet award for outstanding service to the nation, both military and civilian; the medal depicted a portrait of Vladimir Lenin; it was considered second in honour only to Hero of the Soviet Union

Order of the Red Banner: Soviet military award, next in rank to the Order of Lenin; some servicemen and women valued it more highly because it was a purely military award; the medal depicted a red flag emblazoned with a Communist motto

Order of the Red Star: Soviet military award, next in rank to the Order of the Red Banner; the medal was a red star with a depiction of a soldier at its centre

Peshka (Pe-2): versatile Soviet light bomber, with two engines and a crew of three

Petrushka: traditional comedic character in Russian folk puppet shows; usually depicted as a court jester

pilotka: foldable military cap; it has a triangular appearance when viewed from the front; also known as a side cap

Pravda: Russian for "Truth", this was the name of the official newspaper of the Soviet Communist Party. It effectively provided the official news and opinions of the ruling class.

Rama (Fw 189): German reconnaissance plane; *rama* is Russian for "frame;" it had two engines mounted on parallel booms linked by the wings near the nose and a stabilizer near the tail, giving it the appearance of a window frame; a glass-enclosed crew compartment made it ideal for spotting and photographing enemy troops on the ground

Murzilka: illustrated children's magazine founded in the Soviet Union in 1924

Red Army Soldier (*Krasnoarmeets*): the official magazine of the Red Army

Red Star (*Krasnaya Zvezda*): the official military newspaper of the Soviet Union; for the award, see Order of the Red Star

revetment: protective shelter for airplanes, often made with packed earth and sandbags

sirin: mythical creature with a bird's body and the head and torso of a woman; based on the sirens of Greek mythology, it was adapted into Russian culture and came to symbolize joy and harmony

SovInformBuro: *Sovetskoye Informatsionnoye Byuro* (Soviet Information Bureau;) news agency established by the Communist Party at the start of the war to provide a central source for news and propaganda

special officer (*osobist*): the term used by Air Force personnel for an agent of SMERSH (*Smert' Shpionam*, meaning "Death to Spies,") a special department of the NKVD, directed to hunt and eliminate foreign spies and internal opposition

Staffelkapitän: position in the Luftwaffe, equivalent to a squadron commander

starik: Russian for "old man"

Stuka: German dive bomber; with its gull-wing design (resembling a seagull's wings in flight) and fixed landing gear, it was one of the most recognizable planes in the war; to bomb targets, it dived directly at the enemy, dropping bombs with remarkable accuracy, only pulling out of the dive close to the ground

Sturmovik (IL-2): the main ground attack plane for the Soviet Air Force during the war; a combination of cannons, rockets, and bombs made it devastating to ground targets, such as tanks; despite heavy armour plating, the need to fly low and slow in attack runs made it vulnerable; most versions had a tail gunner in addition to the pilot

TASS: *Telegrafnoye Agentstvo Sovetskogo Soyuza* (Telegraph Agency of the Soviet Union;) the Soviet Union's central news agency; during the war, it published numerous propaganda posters to be displayed in store and office windows

The Woman Worker (*Rabotnitsa*): a magazine devoted to women and families founded in pre-Soviet Russia in 1914

Timur and His Team (*Timur I Yevo Komanda*): 1940 children's novel by Arkady Gaidar, about a teenage boy who organizes a secret group of youths to perform good deeds and fight off hooligans

tracer: bullet or cannon shell designed to burn brightly when fired, assisting with aiming; typically, Soviet aircraft loaded one tracer in every four rounds of gun ammunition

U-2: incredibly versatile Soviet biplane used by both civilians and the military in many roles, from crop-duster to air ambulance; it was also the main aircraft used to train new pilots before and during the war

ushanka: fur-lined hat with ear flaps

valenki: traditional Russian felt boots used in winter

VVS: *Voyenno-Vozdushnye Sily* (Military Air Forces;) the Soviet Air Force

Yak-1: the main Soviet single-seat fighter during the war; the 1b variant had a more powerful engine and better armament

yellow-mouth (*zheltorotik*): literally yellow beak, referring to chicks, a derogatory term for novices

zampolit: *zamestitel' komondira politicheskoi chasti* (deputy for political matters;) official representative of the Communist Party within a military unit, responsible for education, morale and propaganda

ZiS: *Zavod imeni Stalina* (Stalin Factory;) Moscow-based automotive factory, renamed for Stalin in 1931 and a major supplier of vehicles and other equipment during the war

CAST OF CHARACTERS

Members of the 74th Guards (formerly 497th) Fighter Aviation Regiment
As of May 1943

    Stanislav Tomenko - "Red" - Regimental Commander
    Firuz Nabiyev - "Frost" - Regimental Navigator
    Leonid Kisel - "Cricket" - *Zampolit* (political officer)
    Ruslan Troyanov - Chief of Staff
    Arkady Muromets - "Legend" - Regimental Adjutant
    Dr. Vera Krupenya - Regimental Doctor

1st Squadron
    David Volusiuk - "Tractor" - Squadron Commander
    Sofia Dolidze - "Sirin"
    Sergei Markov - "Offal" - Sirin's wingman
    Dmitri Lavrov - "Wolf"

2nd Squadron
    Yuri Zadorov - "Baby" - Squadron Commander
    Aelita (Aelya) Makarova - "Mars"
    Damba Erdyniyev - "Lucky" - Aelya's wingman
    Antonina (Tonya) Gorbataya - "Honeybee"
    Bohdan Bronfman - "Vino"
    Tohir Yakhshiyev - "Spam"
    Lev Saponar - "Timur"

3rd Squadron

Mark Akhmatov - "Stitches" - Squadron Commander

Anton Grachev - "Starik" - Stiches's wingman

Roza Kulik - "Lily"

Hagop Demirdjian - "Dema" - Roza's wingman

Masha Petrova - "Stone"

Oleg Malinsky - "Petrushka"

Konstantin Voyevoda - "KV"

Vitaly Yeremin - "Genius"

Technicians

Gavriil Nemchinov - Stitches's crew chief

Duya Ulanova - Stitches's armourer

Zina Borodina - Aelya's crew chief

Katya Kamenskaya - Stone's crew chief

Liza Moroz - Roza's crew chief

Others

Darya Klimentovna Gromadina - Roza's mother

Yelena Kulik - Roza's aunt

Zhora Kulik - Roza's brother

Yevgeny Dmitriev - SovInformBuro Colonel

MAP

Leningrad
Moscow
The
Soviet
Union
Smolensk
Orel
Kursk
Volga River
Stalingrad
Don River
Astrakhan
Berlin
Poland
Germany
Hungary
Romania

Germany and
allied countries
Neutral countries
Territory occupied
by Germany
Front lines, July 5, 1943
German attacks
Soviet counterattacks

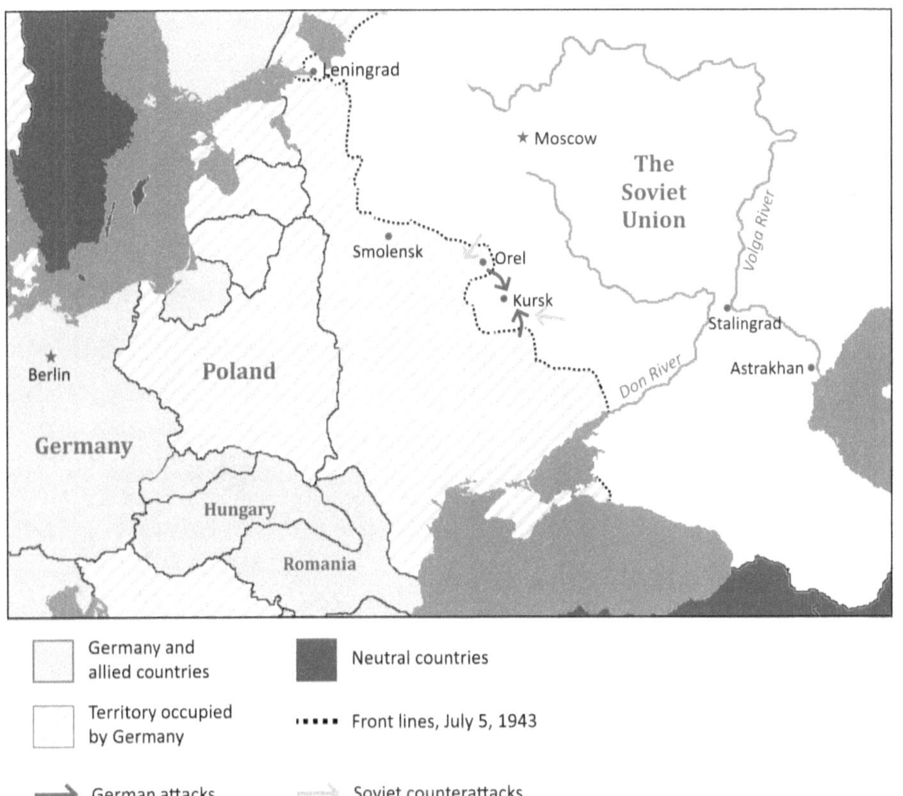

PART I:

Recovery

CHAPTER 1: THE FALLEN

Astrakhan, February 28, 1943

An instant from now, the Bf 109 would be the perfect distance from the red dot. Aelita Makarova—Aelya—stared past the aiming reticule, knowing exactly how long she would have to wait. She couldn't say how many fractions of a second that might be. She just knew.

Her body instinctively counted the number of adrenalin-fuelled heartbeats before she should fire. One heartbeat. Two heartbeats. She pressed the triggers.

The enemy fighter didn't even twitch as she laced it with three thousand grams of armour-piercing bullets and high-explosive shells. It hovered, almost unmoving.

"Stop admiring your shot," Lara shouted in her ear. "Check your six o'clock!"

Aelya snapped a glance over her right shoulder. Brightly coloured posters exhorting defence of the motherland, chipped and worn logs visible between them. The inside of a bunker. Where did the cockpit go? We must be reviewing gun camera footage, her brain decided.

Her attention flicked forward once more. She was in the cockpit. The German plane was still there. It looked so real, suspended in the air. It still hadn't moved, even as its propeller spun at full speed.

That's impossible, she thought, glancing at the control column between her legs. By instinct, she pulled hard and pressed the rudder to break off her attack.

"What are you doing?" Lara asked. "You need to press home the attack, make sure he's dead."

That's not right, Aelya thought. Lara always preached against staying in a straight path for too long and presenting a juicy target to the enemy. She wasn't like the aces in the regiment. Lara was safe and sensible, and everyone called her Auntie for the way she looked after her charges, especially the other women pilots who'd come to Stalingrad with her. As squadron commander, she'd been a pillar of strength for Aelya, reassuring her even in the worst of times.

The cockpit faded. Blackness surrounded Aelya.

"Look where safe and sensible got me," said Lara, appearing next to her.

Aelya stared. Like everyone else, Lara had been ground down by Stalingrad. Beneath Lara's stringy, sweat-matted hair, Aelya thought she could see down to her skull. That was how everyone looked after that cataclysmic battle. But not everyone made it through.

"You're dead," Aelya said, finally accepting that she was dreaming.

"I'm *missing*," replied Lara. That was a major distinction. Missing meant a potential prisoner of war. A potential prisoner meant a potential traitor. True Soviets didn't allow themselves to be captured. Aelya remembered: she'd been forced to denounce her former squadron commander, blaming Lara when the regiment had shot down other Soviet planes by mistake.

She searched Lara's face for the recrimination she thought was sure to be there.

"Would you have done it?" Aelya asked. "Would you have let them destroy my reputation if I had gone missing?" She hadn't done it lightly.

Because Lara had gone missing, her family were refused any benefits and couldn't even cling to the tenuous belief that she had died a hero.

Lara's eyes were soft and filled with pity. "It's your dream. You tell me."

Aelya felt jolted awake. Her gaze darted around, searching for orientation. She was in a corrugated metal maintenance shed. Icy wind whistled through gaps in the walls. Her crew chief, Zina Borodina, hovered over her as she sat on hard-packed dirt, leaning against a wall.

Zina gently patted her quaking arms. "It was just a nightmare."

Aelya wiped sweat from her brow, her pulse racing. It had been nearly a month since their regiment pulled out of the line at Stalingrad, to the shores of the Caspian Sea near Astrakhan. The Soviet counterattack, which had destroyed an entire German army in Stalin's city, churned farther and farther to the west. What Aelya wouldn't give to be back in the fighting. Resting and refitting at a rear area base, pilots like Aelya no longer had to suppress the jitters that came from flying combat missions, so it should have been easier to sleep. But without the vodka rations that came with combat, Aelya was fighting against nightmares as well.

"I'm sorry to startle you," said Zina, "but there's a problem."

Aelya felt backfooted by her friend's words. "I've got nothing else to do, and you were the one who suggested I could nap here."

"Not that," Zina responded. "Remember you told me to watch out for the twins doing anything stupid?"

Aelya rolled her eyes. Sisters Olga and Yulia had also come from the women's regiment. All three were stuck here in administrative limbo, waiting for word on their appeal against being transferred out of the regiment, clinging by their fingernails to their status as frontline fighter pilots. The last thing any of them needed was to entangle themselves in a prank feud with the other regiment sharing this reserve air base.

Zina continued, "Yeah, I think they're doing something stupid."

Aelya was about to ask more but held off. Instead, she said, "I meant for you to go tell someone."

"Who? All the senior officers are away on conference. Legend?" she said, referring to the regiment's adjutant. "Or would you prefer Baby?" She smirked as she named Aelya's squadron commander, the remaining senior officer on base. "Do you really think either of those men should handle this?"

Zina was right. This was something that should be dealt with by the twins' comrades. But even if Roza, Honeybee, and Stone were around, could they really sort it? Roza was too self-absorbed. Honeybee would try to exploit the situation. And Stone would only escalate matters.

"All right," Aelya said. "What's going on?"

CHAPTER 2: FOR THE MOTHERLAND

Moscow

Jutting defiantly toward the sky, the upended tail of the Junkers bomber seemed to deny its crashed state.

"I feel like I'm copying over someone's shoulder in a school exam," Lieutenant Mark Akhmatov, better known as Stitches, whispered through the side of his mouth.

His fellow pilot, Roza Kulik, stifled a giggle. "Call it extra credit, then," she said.

The two of them shivered on a patch of snow in Izmailovsky Park, posing in front of the wrecked Junkers Ju 88, feeling on display themselves. The twin-engine bomber was cracked in half, looking as if it had crashed cleanly in the middle of the park.

Stitches was right in a way—it was cheating. Through their photographs, *Red Army Soldier* magazine would give them credit for someone else's work. The bomber had been shot down the previous year and collected in the park with so many other war trophies. A triumph frozen in time, transported hundreds of kilometres from where it had fallen.

If only I could be shooting at the real thing, Roza thought. She flexed her fingers, grasping on to an imaginary control column. Her body tingled as she remembered the sensation of fighter combat. It was not a joyous or happy business, yet Roza could only describe the feeling as ecstasy, more intense than anything else she had ever experienced. The feeling passed, as the reality of Colonel Dmitriev's propaganda show set in.

"This is hardly the only untruth we'll be a part of," Roza said quietly.

Dmitriev smiled at them, as if he'd heard. Their former regimental commissar was a newly minted colonel, and now a liaison with the Air Force for SovInformBuro. He ensured that the Air Force steadily supplied of all the State's propaganda needs, which included arranging this photo shoot. Untruths are his daily currency, Roza thought.

Behind a tripod, the magazine's photographer, a small, bespectacled man with a thinning brown comb-over, signalled for Roza to remove her *pilotka* cap. She did so reluctantly, exposing the unbleached roots that had been carefully hidden underneath. Stitches was about to do the same with his peaked officer's cap, but the photographer shook his head. He leaned forward to look through his viewfinder, then screwed up his face in disappointment. He stepped around the tripod and reached for Roza's hair. She recoiled reflexively, but held back a retort as Dmitriev glared at her and gave a barely perceptible shake of his head.

"Let your hair down," the photographer said. "Try to make yourself more feminine."

"How about me?" asked Stitches. "Should I look more feminine as well?"

"Look heroic, smartass. Hands on hips. Like in a TASS poster."

The photographer returned to his spot to snap pictures. As soon as Roza untied her bun, the wind whipped her hair in her face. Whatever he was expecting, Roza wasn't going to give it. She stood, arms crossed, her smile lopsided with a glimpse of gritted teeth.

"This is not working," the photographer said with a frown. "Let's try this with just the lieutenant."

Stitches chuckled at Roza, then shrugged.

Dmitriev pulled her roughly out of frame. "Show a little gratitude, Kulik."

"For what?" Roza said. "Getting a ride in the Li-2?" The flight back to Moscow had been much better than the alternative: scrambling between three or four trains loaded with a mix of wounded soldiers, refugees, supplies, horse feed, and who knew what else. But she wasn't about to admit that.

"At least you could have touched up your hair."

"When have I had time?" She'd managed only token efforts to appease her vanity, the situation made worse because she couldn't access the beauty supplies Honeybee usually provided. "I've had to give talks at factories, meet with random officials from departments I've never heard of, and constantly rehearse my story of a blissful Soviet home life for press consumption. I had an easier time looking good at Stalingrad."

"Go see my secretary at the SovInformBuro office this afternoon."

"So you're not hustling me back to the Air Force barracks?"

Dmitriev didn't say anything, but a sly smile crept across his face as the photographer signalled that they could chat while he checked his equipment.

Stitches exhaled loudly, blowing out icy vapour, and exaggerated a slouching posture as he stamped his feet.

Roza sidled over to him. "At least you get to fly when this is over. All I get is more handshaking, smiling, and waving."

"I'd gladly trade. This is the first time they've let me out of the school at Lyubertsy." For the past two weeks, Stitches and his wingman had been sent to the higher air combat school outside of the city.

"I miss flying so much," she said. "What do they have you doing at aces' school?"

"Oh, it's all terribly dull. We spent last week putting the new Klimov engines through their paces. They're nothing special. They top out at just over twelve hundred horsepower," he said with a wink.

"If that's what it takes for you to finally catch up with me . . ."

"Very funny."

"I'll take that as an insult," she said with a smirk.

They turned face to face and laughed. That almost psychic connection they'd forged through combat in the same squadron had kept them alive. Bantering with him now after weeks of dreary propaganda work was like stepping into sunshine from out of a cave.

"I miss this," Stitches said. He cleared his throat. "Being with the regiment, I mean. Don't start thinking you're anything special."

"Of course not. That's why I wasn't invited to Lyubertsy."

She pouted and his eyebrows furrowed as if he was trying to figure out how serious she was about being disappointed. She wasn't sure herself.

"You should be there with us," he said. "You're twice the pilot some of my classmates are. Anyway, the school's really not anything special. It's mostly learning to work better with my wingman. The best part is that I'm close by and can see you."

Roza's chest tightened. Stitches's comment reawakened something in her. On the battlefield, his flippant flirtatiousness had just been a form of tension relief, part of their camaraderie. But now, without the threat of enemy fire, it held the promise of something more.

She'd known of this promise ever since she'd heard Stitches would be at this event. It had kept her spirits up through the cold morning. She was pleased to be pursued, as she had been in high school. She remembered Daniil . . . and Pavel. That one hadn't ended well; she pushed the morbid thought away. This was a game she hadn't played for a while, and she liked it.

"I guess you must be so good that you don't need to show up for classes," she said, her voice dripping with jovial sarcasm. "Win a gold star and now it's gone to your head."

Stitches didn't take the bait. "I'm only here because Dmitriev wanted to use me. Seriously, you should drop this. Come join us at Lyubertsy."

Roza looked away. "You know that's not possible." Photos and meet-and-greets were what the higher-ups wanted her doing, not learning advanced tactics. But Stitches saw her as more than propaganda fodder. She felt guilty for wanting to toy with his emotions a moment ago.

After inserting a new roll of film into his camera, the photographer barked at Roza to try another series of poses, this time against a back-drop of evergreens. His mood soured rapidly as she failed to give him some combination of determined warrior, glamorous femme fatale and maternal caregiver. Exasperated, he complained to Dmitriev. The colonel placated him with promises of better opportunities once Roza cleaned herself up.

"Right, I think we're done here," Dmitriev declared, then waved at Stitches. "You can return to Lyubertsy. I'm really happy with how you balance each other in this composition, but you won't be needed for the rest of the day. Kulik, it's on to our next appointment."

"Everything for the motherland," she said flatly.

Stitches stood in place for a moment; then, as if remembering some-thing, asked, "I'll have another free day on Sunday. Will you join me for lunch?"

Her lips twisted as she considered this. She really did want to see him. "Propaganda's tough work. And I have no idea what Dmitriev has got planned, though I suppose it will be around Moscow. Maybe I can get away. I don't know." She was so used to keeping a part of herself inac-cessible. It was comforting, even, and she didn't want to let go of the game.

"I know you'll find a way," he said, as if completely seeing through her reticence. "How about the Rublev? It's off Teatral'ny Proyezd."

"Fancy," she said, smiling ever so slightly. "I suppose it might be our last chance to see each other."

"You mean until we're back at the front."

Roza tilted an eyebrow. "Always the optimist."

"Come on. This is *you* we're talking about. Orders or no, I'm sure you'll find a way back to the regiment."

The supreme confidence he showed in her made her shudder with unfamiliar excitement. It reminded her of getting at the controls of the Yak fighter for the first time.

"How about eleven o'clock?" she said.

"That would be perfect," he said before kissing her hand in a showy flourish that made her roll her eyes.

Stitches waved as he backed away.

"And Stitches . . ."

"Yes?"

"It's really good to see you. Another comrade from the regiment, I mean."

He winked.

Dmitriev tugged her arm. "Right, Comrade. We're going to be late if we don't hurry. There's still a chance to redeem yourself." He hustled Roza out of the park, and they crunched across the snow-encrusted footpath. On the street, his chauffeur had the door open to his car, provided by SovInformBuro.

Roza plopped down in the rear seat next to Dmitriev. "They want some doll they can dress up and pose. It's not my fault I couldn't be that for them."

Dmitriev wrinkled his nose. "You and your womanly moods. While you were with the regiment, you couldn't wait to get your dress and makeup on. What's wrong?"

Sensing an opening, she smiled slyly. "Well, that's just the thing. I'm not *with* the regiment."

"Ah yes, about that . . ." Dmitriev shifted in his seat to face her. "You're not an ordinary pilot anymore. Going to the front line . . . well, is that really the best use of your time?"

"What do you mean?"

"You're more than a fighter pilot now. You're a symbol. You need to be seen, so the people can see just what our fighting forces are made of. You can tell the workers how they're helping in the war effort. Little boys and especially girls can look at you and think, one day, even I can make a difference. But you're not helping by moping around."

"If I could see some end point and know I'll be back in action, then I promise, I'll be everything you need me to be. But I just . . ." She shook with frustration. "I can't be here too long. I need to be back in action."

He placed his hands on her upper arms. It was neither warm nor threatening. "That's just not possible."

"But you promised you'd help me get back to the front line."

"That was before I moved to SovInformBuro. I'm not risking my prize."

"You won't have a prize, then. I won't do it."

"You're not that valuable, you know. In fact, I'm giving you a great opportunity. Don't squander it." He hefted a leather briefcase from the floor of the car, making a show of rifling through some papers without looking at her, as if he had more important business to tend to. "Face it, your fighting days are over."

CHAPTER 3: POISON

As the ball peen hammer struck a piece of scrap metal, Aelya flinched, feeling the impact in her heart. The metal-on-metal clang reverberated around the cold concrete interior of the former workers' canteen. It was too similar to the sharp crack of a bullet striking an engine block and reminded her of metal tearing into flesh. Too much time away from combat gave her mind the opening to dwell on these things that gnawed at her.

Ulanova put down the hammer. The short Asian technician was seated at a desk at the front of the room. She called out, "I hereby declare the Workers' Committee of the 497th Fighter—"

A staff officer seated next to her elbowed her.

Ulanova scowled, but nodded, declaring, "That should be written into the record as the 74th Guards Fighter Aviation Regiment."

The name change not only acknowledged the regiment's honour and elite status, but also meant higher pay for its personnel.

"I now declare us in session." Ulanova hammered on the metal once more. "Guards Senior Sergeant Duya Ulanova, armourer, presiding. We are convening to review disciplinary action against Guards Sergeant Yulia Yunevich, Guards Senior Sergeant Olga Yunevich, and Guards Senior Sergeant Aelita Makarova."

Low afternoon sunlight streamed through drafty windows, throwing the dozen or so technicians, pilots, and staff officers comprising the workers' committee into silhouette. They formed a semicircle around

Aelya and the twin pilots, Yulia and Olga, as they sat on a bench behind a canteen table, their backs against the wall. Yulia stretched out her long legs, her foot tapping furiously against the table leg, the vibrations causing several models of the latest German warplanes to skip along the table's surface.

Once used to feed the facility's workers, this damp and musty hall southwest of Astrakhan now served as a makeshift classroom. While its proximity to rail lines and long grassy stretches of countryside made this former fish processing plant workable as a reserve air base, little else about it made sense to Aelya. Beyond the unsuitability of many of its buildings, the odour of rotting fish permeated everything. Technicians had been scouring the compound to find the source of the stench for weeks, to no avail.

Baby, Aelya's squadron commander, stood to address Ulanova. "Before we begin, Comrade Chairwoman, I'd like to once more raise my objection." Nicknamed for his chubby build, he was a perfectly adequate fighter pilot, but Aelya had never warmed to him as a commander. He was fickle and frequently condescending to subordinates, while bowing with slimy obsequiousness to higher-ups. With Red and the other senior officers away at a conference, Baby was nominally in charge.

"I think you would all agree that our comrade commander," Baby continued, "wouldn't want military command to be undercut by this workers' committee, no matter how well meaning."

The regiment's political officer, Captain Kisel, raised his hand. "Strict military control made sense in those dangerous times before Stalingrad," the sandy-haired, round-faced captain said in a soft tone. "But now it would be good to remember that such egalitarian assemblies are what make us Soviet. And in my judgment, it would be better for discipline, which is within my purview. I've also spoken to my counterpart in our sister regiment, and he has agreed."

The political control of the regiment had changed, as it had for all the armed forces. No longer were commissars, like Dmitriev, of equal rank and authority to military commanders. The new political officers, called *zampolits*, were fighting men and women who looked to the education and morale of their comrades in arms.

Ulanova responded, "The committee recognizes and accepts Captain Kisel's explanation, and we will proceed with the hearing."

"Excellent." Kisel winked at the accused pilots as if to say, "I'm one of you, too." The fact that he flew fighters with them, instead of sitting in an office conniving ways to award himself medals, had endeared him to the troops already. The *zampolit* even went by the nickname Cricket. How he'd earned that, Aelya had no idea.

Ulanova motioned to begin and read the charges. Aelya and the twins were accused of trying to poison the pilots of the 466th Fighter Regiment, who were also based at the former fish plant.

Olga stood. "Poison? It was just going to give them diarrhea for a bit."

Cricket let out a sharp laugh but Ulanova shot him a glare. Olga sat down.

It grated on Aelya to be included in these charges. She was getting it from both sides. The twins blamed her for their getting caught, but she had prevented things from escalating out of hand. Aelya knew they had been planning revenge against the 466th for a previous prank. With the women pilots appealing their transfer back to the women's regiment in Air Defence, priority for training activities was given to the men. That meant a lot of free time to get into trouble.

After waking her, Zina had told Aelya that Dr. Krupenya discovered certain medications missing, presumed stolen. Putting two and two together, Aelya raced to catch up to Olga and Yulia as they were about to lace the 466th's soup with a drug meant to purge the digestive system. Unfortunately, while they argued, the bottle dropped and shattered, catching the attention of an officer from the 466th.

"Do the accused have anything to say?" asked Ulanova.

Beforehand, Aelya and the other two agreed on a united front, and that Aelya would speak for them.

"We admit that we've done wrong. But we did so to defend the honour of the regiment. A couple of days earlier, while Olga and Yulia were in the bathhouse, some members of the 466th stole their clothes and threw them into a pond. They were forced to parade naked in the snow across the whole compound to get to shelter."

Most grating of all had been the fact that the men of their own regiment, their supposed brothers in arms, were more amused than angry and had done nothing to help. Even now, Yulia turned bright red as a few of the men quietly tittered. Olga looked plaintively at the women of the committee. Perhaps gender solidarity would help them, but Aelya didn't want to resort to appealing to that. Weren't they all supposed to be equals?

Zina, sitting as one of the committee, raised her hand. "Is it true you tried to stop the others from taking such rash action?" As crew chief, she always made sure Aelya's fighter was in top shape, and even now she was trying to protect her.

Aelya wavered. Agreeing to face the charges together with the twins had been easy at the time. They were all part of Sparrow Squadron, three of the six surviving women who had flown down to fight at Stalingrad last autumn. They needed to support each other. But now, with the immediate threat of punishment looming, Aelya worried about being removed from frontline duty permanently.

That was why she'd been so keen to keep the sisters out of trouble. With the other women pilots—Roza, Honeybee, and Stone— all away, it rested with the three of them to cling to the beachhead they had made for women to fight in a frontline fighter regiment. Every day, she'd been hoping the appeals of their regiment's commander, Red, might reverse the Air Force's decision, or that they might simply get lost in the VVS's bureaucracy. Her uncertainty had lingered, twisting in the pit of her stomach for the past month.

There was also the threat to her new Communist Party membership. Whereas Olga and Yulia were still only candidates, Aelya had been welcomed because they'd confirmed she had killed a German. That counted more than knowledge of and dedication to Communist thought. Although membership no longer held any allure for her, Aelya wasn't blind to the privilege and protection it provided, however minimal.

She composed herself, tamping down any temptations to cut the twins loose. She remembered what Roza had shared with her during the worst days at Stalingrad: all they had to keep them going was each other.

"I was aware of the plans and take full responsibility for my complicity in our actions, which again, I stress were for the highest of intentions, to defend the honour of the regiment."

With no other questions, Ulanova excused the three accused pilots. They filed into a corridor outside, observed by a guard, while the committee deliberated.

Olga huffed and paced. "I can't believe we have to sit through this humiliation, on top of everything else."

"It's better than going through military discipline," said Aelya. "I think we have a chance."

"If we weren't women, they would have just laughed everything off. Sometimes I think we'd be better off in Air Defence, back with a women's regiment."

"There shouldn't be women's or men's regiments. We've fought for the right to be here. But sometimes, as my mother says, we have to bear a greater burden, if only to prove how much better we are."

Olga shot her a nasty look, then whispered to her sister, who so far had just stared at the wall. Then they were called back in.

They stood to attention as Ulanova announced the committee's decision. "Because the accused acknowledged their responsibility and caused no actual harm, the committee has decided that their Party membership and candidacies should not be affected, nor their status as active duty personnel of the VVS. Cricket, er, our comrade *zampolit*, has suggested absolution through good works, and we agree. The accused will perform five days of hard labour."

Aelya sighed, breathing freely for the first time since the hearing began. They were still part of the regiment, for now. Olga patted her on the back. Zina was the first to come over and embrace them.

As they filed out, Baby put his arms around Aelya's and Olga's shoulders. "See, I told you it would just be a matter of boys being boys. Or in this case, girls being girls." He slapped Olga on the butt and practically skipped out of the room.

CHAPTER 4: FAMILY PHOTO

The thought of seeing Stitches in a few days gave Roza some hope to cling to as the car weaved through a city turned over to war. The streets were inundated with military vehicles. At the direction of Red Army traffic wardens, mostly women, the black Packard turned awkwardly around X-shaped steel tank traps. Waves of ghostly human beings streamed along the snowy footpaths, their grey faces masks of grim determination. Even after the victory at Stalingrad, Moscow was girding for German attack. Signs indicating bomb shelters and enforcing nightly blackouts showed how near the danger still lay.

It was not the city Roza had expected to return to; there was little sense of home here, the place where she'd grown up. She had been more welcome in the Air Force barracks at Monino, where she'd billeted east of the city. With a lack of accommodations for women, they'd made her sleep in a coatroom, but at least she still felt connected to the Air Force and her comrades at the front.

"Don't be so glum." Dmitriev nudged her shoulder. "I've arranged a little surprise, just for you."

Dmitriev's strained levity made her nervous. There was no surprise he could offer that she was interested in.

The car halted before the entrance to the recently opened ZiS metro station, named for the nearby massive automobile factory now churning out all sorts of war material. After they exited the car, Dmitriev guided her past crowds filing down the stairs. Roughly shoving a woman aside to speak with a ticket collector, he flashed a letter, and a guard was summoned to escort them farther into the depths of the station. Queuing commuters who wore the ubiquitous mask of defiance against the invaders turned nasty glares on Roza. In response, she puffed out her chest, displaying more fully the Order of the Red Banner. She had earned this privilege.

The large pink marble-clad concourse of the station was cluttered with supplies for use in air raids. Folded metal cots, blankets, and large canisters of water had been piled up between the pillars, narrowing the already congested hall. War-themed mosaics adorned the walls. Dmitriev greeted a cluster of officials emerging from a side door.

Roza gasped to see who was with them, alarm flooding her mind. No, not her.

"Ah, my little surprise," Dmitriev trumpeted.

The plump middle-aged woman with fading blonde hair smiled at Roza. She held her arms out, though she maintained a haughty demeanour. Roza only just managed to force a smile.

"I arranged for your mother to be relieved from her shift," continued Dmitriev. "Thank you for obliging, Yelena Borisovna. And Kulik, your things are being transported to her apartment. You're going home."

Roza's heart skipped a beat and her body twisted into knots as she struggled to show the happy face Dmitriev wanted.

"Hello," Roza said. "Mother." She'd almost messed up and called her Aunt Yelena. She exchanged a quick double kiss with her, wary of Dmitriev scrutinizing their relationship. All this time away from Moscow had dulled the constant fear of her true parentage being discovered. Of some careless slip letting the world know that she was really the daughter of an "enemy of the people."

Dmitriev crossed his arms, frowning. A bright flash startled Roza and she reflexively tensed and scanned her surroundings for threats. It was only a photographer accompanying the officials.

"It's not like this is for *Pravda*. It's for *The Woman Worker*," Dmitriev said. "They want images of a strong family."

The reporter accompanying the photographer clasped her hands in contemplation. She had a narrow face and pointed nose, and when she tilted her head Roza thought of a mouse sniffing at cheese.

She moved Roza and Yelena around like store mannequins. "You should be embracing each other. Both arms," she barked. "No, not that way. Over here. Let's try this instead."

Roza felt the cold coming from her aunt with each change of position, and the feeling was mutual. After the series of poses, the reporter's lips curled.

Roza noticed Dmitriev's eye twitching in exasperation. She kept a straight face but laughed inside. If she couldn't get what she wanted, then he couldn't either.

Dmitriev cleared his throat. "I've seen this before. Sometimes the reunion of families under wartime conditions can be difficult. Kulik, perhaps you should spend a night at home with your mother first. Warm up to each other."

The reporter nodded. "I can work with that. We just need to show the transformation after you get home."

Dmitriev waved the magazine crew away, put his hands on his hips, and approached Roza and Yelena. "We'll do a much better job tomorrow, won't we?"

"The struggle continues, Comrade Colonel," Roza quipped.

Dmitriev sent them with his driver to Yelena's apartment, which was nearby. He admonished Roza to get a makeover from his secretary later. After arriving at a four-storey housing block, the driver dumped Roza's suitcase on the sidewalk and left the two women without a word. They trudged up the stairs in silence. Roza lagged behind the other woman, carrying her suitcase, dragging out her steps.

It had been a year and a half since she'd had to show daughterly affection toward the woman. She was out of practice and not in the mood to try harder. When the State had turned against Roza's father, Roza, her little brother, and her mother were left friendless and homeless in Moscow. Yelena was only too eager to remind everyone she wasn't a blood relation; Roza's mother was the sister of Yelena's husband. Only later, when it proved useful, did Yelena take Roza and her brother in, pretending to be their mother.

On reaching the top landing, her steps still echoing in the drafty stairwell, Roza felt a wave of trepidation wash over her. "Does Zhora know I'm here?"

Yelena shrugged, then moved to open her front door. Roza's heart pounded at the thought of seeing her little brother, but as the door swung wide the other woman spat, "He likes to stay overnight at the ZiS plant."

Roza relaxed involuntarily, forced to admit to herself that she was relieved. "The ZiS plant?"

"The boy's thrown himself into the war effort."

In the foyer, Roza's eyes darted around the familiar layout of the apartment, roomy by Moscow standards. "I'm sure you appreciate the extra money but he should be in school."

"Not so loud," Yelena snapped. From the kitchen and dining area that opened out from the foyer, Roza noticed an older couple in dusty, dark clothes watching her curiously. "The schools shut down when the Fascists were on the doorstep, so he found work at the factory. He wouldn't go back when they reopened. Maybe you should have done the same, but instead you pranced off on your adventure with the aeroclub."

She spoke as if Roza's evacuation from Moscow had been a picnic, as if all her experiences at Stalingrad counted for nothing. Perhaps Yelena hadn't bothered keeping up, hadn't read any of Roza's letters, which she was supposed to have relayed to Zhora, but it was doubtful she'd passed them on.

Without acknowledging the couple, Yelena motioned toward a long bench beside the stove. "You can sleep there."

Roza put down her suitcase and glanced at the door to the old room she'd shared with her little brother.

Yelena leaned in close. "If you want to, you can ask to sleep on the floor in the Mandelbaums' room. Just keep an eye on your things." She gave a knowing glance that dripped with disdain, which Roza did her best not to acknowledge. "Lord knows they've taken up all the available space in here," she said a little louder.

Roza smiled weakly at the Mandelbaums. Though they weren't much older than Yelena, their skin was splotchy and withered. Even before she'd left Moscow, refugees had been trickling in to the apartment block, to be placed in the few homes that had extra space. She'd envisioned that the apartment would be the same, though with Yelena's husband in the army and Zhora at the factory, it had become a prime candidate for shared housing.

She tried to suppress her surprise at the newcomers. "Where are you from?"

After a long pause, the man replied, "Vitebsk." With the name Mandelbaum, they were lucky to be alive. The town was in Nazi territory, and stories had trickled out of a terrible massacre of its Jewish population.

"Settle yourself in," said Yelena. "What's another body in here? Fine thanks for my husband putting his life on the line."

"Uncle Kolya delivers military mail," Roza snapped. "Anyway, if this is too cozy for you, why not move to Vitebsk? I'm sure the Mandelbaums will trade you their home. The Nazis have lots of space in their lands."

Yelena put a hand on her heart, playing up being offended.

Roza picked up her suitcase. "Well, you needn't worry about one more body. I'm going to stay with my mother."

CHAPTER 5: SHIFT

Roza wended her way around the long tables and pillars that divided the workshop. It was a relatively snug affair compared to the cavernous main assembly areas of the vast ZiS automotive complex.

"This is my spot," said Zhora exuberantly. With a skinny arm, he pointed at a half-made PPSh submachine gun slowly rolling along a conveyor belt. An elderly woman seated at her station picked up the gun and probed it with some sort of customized metal tool. Other workers seated along the line were adding their own parts, their tables separated from each other by low wooden barriers. "Can you believe they used to make speedometers here?"

At the end of the line, Zhora twirled a tall wheeled trolley with multiple submachine guns stacked on its shelves. He placed his arms around two workers standing by the trolley, one old enough to be his grandfather, the other a girl around his age. He'd grown so much since Roza had left Moscow. Tall and spindly like a larch, and heavy and awkward in his movements.

In the same way the car plant had been turned over to military production, the workers putting together whatever scraps they could find for the war effort, the labour force had been built with the same incongruous, patchwork expediency. Women, the elderly, and children all took part, although Zhora was among the youngest.

"Doesn't my sister look distinguished in uniform?" he said, beaming. "Hero of the socialist cause. Scourge of the Fascists." He nodded toward the girl. "Anya, you might soon get a merit badge, like my sister." Anya scowled.

Zhora clapped his hands. The workers put down their tools and he gathered them around. Roza had to marvel at the way he commanded their attention. For the past five years, he'd been forced to grow up fast, seemingly without pause. It was gratifying to see him this self-assured, but she no longer recognized her little brother within the fourteen year-old body.

The workers muttered in low voices to each other. Some flashed Roza relaxed smiles. It had been Roza's idea to come at the end of their twelve-hour shift, to avoid any disruption that might get her brother in trouble. She wondered if the warmth they showed was merely the relief at the end of a long day.

Zhora declared, "Comrades, this is the great Soviet hero, Roza Kulik. She's my sister, so you can think of her as a sister too."

He barked the words like a call to arms. But for all his talk of family, Roza sensed a cold detachment in his voice. He was growing up and growing further away from her. She suppressed the anguish welling inside her. This is better for him, she told herself. He's found his place, and maybe he might find the capacity for forgiveness as well.

"Comrade Kulik has been doing great things for our cause . . ." He continued in this manner for a minute, extolling the glory she had brought to the Soviet Union.

"I serve the Soviet Union." That was the mandatory response to receiving awards. It had tasted bitter coming out of her mouth when General Platonov pinned the Red Banner to her chest at Stalingrad. The taste lingered now.

She had been fooling herself when she and her brother had first laid eyes on each other this evening. Had she expected some vulnerable moment with him, perhaps hugs and tears? He brightened immediately, but now she knew his enthusiasm was one of revolutionary fervour, not joyous reunion.

The workers applauded.

"We salute your efforts on behalf of the motherland," a portly man in a grey suit called out from the back of the room. "And we salute our guiding light, without whom we would all be lost: Comrade Stalin!" The applause was louder this time, and the workers spontaneously sang "The Sacred War." Roza saw genuine enthusiasm in the faces, young and old. She refused to be carried along, even as she fondly recalled Red Army *makhras* singing it on their way to the front.

Perhaps she was supposed to be overcome with a sense of unity, a sense that the workers were behind the soldiers. But she saw in this enthusiastic chorus only mindless followers of the system. The same ones who'd been so eager to turn on her family and believe the worst of her father.

The workers continued into the second verse as they began the process of switching over the line to the next shift. The man in the suit approached.

"Comrade Vronsky," Zhora said with deference. "I would like to introduce Comrade Kulik to the workers' committee." Comrade Kulik. That was what she was to him. "Perhaps she could suggest improvements in our processes to help the brave fighters on the front line."

The factory. The factory always came first.

While Vronsky nodded enthusiastically, Roza tamped down his expectations. "I fly fighters. I don't use submachine guns." The last thing she wanted to do was glad-handing more model workers and Party acolytes.

"That's a shame," said Vronsky. "Even if you have no ideas for our manufacturing, the workers I supervise would appreciate news from the front. I'm sure they have many questions."

I'm sure they do, thought Roza with unease. "I don't really think I can say much."

They shifted uncomfortably in silence. Vronsky cleared his throat. "Yes, I'm sure you're very busy. If there's anything we can do for you—"

"Actually, Comrade Vronsky," Roza said, "it's the end of the shift. Can you spare a moment of my brother's time?"

Vronsky agreed heartily to her request. Taking her brother to one side, Roza said quietly, "Zhora, can't we leave this place?"

Boots stomped past as the evening shift entered to exchange places with their daytime counterparts.

Zhora frowned. She knew he was disappointed by the inconvenience to his work. She hated seeing this side of her brother, which had become more pronounced over the years as he came to terms with their father having been purged. She hated that he was becoming someone she needed to be guarded around. Someone who might turn on her, declaring her an enemy of the people. That was what his socialist heroes did. Worst of all, she began to see in his face the same shadowy man who had taken their father away. Perhaps the only thing stopping him from revealing her secret past was the shared shame of being descended from a "traitor."

She said, "I was just hoping I could spend more time with you. And with Mama. Dinner, maybe?"

They stared at one another for a moment. His eyebrows lowered. "I get my meals at the factory."

"You should be in school. This is no life for you."

"So you can make a contribution to the war effort, but I can't?"

"You'd prefer to go to the front—is that it?"

"I'm only a few years younger than you. And I won't sit back while my sister fights for me."

Roza inhaled to calm herself. "Mama needs you."

He stepped close to her. "Don't talk to me about that traitor."

"Don't you ever see her?"

He was silent. Roza put a hand on his shoulder, but he shook it away, casting his gaze down.

She said softly, "That's not fair to her. Just come with me and see her."

"You can go without me." He shook his head. "Now I'm going to be late for the workers' committee."

She tried to catch his gaze, her eyes wide, pleading. She hated this vulnerability, being forced to beg from her baby brother. "Then tell me where to find her, at least."

Zhora's shoulders slumped and he said, "Last I checked, she was staying in an apartment along Central. Number 18. I'm sure she's still there. She has no reason to leave."

Snow blustered and whirled around the ZiS plant's smokestack, which loomed over rows of workers' apartment blocks. Tired and grubby, Roza pushed sweat-matted hair away from her face with some effort.

In blackout conditions, she could barely make her way down the street. Finally, she reached number 18, as Zhora had instructed. If this doesn't pan out, she thought, I'm sleeping in the doorway.

Inside, there was little relief from the winter. The stairwell was scarcely warmer than outside. Only the exertion of taking her suitcase up three flights kept her warm.

Roza paused at the landing, staring at the door. After knocking, she was greeted by a gruff, unshaven, stone-faced man.

"Darya Klimentovna?" she asked, huffing a cloud of vapour into the cold air of the room. Paper and scraps of wood burned in a small tin stove by a window, which was all that kept the room from freezing over completely.

The man grunted and nodded to a corner, separated from the rest of the room by a flimsy curtain. Roza had to pass a bed next to the stove, where a woman she assumed was the man's wife sat glaring at her.

Nudging her head behind the curtain, she saw another older woman with stringy dark hair streaked with grey lying on a metal frame cot. The sheets were threadbare and stained. Even with two layers of blankets, Roza's mother looked ten kilos lighter than when she'd last seen her. Roza knelt on the filthy floor, where empty bottles, reeking of homebrew, lay on rotting floorboards. She gently stroked her mother's soot-stained cheek. Her mother's eyes were open and puffs of vapour fogged the air between them with each breath, but she didn't react to Roza's presence.

She shook Darya. Her mother squinted, recognized her at last. She recoiled, shrinking farther into her bed, as if trying to hide from her daughter.

Roza lowered her head, her eyes clenched shut, determined not to show her mother weakness. Four years before the war, the family had been evicted from their apartment after the shadowy men in their black vans took her father away. "Enemy of the people," they called him in the notice they gave Darya. Even now, Roza could only guess at their true reasons. Her mother had once mentioned corruption at the Moscow waterworks where she and Roza's father worked. In an unguarded moment, she told Roza she regretted confiding in her husband about what she'd seen at their workplace. Perhaps he'd spoken up, only to be denounced by the culprits. Then again, it was equally feasible that someone had denounced them just to get their hands on the family's apartment.

In his first letter from prison, Roza's father had insisted that Darya divorce him to save herself from arrest, and she complied. To survive, Darya went by her maiden name and wandered the city in search of work and lodgings while friends and family turned their backs. Eventually, Roza and Zhora found refuge with Darya's brother and sister-in-law,

Nikolai and Yelena. The children's presence proved useful in claiming a larger apartment.

Yelena had wanted them to have no further contact with their parents, but Roza still managed to sneak off letters to her father. He'd been fond of doing word puzzles with Roza, so they worked out a code in order to write honestly to each other while he was incarcerated. She thought she'd be writing a lot and had sharpened her puzzle skills. They exchanged only two letters before responses from the prison camp ceased. Perhaps he hadn't wanted Roza to be implicated either. Or perhaps he'd already been killed. She kept writing letters anyway, until Yelena found one in her schoolbag. Yelena burned it, and that was the end of that. No one in her aunt's household would be seen as sympathizers to a traitor.

After that, Roza simply walked out the door. She would still pretend to the outside world that she lived with Aunt Yelena. But she tracked down her mother, who had managed to find lodgings on the other side of town in a cramped communal apartment in Dzerzhinsky District. It helped that Roza could be closer to Tushino and its Chkalov Aeroclub and listen to the drone of planes landing at Central Airfield. Most of all, she could pretend at least part of her family was still together.

But she could see the signs then. Her mother would often return home from a trip to the unsanctioned markets at the train station, a bottle of vodka tucked under her coat. It wasn't surprising, though no less upsetting, that in Roza's absence she couldn't even manage to stay in that modest apartment.

Now, she calmed her mother down and lay down next to her. Clasping Darya's hands, she tried to rub some warmth into them. Her cheek rested against her mother's and the cold permeated her skin. Roza lay with eyes open, lashes icily sticking together every time she blinked in the mortuary-like chill.

A shadow flickered against the curtain, dimly lit by the apartment's stove. My mother is going to die like this, she thought. Maybe she needed to stay in Moscow, somehow take care of her. Her drive to return to the front lines began to disappear. She saw a shadow watching over them, taking on the shape of a man before fading into the growing nighttime darkness.

CHAPTER 6: THE SIRIN

Even though she was wrapped in a greatcoat, *valenki, ushanka,* and woollen scarf, the wind found its way onto Aelya's skin, biting into her flesh. Still, the cold was bracing. Cricket was right: labour had a cleansing effect. After plodding through a lawn made muddy by freezing rain, she loaded the last brick into the wheelbarrow for Yulia to take away.

She didn't mind being punished for the sisters' transgression. At least they were all together. The last time they'd been given labour duty, Aelya had been accused of being an informant and had been ostracized by the rest of the squadron. What they'd experienced together in combat made that sort antagonism, if not impossible, meaningless now.

They moved construction debris from one side to the other of a large fish butchery facility, now used for storing aircraft parts. Aelya had a sneaking suspicion there was no purpose to this work, but it was better than guardhouse duty.

A high-pitched buzz cut through the winter air as other pilots practised their manoeuvres. That hurt the most. They were trialling new Yak-1b fighters, upgraded versions of what the regiment had flown over Stalingrad. A bigger engine. Better armament. Cleaner lines. A bubble canopy that gave a better view of the all-important six o'clock area behind the plane, where enemy fighters liked to lurk. It had been a pleasure when Aelya first took one up. She closed her eyes and wistfully remembered seeing the dark waters of the Caspian hovering on the horizon as the Yak nimbly responded to all her commands. She had never seen the sea before and had been sorely tempted to deviate from her flight path to get a closer look.

Metal clanged, snapping Aelya to attention. Olga was hauling a tarp covered with rusty parts. Aelya helped load them into another wheelbarrow. Her steps were a little heavier now. An unease crept over her, and she wished more than anything to escape the dreary earth in a plane.

A three-ton ZiS truck rumbled up the road leading to the air base. After checking in with the guard, it was waved through, trundling past Aelya and Olga, flicking slush onto their coats.

Aelya turned back to her work, but a commotion caught her attention once more. The truck parked outside the classroom where they'd been disciplined, and several pilots filed out, chattering excitedly. They surrounded the truck as it disgorged a half dozen uniformed passengers. The pilots were jeering them.

"The replacements are here," said Olga.

"I was actually looking forward to scaring those yellow-mouthed newcomers," Aelya said.

"Don't you think that's cruel?" Yulia asked, returning with an empty wheelbarrow.

"I used to."

They turned back to their work. Olga and Yulia were both exceptionally tall, leading to their nicknames, Everest and Elbrus respectively. Their lanky frames belied a wiry strength, another reason Aelya was grateful to have them labouring by her side. It took only four more wheelbarrow trips to finish. Rather than ask for their next task, Aelya and the others decided on a break, quietly sharing a canteen of water.

A chipper voice cut through the silence. "Oh, wow. You must be the famous girls' squadron."

One of the new pilots, also dressed in a greatcoat and *ushanka*, extended a gloved hand. Aelya thought the pilot unusually small and soft-spoken, until she noticed the shoulder-length black hair flowing from under the cap.

Olga stood open-mouthed. Yulia asked, "They're sending more women pilots?"

"Sofia Davitovichna Dolidze," the newcomer said, smiling broadly and shaking their hands. "I'm so excited to meet you." The Georgian name surprised Aelya, as after taking a closer look she saw that the girl had a markedly Asian appearance. "You can call me Sirin."

Aelya raised an eyebrow.

"The boys at the academy called me that," Sirin said. "In myth, sirens have an irresistible voice, tempting men into danger. I think they meant it as a joke. Apparently, I sound shrill over the radio. But I like the name."

Who was this fresh-faced woman, surely only a year or two older than Aelya, to already claim a nickname? That was something that should be reserved for pilots who'd made it past a dozen combat sorties. Survivors.

"Which academy would this be?" Aelya asked.

"Chuguev Military Aviation School, in Kharkov. Well, that was before we got moved way out to eastern Kazakhstan when the war started. It was quite the trip getting here. Although I'm sure it's nothing compared to what you've gone through. "

"You got into Chuguev?" Yulia asked, wide-eyed.

"I was an instructor. Actually, I sent a couple of graduates here. Voyevoda and Bronfman. Oh, you call them KV and Vino. They were the ones who told me where to find you." She scanned them from left to right. "I kind of thought there were more of you."

"Stone and Honeybee are on an officers' training course," Aelya said. She should have been on that training as well but had been sent to ferry new planes from the Saratov factory instead. She'd complained to their bookish adjutant about being left out and Legend, as everyone called him, assured her that Red had high hopes for her and not to worry. Apparently, high hopes meant idling in a fish plant, existing on minimal sleep, and getting into trouble. It rankled her.

"Such delightful nicknames." Sirin beamed.

"We had to earn them," said Aelya.

Something didn't seem right about this woman. Her cheery mood almost offended Aelya, as if Sirin should be feeling the same anxiety that permeated her own restless existence here, this limbo between the front and home.

"Stone's real name is Masha Petrova," Aelya continued. "We call her Stone because that's what her heart's made of. The Fascists murdered her family, and there's nothing she likes better than killing Nazis. I hope you're good at that. That's pretty much the job."

Sirin smiled in a puppyish way that grated on Aelya even more. "And who's this Honeybee?"

"Tonya Gorbataya. I . . . think you'll get along."

Sirin lifted her *ushanka* to scratch her head. "Honeybee . . . oh yes, Vino used to fly on her wing. He told me she was the one to know. Is she your top ace?"

"Ha!" Olga laughed. "Don't get us wrong—she's good, but not half as good as she thinks she is."

"So who's the best here?"

That was hotly disputed in canteen banter. Olga and Yulia glanced at Aelya, not because she was the best but because they were probably expecting her to give the most diplomatic answer. Either way, she found it flattering.

"I have three victories. But our ace is Roza Kulik. She's also probably the best pilot in the regiment."

Sirin playfully slapped her forehead. "Of course. How could I forget the White Lily?"

"These introductions are all well and good," Aelya said, "but don't expect to stay here long. We've been ordered to transfer back to the 586th in Air Defence."

"Oh, I don't think that will apply to me. I was never part of Air Defence in the first place."

Aelya narrowed her eyes. "I'm pretty sure the order was meant to remove all women fighter pilots from the front. They're ending the 'experiment.'"

"But there are orders and then there are *orders*. These things tend to be more flexible than you think. I have a feeling this all might get sorted out in your favour." Sirin poked her lightly, and Aelya had to resist the urge to slap her hand away.

Although Sirin was a yellow-mouth just off the truck, she was still a full lieutenant, complete with the new shoulder board insignia, leaving Aelya unsure of how far she should push her veteran status. She settled on saying, "Oh really? You know some sort of magic fairy to wish the transfer away?"

Sirin shrugged. "Who knows? Maybe I do."

CHAPTER 7: PREFERENTIAL TREATMENT

Roza had to ask several passersby before she found the Rublev, hidden down an alley off Teatral'ny Proyezd, a wide thorough-fare of opulent hotels and cafés. Although the interior of the Rublev was more modest than that of its neighbours, it hinted at a by-gone czarist age in its plaster details along the ceiling and its fine stained glass windows.

She forced her way through a crowd that started at the door, which was unable to close, letting in the bitter wind. Away from the entrance, the air was hot enough for unbuttoned shirts and dresses with exposed shoulders. In spaces between all the people, little round tables and metal chairs covered the varnished wooden floors.

Roza's eyes widened at the baked delicacies on display at the L-shaped bar. How could they have managed this with rationing? Before the war, sometimes sneaking in with a group, sometimes bluffing, she'd managed to visit special stores meant for families of high-ranking man-agers. But this display reflected a whole different level of privilege.

She'd never visited this part of Moscow. She had no time for the theatres that gave Teatral'ny Proyezd its name. And most hotels were for foreigners or high dignitaries. But the Rublev was different from that. The men in civilian attire had an easy confidence, as though they were used to such luxury. They were fixers, men who trafficked in *blat*, the connections and corruption that ran everything. Some might even be gangsters. She noticed a fair share of military uniforms as well. But it was the women who set the Rublev apart. These didn't resemble dour Party members or bohemian intelligentsia; even mid-morning, they were dressed as if going to a ball.

Dmitriev's secretary had done her best at Roza's belated beauty appointment, grousing over the limited supplies that even a well-connected commissar could scarcely get a hold of during wartime. Still, Roza's hair was finally blonde again, though a dirtier shade than she preferred, and her makeup passable. But the uniform clung to Roza like a bad odour. It wasn't just that she was the only woman in here wearing one; something about it changed the way she carried herself, the way she felt about herself. Another time, perhaps, she might have tried to blend in. There was no chance of that now.

This was her only free time before Dmitriev started her on a new round of propaganda events. And she could feel the gravity of that filthy hovel her mother called home also dragging her down. They had established a routine over the past few days, aimed at sobering Darya up. Her mother had readily gone along. Perhaps it was easy to fall into the habit of depending on her daughter again. Every day, Roza helped her mother to the washroom to clean up. She fed her leftover porridge from the communal kitchen. She gave other residents her mother's homebrew in exchange for extra blankets.

But all that effort would be wasted without work to keep her mother occupied. Maybe Dmitriev could help with that, but Roza was already fighting him to get transferred back to the front. Even if she succeeded, where would that leave her mother? Yelena certainly wouldn't be lending a hand. It was just too much to think about.

A woman jostled her, spilling coffee on her wool coat, the liquid mingling with slush stains. The woman stared at Roza, then flitted away laughing. Where is Stitches? she wondered.

The sheer number of people was stifling. She took off her coat. Feeling it was easier to manoeuvre now, she circulated through the crowd, who were mostly standing around in groups while the few lucky seated ones took their time. She looked past everyone, as if she were meeting someone more important than them. But how long could the pretense last? Before the war, she could armour herself in hand-sewn dresses mimicking the latest trends, luxuriant bleached-blonde hair, and high heels deftly emerging from underneath *valenki*. That was lost to her now. The uniform made her sweat.

Why on earth had Stitches suggested such a place? It must have been a mistake.

She turned back toward the door and nearly stumbled into the very man at the top of her mind. Stitches's heavy brow perked up. He hugged her and they exchanged kisses on the cheeks.

"There's no place to sit," she complained.

"We'll see about that." He strutted into the room, exactly the way she might have before the war.

An oily man in a black suit and tie seated at a table spotted him and shouted. "Gold star! Over here."

Stitches winked and led her over. They sat next to him and his be-spectacled companion, who looked as if he could be a government official.

"I'm Denisov," the oily man said, "and this is Nikolishin." He flagged down a passing waitress. "What will you have, coffee? Nothing but the best for a Hero of the Soviet Union and his beautiful compan-ion."

Roza shrugged and sneered. Did they think her some field wife, a mistress kept by her officer?

Stitches introduced himself and Roza, calling her a senior pilot, and she softened. Neither of their new acquaintances reacted to his state-ment, however. Was it that common now for women to be in the Air Force? Or did they assume it was just another story to cover for an illicit relationship?

Denisov loudly asked the waitress for two coffees, then sent her away. "May I?" he asked, gently examining the gold star pinned to Stitches's chest.

"Of course. Premier Kalinin himself gave it to me."

"Kalinin," Denisov said with loud admiration. He leaned back in his chair, smoothing his hair. He held his arms wide, as if to bask in the reflected glory of a war hero. "So, you must know a thing or two of the war. What do you think will happen next? Is the big fight to continue in the south, or will we finally get them away from Moscow's doorstep?"

"Maybe we'll even throw the Germans back across the border by the summer," said Nikolishin.

It was a ridiculous supposition after the experiences of the past two years, but anything less optimistic could be called defeatist.

Roza leaned forward conspiratorially. "If he told you, he'd have to kill you." Then she smiled and looked at Stitches. "So go ahead and tell them."

Denisov slapped the table, laughing boisterously, almost making the waitress spill the coffee she brought over. "Not just a pretty face, then!"

Stitches said, "It's easy to forget how pretty she is when you're fighting side by side."

Roza raised a cup in salute, briefly touching the Order of the Red Banner on her chest.

With a thin smile, Nikolishin raised his cup. "I'm looking forward to this war business ending as quickly as possible. It's been terribly disruptive."

"Come, now," said Denisov. "Sure it's been bad for some, but we're an adaptable people. Our history is all about rising from harsh circumstances. There's much opportunity in war, if you know how to look for it."

Roza said, "And what opportunities have you found to contribute to the war effort, Comrade Denisov?"

"Ah, some of us were not made to fight, at least not with weapons. But as you're with the Air Force, you should know that those who produce more planes than the enemy, well that counts for something."

I'm sure you get your hands dirty, Roza thought, but bit her lip. Stitches grasped her hand, then looked at the two men's empty cups. He raised an eyebrow.

"A war hero needs time to relax while he's back home," Denisov said, taking the hint. "Please, stay at our table and enjoy. We'll of course take care of the payment."

Roza made sure her smile looked insincere as they left.

Stitches relaxed his hold and she took her hand away. "At least we got a table out of that," he said.

Roza grimaced at him. "How did you find such a place?"

"One of the instructors at Lyubertsy is a Hero of the Soviet Union as well. He told me about the special treatment we could get."

"Doesn't it seem too . . . decadent?"

"The people in here are among the elite of the Soviet Union. It can't possibly be un-Soviet, then, can it?"

"I don't know."

"Let's make the most of it. I rather enjoy the treatment."

The waitress came to check on them and flashed a smile at Stitches. She suggested almond tarts, which she assured him were set aside for special customers. He ordered two. The waitress looked sharply at Roza but forced a smile.

After she left, Roza said, "These people would just as soon spit on us if it weren't for your gold star."

"They can't now, can they?"

"You enjoy mingling with them?"

"They'd be living it up like gluttons, with or without us. Might as well have some of the sweets come to us."

She smiled wryly. "I just . . ." He was right. Why was it so difficult to keep her composure? Five years of playing the part so effortlessly, and now it suddenly seemed so difficult. And when the waitress came back with the pastries, she had to force her hand to touch one. Was she betraying her father? Betraying her mother? Would she become one of those parasites for whom the system always worked? These were the people who'd murdered her father. These were the people her brother had given his life over to support with his toil.

"I don't think I can stay here," she said, drumming her fingers on the table.

"Don't be so glum." He took her hand. "You're as bad as Dema."

She had to laugh at the comparison to her fatalistic wingman.

"Don't let these people make you feel guilty," he continued. "You're not like them."

"Aren't I? I'm sitting in their seats. Eating their cakes."

"We deserve this as much as any of them. More." He let out a long sigh. "I've long ago made peace with the vastly unfair fortunes visited upon people, good and bad. So let them treat us well. We deserve it. And we'll never lose who we are . . ."

She caught something in his look. Something she recognized. He was a kindred spirit, with a past also hidden.

Stitches raised his cup of coffee. "To the 497th," he said.

"The 74th Guards, you mean." She smirked, then drank up. She couldn't bring herself to eat the pastry. "Do you miss them as much as I do?"

"I miss being at the front. The people, not so much." He broke into a smile, and Roza punched him playfully on the arm.

They both knew their comrades meant everything to them. As hellish as the front lines were, this cushioned lifestyle in Moscow was even more discomfiting. She even missed Dema's pervasive pessimism. At least there was a grain of humour to it. It was necessary, even, to keep her sane at the front. Here, her mother's struggles and Dmitriev's demands were suffocating. She sighed.

"What's wrong?" Stitches asked.

She related Dmitriev's declaration that she was out of the fighting for good. It was liberating to share at least one of her burdens.

Stitches brightened. "I know that's not what you want, but don't overlook your propaganda work. And—"

Roza shook her head, running her hands through her hair, ruining the hard work Dmitriev's secretary had put in. "I just want to go back. I don't know if I can do this. My mother is a wreck. She has been since . . . she cut herself off from my father."

They stared at each other. That comment could be taken any number of ways. They sat silently, sharing the same look as before. She hoped to somehow will him into exchanging the unspoken. She remembered the look her mother had shared with a neighbour who'd also lost a husband to the Great Terror. She had seen the same unspoken energy, the nervous tension, the hesitant communication where the slightest misstep might mean life or death. There was a fellowship among the families of the persecuted.

Stitches brought his face close to hers. "You know my family were descended from Tartars. Heirs to the Golden Horde and Genghis Khan. We used to be proud of that fact, or so I'm told. But that's all in the past. We call ourselves the Kryashen. For more generations than I can count, we've been Christian. And good Russians."

Roza nodded. But not good enough, she well knew. Not for a revolution that had enemies in all directions, inside and out. Comrade Stalin had warned them all to be vigilant. To ensure the revolution's survival, every person or group who showed the slightest hint of anything that might not fully align with Stalin's vision of loyal Soviet citizens was under suspicion. Like people who were proud of a heritage that wasn't wholly Russian. Or those like her father, a clerk at the waterworks who made too much noise about corruption.

His voice dropped to a whisper that forced her to lean in close. "My parents, my uncles, everyone of that generation, rounded up. I was fourteen. Old enough to be sent to prison. I had to . . ." He sighed. "My parents and I, we agreed . . ." He trembled, unable to get the words out.

She stopped him. She knew the answer all too well. He'd had to denounce his parents. Deny himself any contact with them. She knew the answer, but she didn't want him to say it. It would be too painful.

He pressed on. "They might be gone, but I still bear the scars, and I can't do anything to make it better. But you, you have a living mother. You have a chance now. Take it."

"Stay in Moscow?"

He nodded.

She picked up the pastry, tired of denying herself. She turned it over in her hand, delighting in the squishy feeling of the icing and licking it off her fingers. "How did they ever manage to get these ingredients with all the rationing?"

Stitches squeezed her hand. "Moscow's not all bad. I'm glad I got to share this moment with you."

She didn't want to look at him. How could she still play games with him after all he'd shared? she wondered. And yet, she did.

"Your optimism's almost embarrassing," she said.

"Why shouldn't I be optimistic? I've learned to fly. I've met you. My life is . . ."

An awkward silence followed as they smiled at each other, and they both leaned in to kiss. A second later, they drew back from each other, though their faces hovered close together.

It was nice but not extraordinary. Roza found herself disarmed by the pleasantness of it, as if it were completely incongruous with everything else that was happening.

He leaned in again, but the waitress came to take their cups away.

"I could live like this for a long time," Stitches said after she left.

"I suppose I'll be enjoying it for a while," she said, pulling her hand back a bit but not letting go. "Dmitriev's determined to squeeze every last bit of propaganda value out of me. I think he wants me to visit the Yak factory in Novosibirsk."

"At least you get to see the country."

"But what's going to happen to my mother? She needs to learn to look after herself. I think she needs a job."

"So put Dmitriev on it. I'm sure he has the connections."

"He said I wasn't that important."

"Then he's small-minded."

She patted him on the arm.

"I'm serious," he said. "People like Dmitriev, they're part of the past. Change is coming. I can feel it. And you're a big part of it. You just need to make him see it."

"You think about the future?" she asked. "How can you?"

"How can you not? What else is this war but a fight for what the future will look like?"

He looked a bit moon-eyed. The look of a hopeful admirer, the sort she'd mocked in high school. But somehow, this was different. Perhaps she was changing too.

What did the future look like? She thought of a nice, spacious apartment like Aunt Yelena's. Except this apartment would have her mother and brother in it, together again. And in her vision, Stitches was there too. She remembered how Dmitriev liked how they balanced each other. They looked like the perfect image of a family, the sort Dmitriev would salivate over.

She had an idea.

"Sorry, Stitches—"

"This isn't the regiment. Call me Mark."

She grabbed the rest of the almond tart. "I need to catch up with Dmitriev."

"I thought we'd have more time than this."

"So did I," she answered between bites. "But I need to make an extra stop."

CHAPTER 8: BOUND TOGETHER

Dmitriev, a photographer, and the mousy journalist from *The Woman Worker* would already be at Aunt Yelena's apartment by the time Roza got there. That was for the best. Their being there would force Yelena to suppress any explosion upon seeing her sister-in-law behind Roza.

Darya's lids rested heavily over her eyes, which were glazed over anyway, but at least she was upright.

It was Dmitriev who answered the knock. Roza waltzed in lightly with her mother in tow.

"Tardiness is unacceptable in a—" He cut short his scolding, confused at the presence of a newcomer. Behind him, Yelena shuddered like a pot of soup about to boil.

Roza made straight for the reporter, who whipped out her notepad. "May I introduce my mother, Darya Klimentovna?" Darya barely lifted her eyes, still partly shielded by a headscarf.

Yelena managed to get control of her jaw, which had been agape, and forced out a courteous "Daryushka, what an unexpected surprise."

"This"—Dmitriev pointed a hesitant finger at Darya—"is your mother? Then . . ." He turned to Yelena, who had grown pale.

"My lovely aunt," said Roza. "Thank you so much for hosting us. My mother's housing situation, as you can imagine, Colonel Dmitriev, is in a transitional state. As it is for so many in our resilient capital."

Yelena was about to say something when Dmitriev interjected. "Yes, of course. We all make sacrifices for the greater good in wartime."

Roza smiled. She might just get out of this predicament she'd created. The risk was energizing. Almost as good as being in a fighter, Roza thought. "Ultimately, however," she said, "the State always ensures that its most prominent contributors are well looked after." She turned to the journalist and photographer. "Would you like a tour?"

She pushed open one door and peered in impishly. All signs of occupation by the former refugees, the Mandelbaums, had been removed. Dmitriev must have moved them out in anticipation of this photo opportunity.

"So spacious, this apartment," Roza said. "Amazing that even in these times a room can remain unoccupied."

Dmitriev stepped in. "Of course, for the time being Comrade Kulik is staying here—"

"No, I'm staying with my mother."

Dmitriev screwed up his face, then guided the two press people back toward the landing of the outside stairs. "Er, there are a few other details I forgot to go over with you." He glared at Roza, who smiled back.

Dmitriev spoke quietly with the press. Yelena stared at her sister-in-law, who wouldn't meet her gaze. "You have a lot of nerve," she told her.

Darya turned to leave, but Roza stopped her. "Stay. You should at least catch up." She grabbed two teacups that Yelena had left for her guests and guided her mother and her aunt to the main bedroom. "Let me take care of this."

"You'd better," Yelena said irritably.

A moment later, Dmitriev had returned, minus the media. "I can't use any of this, you know."

Roza shrugged.

"What do you want, Kulik? If that's even your name."

"I'm sure you had an inkling. You just didn't want to dig too deeply."

"I always knew you couldn't be trusted."

"Not true. My whole family could be trusted. We were loyal comrades of the struggle. We still are. I go out there and I kill the invaders. How much of a contribution do you make?"

Dmitriev waved dismissively. "Is that what this is about? You want to rehabilitate your name? That sort of thing is out of my hands."

"My mother did everything right in divorcing and denouncing my father. I took my uncle's name in solidarity." It hurt Roza to say such things, but she reminded herself that she needed to do this for the greater good. "I just want a normal life for my family—the ones who remain."

Dmitriev laughed. "I'd rather just move on. There are always new heroes, even women."

"Move on to your next female fighter ace? You're not going to do that. You know what I want, but I also know what *you* want. Do you have someone else on the cusp of becoming a Hero of the Soviet Union? I'm only three kills away."

Dmitriev wasn't stupid. He must have noticed that there were too many inconsistencies in her record. Aunt Yelena and Uncle Kolya were listed as her parents on her forged birth certificate, and the deception had flowed from there: her school records, her Komsomol membership, her internal passport. But the NKVD had access to other records that listed her true parents. Nevertheless, Dmitriev seemed not to have investigated. Roza gambled that he'd been too blinded by her potential to look deeply. He'd surely figured out the truth now, however: Roza's mother had been ostracized.

She leaned closer to Dmitriev, lowering her voice almost seductively. "You need your propaganda star, and I'll give you one. I'll be your hero and your glamorous exemplar of femininity. I could be your Pavlichenko. Except I'll play along."

She could imagine the gears working in Dmitriev's head, his ambition overcoming his caution. The female sniper Pavlichenko was such a propaganda asset that she'd been sent to America to meet the wife of the president. But she was uncomfortable in the spotlight, and stories of her stubbornness and coarse manners rubbed eager bureaucratic climbers like Dmitriev the wrong way. Pavlichenko seemed to be in the news a lot less of late.

"So you want back into a frontline regiment?" Dmitriev asked.

"Back to *my* regiment. The 74th Guards. But before that, if I'm supposed to play along and go to all your picture sessions, I'll need a clean record and a model Soviet family home befitting a hero."

This was a dangerous game she was playing. Too many people already knew about her father. People had been sent away in black vans for less.

Dmitriev paced around the small kitchen, pinching the bridge of his nose. "Where is your mother staying?"

She had him. "Some dilapidated ruin on Central in Danilovsky District."

"That can be corrected. As for anything else in your family's record, that will be more difficult. Prove yourself worthwhile and we'll arrange it."

"It's not a question of worth. You're going to be stuck with me. We're bound together, but that's a good thing. We rise together and we fall together. True comrades. Just as if we were back at the regiment."

"I need you to be the model Soviet hero. Nothing less. And no unnecessary risks. Get your three kills, we'll put you up for the award, and then I want you out of there."

Roza stumbled. What would happen after three more kills? She hadn't thought that far ahead. Of course, Dmitriev would want to protect his investment. When she'd told Stitches she missed being in action with the others, she meant it, but if the opportunity came to finally wipe clean the stain of treason from her family's name, could she just abandon the regiment? The women like Aelya who'd been with her from the start? Stitches?

"I'm a fighter pilot," she said. "If you want me to be a star fighter pilot, you need to let me do fighter pilot things."

"Just come back in one piece." It was an implied threat. She should under no circumstances allow herself to go missing like her former squadron commander, Auntie.

She patted Dmitriev on the cheek, pushing the limits of his tolerance. "I'll be a bigger star than you ever imagined."

And with that, he called the journalist and photographer back into the room.

The street in front of Aunt Yelena's apartment block was lit only by the half-shuttered lamps of Dmitriev's car by the time Roza returned after settling her mother in a new place. The colonel had needed to pull more strings to exempt her from curfew. She hated owing him for yet another favour, but she'd needed to ensure her mother wouldn't spend another night in that miserable apartment. Yelena had flat out refused to take Darya in. After a blazing row that dredged up every slight and resentment over the past two decades, Roza had to admit that bringing the two women together at home would never work. So Dmitriev arranged a temporary stay at a convalescent home for Roza's mother while he sorted out a job and corresponding worker's apartment. A tiny glimmer of peace had shone in her mother's eyes as Roza kissed her goodbye.

Dmitriev's driver left her to stumble to the doorway of her aunt's apartment block in darkness. A shadow stirred in front of her. Startled, she reached for her pistol, forgetting she'd handed it in when she left Stalingrad.

"It's just me," Stitches said in a pleading tone.

"Are you nuts? How long have you been there?"

"Dmitriev's secretary told me I could find you at this address. I just didn't know when you'd appear," he said casually, as if he'd only just arrived.

She didn't know how to react. Was he following her around like a puppy, like Daniil had in high school? That didn't fit with the confident, borderline-arrogant Stitches she knew from the battlefield. He still sounded self-assured. He was playing a game too.

"Aren't you due at the academy?" she said.

"Having a gold star has its privileges."

"I should report you."

"Maybe you should." He was challenging her. A thrill coursed through her like a current of electricity.

She swallowed. "I'll have to give it some thought. Maybe sleep on it."

"I'll be right here."

"You're liable to be picked up for violating curfew."

"I'm willing to take that risk." He took a step forward, close enough that she could feel his warmth. She had the urge to take hold of him, cover his body with kisses.

"Did I mention I have my own private bedroom?" she asked.

"I didn't think such a thing existed in Moscow."

"Come here, you fool." She pulled him in and planted her lips on his.

CHAPTER 9: STRAYS

The smell of fish permeated the marketplace in Astrakhan, but unlike the makeshift air base, it had a salty rather than putrid quality. Salt and rust stained the metal posts supporting the open air shelter's roof. Aelya imagined that before the war the hall had been lively with vendors hawking the famous local seafood. Now most of the market had been turned over to refugees and war profiteers, and all the goods and contraband that entailed.

"Oh, look, there's a stall for the fishery collective." Olga pointed to a corner of the hall where a thin layer of snow blew in. "Do you remember how to tell if the caviar is the real thing, or just dyed to look like it?"

Aelya glared at her side-eyed.

Their last appeal had been exhausted, and now the transfer order was official. They had been removed from active duty while awaiting arrangements to take them back to the 586th regiment in Air Defence. With nothing else to do, the twins had successfully lobbied to be allowed liberty in Astrakhan.

The flood of refugees, the scars of air raids, and the shortages brought on by war made this place feel transitory, with little connection to the exoticism of the ancient city. It was just somewhere to stop on the way to something better.

Aelya felt an affinity with the aimlessness of the refugees. It was one thing to be given occasional liberty, as she had when ferrying the airplanes from Saratov, but now she was distinctly marginalized from the regiment. The rest of them, even the female technicians, were busily preparing for the move back to the front. While the women technicians were accepted out of grudging necessity, she, Olga, and Yulia had been cut adrift, waiting until arrangements could be made for them to catch trains back to wherever the 586th was stationed now. Sirin had been right; the order hadn't mentioned her.

"I think Sirin said caviar should smell like smoked salmon," said Olga, the taller of the twin sisters, wringing her hands. "Or did she say it shouldn't?"

"Why do you think Sirin knows what she's talking about?" Aelya snapped.

"She's seen so much," Yulia said. "I heard she even spent a few years in Finland. I've never been, and I could see it from my hometown." With a sharp intake of breath, she was no doubt thinking back to her life in Leningrad, its people now starving and besieged by Germans.

It had become a game of sorts for the pilots to guess at the mysterious, possibly exotic past of their newest member. Sirin seemed to come from an important family, given her confident, carefree, almost aristocratic bearing. But as Aelya had learned with Roza, people were good at disguising their nature when their survival depended on it.

Zina had passed on a story that was making the rounds. Apparently, Sirin had been at an Air Force base near the border, running an errand in a U-2 on that first Sunday of the invasion. The base got hit by enemy bombers, but she'd made it out in her little biplane before the runway was cratered. She didn't get away cleanly, though—a Bf 109 fighter had homed in on her. To escape, she flew close to the ground, so low that she made the vulture crash before getting away. Zina had the decency to remind everyone that Aelya had done something similar at Stalingrad.

Aelya smiled, thinking fondly of her crew chief defending her reputation. Aelya would need to make peace with separating from her—or not, she thought.

It was strange being free of any schedule. Aelya couldn't suppress her nervous energy.

"We need to do something about the transfer order," she said.

"Like what?" said Olga.

"You sound like you don't want to stay with the regiment."

"Of course we do," Yulia said. "Why don't we write to Kalinin?"

"That's your solution to everything," Aelya said. In addition to being lankier and more awkward than her sister, Yulia was also more reticent in standing up for herself and more likely to fall in line with authority figures.

"I've only ever said it once," Yulia said. "My aunt wrote to him when she was evicted from her communal apartment before the war." Kalinin, the Soviet Union's premier, was the patron saint of the petition. Stories circulated everywhere about the benevolent figure who could save those in need. These had acquired an almost religious aspect during the Great Terror, when everyone was getting arrested.

"You're thinking too much within the rules," Aelya said.

Olga reddened. "Some of us can't get away with anything else."

"What's that supposed to mean?" said Aelya.

Olga laughed mirthlessly. "Of course, you wouldn't know. I follow the rules and still it's not good enough. Everything I say gets second-guessed, or worse, ignored. When I kick up a fuss, they say I don't work well in a team."

"I've had to prove myself just as much as you," said Aelya. "My mother had to deal with the same things. She said all women have to push past it."

"It's easy for you to casually talk of rule breaking when Red and the other officers like you. You're a girl to them, not a woman, so you're not a threat."

Aelya didn't know what to say to that. She thought of the men as brothers or uncles. Weren't those feelings mutual?

The three of them strolled uncomfortably past the first row of market stalls, their eyes ahead, tension hovering over them. There were so many refugees, displaced and damaged from the war. Stragglers lolled around in miserable, dirty piles near the market, hoping for scraps of food or money. Some beggars wore khaki too, with the coloured piping and facings of the Red Army. Missing arms. Missing legs. Missing eyes. They were broken in body and spirit.

A young man rolled across their path, kneeling with his two stumps on a low-wheeled platform made from planks. He held a tattered *pilotka* cap upside down.

Yulia knelt down to give him some money, catching the attention of other beggars from the margins of the market. They closed in like stray dogs converging on scraps.

Olga shrugged at her sister's indulgence. She mumbled something about seeing caviar and hurried to the other side of the market. Aelya lost sight of her as another wave of bedraggled refugees crossed her path.

The press of bodies in the market felt confining to Aelya. She stumbled through slush-covered ground out to an open square sheltered in the lee of the market. More refugees lingered here, mainly civilians. They were a ragged mass, women, children, and the elderly, clinging to each other yet still trying to sell randomly collected wares laid out on little scarves and blankets.

A wave of outstretched arms surged forth with the arrival of every civilian in freshly laundered clothes or every soldier in a pressed uniform. They clamoured for attention.

"Comrade, comrade, I have the perfect thing for you . . . Auntie, a moment of your time . . . You look like you have discerning taste . . ."

Aelya recoiled from a tug on her sleeve. A little dirt-smudged girl, perhaps eight or nine, looked up at her with wide eyes. A mangy cat hid among the folds of her ragged dress. She held out a postcard-sized ink drawing of a deer. Behind the girl, a woman, presumably her mother, sat on a blanket with more drawings.

If she walked away, Aelya would be haunted by the look in the girl's eyes. Intrigued, she allowed the girl to pull her over to examine her wares. "Did you draw these yourself?" Aelya asked as she scanned the cards. The girl nodded. "You're very talented." They were simple line drawings, though the shapes had a certain elegance.

Aelya stopped at one card. "What sort of bird is that?"

The mother looked at her daughter, who shrugged.

"Could it be a sparrow?" Aelya asked.

"Sure, it's a sparrow."

It was the first time she had felt like smiling in a while.

Olga called her name. Aelya mumbled an apology and backed away into the centre of the square to meet her comrade. "No caviar?" she said.

"I couldn't go through with it. What if I got it wrong? What would Sirin say?"

Aelya groaned. "We'd better go find your sister."

When they did, Yulia had a wide grin. Behind her, a familiar face emerged from the crowd.

Aelya cracked a smile. "Petrushka!"

The perpetually jovial pilot seemed to have put some weight on his thin frame. Having missed most of Stalingrad, he looked rounder, more normal than the other pilots, reminding Aelya of how gaunt, drawn out, and haunted the rest had become.

"Ladies." Petrushka bowed. "I was waiting for a ride back to base and thought I'd look for a souvenir. This is the first decent market I've seen in months."

"When I first saw you," Yulia said, "I thought the worst."

"After running afoul of Stone, I thought I'd lose *my* leg too." Memories of playing soccer and the unfortunate collision between him and Stone made Aelya shudder. A leg should never bend at that sort of angle.

He grabbed Aelya. "How is Stone? Is she . . . ?"

"She's an ace now. And off to officer training with Honeybee. She even got to take Volkov with her." The little stray dog that had attached himself to Stone had become a regimental mascot. His absence probably contributed to the malaise affecting the pilots on base.

They quickly rolled through the names of other pilots. He knew Stitches was all right, having read about his Hero of the Soviet Union award in the military newspaper. There was relief over those who were still flying, and a moment's hesitation, a shadow of grief, over those who weren't.

Goosebumps prickled Aelya and she hugged Petrushka fiercely, as if he could connect her to a happier time, connect her to those who'd still been alive before he'd left with his injury. As Yulia and Olga joined in, she felt the hard edge of the book she kept in the breast pocket of her jacket. *Aelita,* the book she was named after. Once her lucky charm, it had been a long time since she'd thought of it, though it was always on her.

When she finally broke free, she asked Petrushka, "How's the leg?"

He danced a little jig.

"Took you long enough to get back to duty. Are you sure you weren't milking it?" Aelya said, feeling in better humour from his mere presence.

"It wasn't the leg that kept me away. When I was discharged from the hospital, a navy major was picking up one of his own flyers. He saw my pilot's badge, found out I flew fighters, and ordered me onto a truck. They'd been waiting for a replacement for weeks and decided to speed up the process."

"They can just do that?" Aelya asked.

"It's worse at the transition points. I've heard stories of wounded pilots written up as missing and simply getting drafted into other units, no matter the qualifications. Everyone just needs bodies."

Aelya silently gave thanks that the arm injury she'd suffered at Stalingrad hadn't been serious enough to take her off base. Who knows where she'd have ended up?

Petrushka continued, "The naval regiment just converted to Lavochkins, so when I arrived, I was stuck on base doing a lot of training. Then one day a divisional liaison was visiting the regiment. He left his U-2 unsupervised, and so off I went to Astrakhan. I hitchhiked the rest of my way here. I'd been planning on spending some time at the market and bathhouses before finding my way to you, but it was fate we should meet now."

"Weren't you worried about stealing the plane?"

"Nah. People steal planes all the time. It's war. They let you get away with anything, pretty much. As long as you kill Fascists."

Aelya thought it was ridiculous and unfair for the women to be sent back to Air Defence when Petrushka had stolen a plane. If anything, they should be sending him away.

"Maybe I should run away to another regiment," she muttered. "That would solve everything."

"I'm back for five minutes and already I'm driving people away," Petrushka joked. "Well, I'm here to help. There's a navy regiment missing a pilot, I hear."

She nudged him on the arm with her fist. They all agreed they needed to get something to eat and warm up. And yet they lingered in the glow of the reunion a while longer, silently basking in the comfort of knowing they'd been together through hell.

"I can't wait to bring you back with us," said Olga. "The yellowmouths could do with some ridicule."

"That's what I'm here for," said Petrushka.

Aelya had a thought. "Petrushka, you went to Chuguev School, didn't you? You remember a woman instructor there?"

"You're digging into ancient history. I barely remember what I had for breakfast. But yeah, we had a couple on the base, though I finished just as they were starting."

"This one you might remember. She looks Asian. She just joined our regiment."

He doffed his *pilotka* to scratch his head. "She has a nickname?"

"Sirin."

"Yes, that's it." He whistled. "Sirin's in the regiment? Yeah . . ." After a pause, he drew them all closer, saying quietly, "I'd be careful not to be around her that much."

"Is she that much trouble?"

"Not her. Her father. He's very high up in the NKVD." He looked around, spooked. "So, you know . . . don't get her angry"

Aelya chuckled.

"I'm serious," Petrushka said. "I heard that one of the students pissed her off, and next thing I know, he's being assigned to a penal battalion." He laughed it off. "I think I've had enough of this place. Can you help me find a ride back to base? I can't wait to see everyone again."

Before they left, Aelya went back to the little girl. She bought the card with the sparrow drawn on it.

"It's not over," she said, to no one but herself.

CHAPTER 10: PARTING

Joyful cheers, songs and clinking glasses drifted from the canteen as the regiment gathered for a farewell. Air Force bureaucracy had decided the perfectly functional workers' canteen should be a classroom, so the regiment ate in a flimsy tent set up in the yard of the fish plant. Even with all the pilots packed inside, it was a chilly affair. Early spring rain pelted the ground outside, transforming the snow into a lake of slush.

After the regiment's political officer, Cricket, opened with a salute to Comrade Stalin and the women pilots, he urged them to get on with the vodka, which did nothing to harm his popularity.

Next, Red stood to address them for the first time since he'd returned from his conference, greeted by a rousing cheer. He was a tough, demanding commander, but he fought hard for them and with them. The regiment had won more than it had lost at Stalingrad under his command. For that, Aelya respected him. Love was too strong a word, but she was gladdened by his return. The new shoulder boards with two stars and two stripes looked good on him. They marked his well-deserved promotion to Lieutenant Colonel.

Red made note of the absence of three of the nominal guests of honour: Roza, Stone, and Honeybee. "It might be for the best," he said. "If they were all here, we might be too overcome with emotion."

Aelya teared up a bit to hear her commander being so unusually open and his words so heartfelt. It was all so unreal, as if it wasn't actually happening. As if the transfer order was part of a bad dream.

"I don't want to make this a sad occasion," Red continued. "But let us admit that the character of this regiment will change with the departure of our beloved comrade pilots to Air Defence. This war is a grey, stoic journey. Having you with us made it a little less so."

Aelya quavered. The moment was so precious, she almost felt bad that it would be rendered meaningless by her plan. A few pilots cleared their throats in the silence as they tried to avoid showing emotions.

"Come now," Cricket declared. "This parting should be marked with joy at the new possibilities ahead of us, which will allow us each to contribute more fully to our nation's triumph over the enemy."

He went to start the gramophone, but Frost, the regiment's navigator and second-in-command, stepped forward with his guitar instead. He started up a ballad with a bouncing rhythm from his Tajik homeland. The men seemed determined to remain sad, until Olga took Petrushka by the arms and started to dance. Soon limbs flailed and drinks were knocked back.

"Would you like this dance?" Lucky asked Aelya, in a rare break from his usual shyness. She took her wingman's hands.

They had no idea what they were doing. The dance was sloppy and graceless and exuberant. She didn't mind how she looked compared to Olga, who had trained as a ballerina. Sirin and Yulia soon had partners too, and other men showed varying degrees of skill and sobriety while dancing solo.

After a bit of stumbling, Aelya and Lucky slowed down, only performing the barest imitation of a dance, while Frost switched up the tempo.

"You saved my life," Lucky said.

"Lots of times." Aelya grinned.

"Yes, lots of times. Still, I wanted you to know that."

"Don't underrate yourself. You help save me every day as well."

"Maybe. But you're still my senior pilot, so it's mostly you."

"Stay smart and stay alive, Lucky. The regiment needs you."

She realized this was her family now. Not just the women pilots but the the rest of the regiment. The pilots, the staff and technicians. She vowed not to give up on them.

Look at me, she thought, forgetting my real family. Her parents and sister were toiling away out east in Kuybyshev. They'd been evacuated there when the aircraft plant in Smolensk had been dismantled and moved to escape the initial invasion back in 1941. In the intervening year and a half, Aelya's letters home had grown less frequent. And though she missed her family and thought of them often, they seemed less and less a part of her world.

Red couldn't let the party last too long. The regiment had received its orders. They were finally flying back to the front in their new Yak-1b fighters. They were heading somewhere to the northwest, where everyone was sure, or at least hoping, the summer offensive would begin and the Fascist occupiers would be rolled back to Berlin. Just as they'd thought in 1942. And in 1941.

The technicians were already in the throes of the rebasing effort, and so after one more dance, the pilots bade their final farewells and began to see to their own packing.

Airplane engines droned at the foot of the runway, signalling the departure. First the fighters and support planes took off, then the staff in their Li-2 transport.

Aelya, Olga, and Yulia waved from the side of the runway. Afterwards, the three had to make abbreviated farewells to the ground crew.

Busy as always, the technicians packed their gear and hopped onto already moving trucks, trying not to miss their ride. Zina gave Aelya a wink after they blew kisses at each other.

Finally, only the three of them remained, without a regiment. Technicians from the next regiment coming into reserve started to arrive, taking over the base. They had to rush to their barracks to pack.

"What about our other things?" Olga asked as they hustled out of the barracks with just their suitcases and winter uniforms. She meant the trunks full of personal items accumulated over the past year and a half. "Shouldn't they be going to the train station with us?"

"Zina sorted that ahead of time," Aelya said. "They'll probably arrive on base before we do."

Before they reached the transportation pool to hitch a ride to the rail depot, Aelya steered them toward the fish factory's former workshops, which served as the base's maintenance area. To the sisters' puzzled questions as to why they had stopped here instead of continuing to the train station, she replied merely that they would know soon enough.

Once they entered a dusty machine shop, Aelya declared, "This is where we'll be staying."

"Come again?" said Olga.

As she crouched beneath one of the workbenches, Aelya said, "They hardly ever use this shed. And anyway, the full crew of mechanics aren't due for days. We'll be gone by then."

She pulled out a bundle wrapped in a blanket and untied it, revealing a stash of canned food, water canteens, and padded sleeping rolls.

"Are you serious?" said Olga.

"No wait—listen to me. This will work. Zina helped to scout out everything. The trunks with our non-essentials were relabelled and packed up with the rest of the regiment's. We can stay here while everyone else thinks we've boarded our train. None of the personnel here know us. It's all a jumble of different units moving in and out, so everyone will just assume we're with another regiment. Anyway, it's just for a day. First light tomorrow, we grab our ride."

Olga rolled her eyes.

"Take this seriously. It will work. There's a two-seat Yak trainer at the depot." The division had set up a depot to service and repair planes coming through the base. A mass of aircraft and parts sat in rows on the snowy grass outside the fish plant. "The trainer's supposed to be left behind for the next reserve unit," Aelya continued. "It could fit three in a pinch and there's space in the fuselage for our things. And with no ammo, the weight should balance out."

"We're going to fly a broken plane," said Olga.

"A broken, stolen plane," Yulia added.

"No, it's all fixed. Zina's checked it out, and she's altered the maintenance logs so it won't be missed. They'll just think we're taking it back into service." She had always known Zina would support her, despite her misgivings about Aelya's scheme. Zina didn't need to get herself in trouble, and yet she did, without complaint. It was unfair and exploitative, but Aelya needed the help.

Yulia gave Aelya a look, as if this was painful for her.

"I'm doing this for you," Aelya said.

"You're doing this for yourself," snapped Olga.

"Don't you care about this? The regiment where we belong. They're our family."

"And what happens to Lily?" Olga asked, referring to Roza by her nickname. "What about Stone and Honeybee?"

"Let's just get back into the regiment. Once we're there, we can help the others too." She hated to admit that she hadn't thought that far ahead.

"That isn't the only place for us," said Yulia. "I mean, even if it's not with the 586th, there are other regiments."

"But the 497th is where we bled. Two of us died for this regiment."

"This is crazy and we'll all get in trouble," Olga said. She stormed out, pulling her sister by the arm.

Aelya followed, slogging through the muddy yard. She grabbed Olga by the shoulder. "I'm sorry, all right?" she said. "I'm sorry things have been harder for you. But let me do this to help you."

Olga sighed. "Listen, you're a good friend, really. But all of this, it's like trying to use an umbrella in a hurricane. What is it you're really going to achieve?" She put a hand on Aelya's shoulder. "You get fixated on your tiny little quest. Meanwhile, the world doesn't care. Sometimes, things just don't work out. It'll be a lot easier if you can accept that."

Aelya fought against tears. It just wasn't fair. She hated the fact that the two sisters felt their problems were insurmountable. And she hated them because they were going to leave her on her own.

"Just come with us," Yulia said. "Let's stick together."

Aelya was tempted. Just hop onto the train as scheduled and never look back, despite the blood they'd shed for the regiment. But the unfairness of it all just made her more determined.

"I can't. My trunk's already on its way to the front line."

"What a minute . . . what about ours?" asked Olga.

"Um, I guess it's already on its way to the front as well. Zina relabelled everything."

She was expecting an explosion, but the twins gradually broke into laughter. Olga shrugged. "We'll just wait for them to show up. It'll probably take months, but we're used to that sort of thing."

They stood silently for a moment. Aelya thought back to the time she and Yulia had searched a transportation depot up and down for their missing baggage. And she remembered all the other things the three of them had been through, from training to battle.

"You know, I wasn't very nice to you during training," said Olga. "I'm sorry. We both are."

Aelya was taken aback. While she hadn't exactly forgotten, she'd filed those memories away, like everything else that was difficult to talk about, just hoping they would fade with time. A lump caught in her throat. "That's all right. It helped toughen me up." Aelya hugged them both tightly. "It's still going to be dangerous in Air Defence. Stay safe."

Olga started toward the facility's gate, but Yulia turned around and leaned toward Aelya to say softly, "You always think of everyone, even when you're wrong. Stay . . . stay safe, sweet girl." They couldn't openly talk of after the war. They might as well have been talking of life on another planet.

And then she left to join her sister. Aelya was alone.

CHAPTER 11: FLIGHT

Being aloft energized Aelya. As if it was her natural state of being. The moment she cleared Astrakhan's airspace, her burdens lightened.

Slipping into the maintenance depot and absconding with the two-seater Yak had been easy. Zina's doctored paperwork had passed muster. With the confusion of a new regiment moving in, no one took much notice of a lone pilot from another unit flying out.

Aelya wasn't free of anxiety by any means, but nothing seemed insurmountable to her now. She was headed toward a combat zone in a stolen plane on an unauthorized flight and without ammo. But a pilot's fears were ones she understood, so she would constantly check her bearings and be aware of her surroundings, on each side and above and below. If something went wrong, there would be no ambiguity. Everything was always simpler in the air.

She planned her route to follow in the wake of her regiment. Feigning curiosity, she weaseled the information she needed from Legend. After turning north at a planned waypoint, she approached her refuelling stop, at the same airfield in the northern Rostov region that the regiment would have used. It was easy to pretend to the control tower that she was a laggard dealing with mechanical trouble. Eyebrows were raised upon her arrival, which people assumed reflected the usual bureaucratic incompetence, bad luck, and general confusion that followed the Air Force everywhere. She gave Roza's name when she signed the forms on arrival.

Roza could handle any trouble if it came, she thought impishly. Well, there would only be trouble when she got Roza, Stone, and Honeybee back into the fold as well; then it would be a good problem to have.

She still had a lot of flying to do, and it was well into afternoon when she finally made it to the new airfield near a village called Nizhneye Chaynikovo. She calmly used the right call signs and was cleared to land.

One of the swing duty mechanics guided her ride to shelter. A look of recognition, then confusion, dawned on the woman's face as Aelya removed her helmet. But like so many members of the Air Force, the technician just assumed somebody somewhere knew what they were doing and towed the Yak trainer away without another word.

Aelya steeled herself, rehearsing what she would say to Red to force her way back into the regiment. She wasn't due back at the 586th yet, so she technically wasn't absent without leave. That was weak, but it was a start.

As she walked past the row of sandbagged revetments and onto the main dirt track that ran parallel to the airstrip, a jeep pulled up next to her. A doll-like face beneath a crisp new officer's cap, framed by perfectly coiffed shoulder-length dark hair, greeted her.

"Honeybee!" Now a full lieutenant. Aelya observed the insignia on her new shoulder boards with a touch of envy.

After a moment's surprise, Honeybee recovered her snarky quality. "I was expecting somebody new."

In the silence that followed, Aelya felt perhaps she should hug Honeybee, but they had never quite warmed to each other, no matter what they had been through together, and the moment passed. Aelya just gave her a playful pat on the back as Honeybee gestured to her to climb aboard.

Honeybee glanced sideways at her as she pulled the jeep away. "You look like hell and you haven't even been back at the front for two minutes."

Honeybee looked very well put together, as always. Wherever she'd gone to do the officers' course must have been much nicer than a fish plant.

Honeybee was used to chauffeurs, so Aelya wasn't sure when she'd had time to learn to drive. Her lack of experience showed as Honeybee moved in fits and starts, careening along dirt tracks made muddy by spring rains. They drove away from the cluster of Air Force buildings and into the village proper. Honeybee pointed out the ordinary log houses that had been commandeered for their quarters, canteen, and supply stores.

"Where do the villagers stay?" Aelya asked.

"The Germans took care of that. Half of them are dead, so there's plenty of space for everyone," Honeybee said with unfeigned delight.

"So how did you make it back to the regiment?" Aelya asked.

"What are you talking about?"

Honeybee—she made everything sound easy, but Aelya knew how much she fought for what she wanted, often in underhanded, dishonourable ways.

"Didn't you get the order to return to the 586th?"

"Oh, that," Honeybee said. "That's been rescinded. Haven't you heard?"

"But I thought all appeals had been exhausted."

"The boss's son stepped in personally."

"Boss?"

"Vasily Stalin, silly. Wait a minute—what're you doing here if you haven't heard?" Honeybee thought about this a bit, then doubled over laughing. "You sneaked in here, didn't you? That explains why the control tower thought you were a new pilot. Clever. But at the same time, stupid. You are going to be in so much trouble."

The jeep rolled to a halt outside the most important building. Possibly a former schoolhouse, the white wooden hall now served as the pilots' club.

Honeybee gleefully hopped out. "Well, let's have a drink to our happy return."

"Are Stone and Lily back too?" Aelya said as she followed Honeybee out of the jeep.

"Stone's here, but I have no idea where our beloved star is to be found." She didn't seem concerned.

"Shouldn't we go to operations first? I need to sign in," Aelya said, still nervous about what punishment might await her.

"This place is completely disorganized. What's the point? Let Legend sort it out tomorrow."

When they entered the spacious clubhouse, cheers arose from the pilots who were enjoying a drink. Standing on the threshold, Aelya basked in the smiles from the familiar faces of those who approached her. Stitches. Stone. And Lucky, who'd probably thought he'd never see her again.

Everyone stiffened and stood upright, and immediately Aelya knew what was up. She turned and stood to attention as well. She remembered to salute Red, who glowered at her.

"Come with me."

PART II:

The Front

CHAPTER 12: SUFFERING

Roza grimaced from pushing the needle and thread through the lining. The final stitch done, she placed the pair of faded and worn felt shoes onto the bench next to her, admiring her work in the sunlight from a half-shattered window. The smell of cow manure wafted into the little two-storey log house.

"I'm done taking them in," she called out.

This bit of tailoring took her back to her mischievous days in training, when she'd adjusted oversized uniforms for the women's regiment in the night. Taking on that task had ingratiated her to the others at a time when her sheen of arrogance had come perilously close to getting her kicked out of the Air Force.

A wrinkled, unkempt, middle-aged woman tromped down the stairs, an adolescent boy, equally shabby, following in her wake. With little apparent gratitude, they looked at the shoes. Roza didn't expect much from her hosts. They'd done enough for her already.

Roza had hitched several rides to get to this dusty little town near the Moscow-to-Kursk road. The Air Force had taken up occupancy in this village. Unfortunately, it was the wrong Air Force unit. When the officer in charge refused her billeting room, this family had taken her in.

Their home wasn't so different from her grandfather's country house outside of Moscow. As a child, she'd played hide and seek with him,

dodging behind sturdy, handcrafted furniture much the same as what adorned this home.

The boy, Fedka, slipped the shoes on, finding them a snug fit. They
belonged to his father, who had been murdered by the Nazis, along with
most of the village's adult men. His mother had screamed at the murder-
ers and been shot for her trouble. His aunt Nina took Fedka in, even
after suffering her own egregious losses. She had a son who kept to himself upstairs. When Roza saw him, he would lower his eyes and hobble
on one leg. Perhaps he was unable to bear the humiliation of doing do-
mestic work. No older than twelve, he had volunteered to help a "trophy
battalion" responsible for scavenging battle material that the Red Army
could reuse or re-purpose. His leg had been blown off by a mine. These
two boys, along with Nina's elderly mother, were perhaps all that was left
of the family.

From whispers, Roza gathered that the Germans had murdered both
Nina's father and her husband. She had another son, somewhere on the
front lines, and a daughter, taken away to slavery in the West. Roza
shuddered to imagine what horrors were visited upon her. Perhaps it was
better to simply hope that she was already dead.

Outside, peasants made thin from their meagre food and hard labour toiled to plant the sugar beet crop. This land had been fought over
during the early spring, so the villagers had planted nothing until now.
They eked out whatever resources they could find; with luck, they would
manage almost a full harvest. The villagers wouldn't let Roza help with
planting. Their lives had been shattered by the war, but at least by contributing this little bit to the Air Force, they would be fighting back.
Perhaps they thought of her as an angel of vengeance, above such menial
work. More likely they thought she'd just get in the way.

As much as they had suffered, Roza felt her own pangs of loneli-
ness. She was struck by the closeness of this family. In their worst times,
they held each other closer.

Her stomach rumbled. Roza had refused to take any of their paltry food. This existence was a far cry from the gluttonous excess of the Rublev café. Moscow hadn't felt like part of the real world. The time she'd spent with Stitches seemed as if it belonged to someone else. She clung to the warm memories of his touch. With him, she'd been free from the shackles of concealment and deception she'd imposed on herself.

Stop making this into a thing, she told herself. It was just a fling. Hadn't Pavel from the Komsomol declared his undying love for her after just one night? She'd been happy to play along, but once the war started she didn't want him leaving for the front believing in a lie. Her rejection shattered him, and she wondered if that had driven Pavel to his death prematurely. She pushed the guilt away. Pavel was responsible for himself, just as she was for herself.

Now at the front, desire felt foreign to her. Those feelings for Stitches belonged to a different person who couldn't exist here. In Moscow, they'd thought they'd never grow old because they were immortal. Here, they'd never grow old because they might die. No, she wasn't going to lie to herself. Just as there had been no room to love Pavel, there was none to love Stitches, and it was better that way.

A heavy truck rumbled down the dirt road that bisected the village, screeching to a halt not far from the window where Roza sat. At last, my ride, she thought. Two days ago, she'd managed to contact her division using an Air Force telephone. While waiting for the promised pickup, she'd considered hitching a ride to the 74th Guards' airfield but relented for fear of getting even more lost.

She eagerly gathered her suitcase and ran outside.

A few villagers had assembled to see what the fuss was about. A pall hung over them. The soldiers who emerged weren't Air Force. They wore tired expressions and threadbare, mud-covered Red Army uniforms. Men from a labour battalion.

A bearded, bespectacled man in a fisherman's cap, looking like a cheap replica of Lenin, accompanied a frowning lieutenant out of the truck's cab. Murmurs of discontent grew as more villagers appeared. Nina emerged with her mother, who spat on the ground.

"You only ever show up to accept credit for someone else's work or to take away what little we have," the old woman complained. "So which one is it, Comrade Chairman? I'm guessing the latter."

Roza had heard all about the chairman of this farming collective, or *kolkhoz*. He'd fled before the Nazi occupation. Understandable, since Communist Party members were shot out of hand by the invaders. But the villages he'd left behind had been gutted. The Germans thoroughly plundered the town, wantonly raping and murdering, only pausing to take the strongest villagers away for slavery out west. By the time they left, they'd burned down the schoolhouse and the food stores.

Liberation had brought little joy. With the Red Army came Party bureaucracy, complete with heavy demands to feed the army and to supply labourers for the war effort, including children for trophy battalions. What more could this imitation Lenin demand?

"You've hardly been gone a week," another villager shouted. "You've been too long among the bureaucrats if you think beets grow that quickly."

The lieutenant and a pair of soldiers stood behind the *kolkhoz* chairman, sneering contemptibly at the villagers. Emboldened, "Lenin" ignored the accusatory noise and read a note from his pocket. "By order of the District Party Committee, this village is hereby required to lend any and all remaining draft animals for the defence of the motherland."

The villagers glanced nervously at the fenced-in yard where their one remaining cow grazed obliviously.

"We use that cow for her milk," one villager said. "It's the only sustenance we can get after everything you keep taking. It's of no use as a draft animal."

"I decide what's of use or not." Puffed up, he nodded toward the cow. A party of soldiers marched dutifully toward the fence, and the old women of the village backed away.

Then Nina's mother sprang forward and blocked their path. "Don't you dare," the old *babushka* said, staring the soldiers down.

They glanced back at their lieutenant. There were other Air Force personnel staying in the village. Roza noticed them keeping their eyes down, disappearing from the village's main street.

At a signal from the lieutenant, two soldiers grabbed the elderly woman by the arms as she hurled obscenities at them.

Nina ran toward them, but more soldiers blocked her. "We've lost so much already," she begged. "Please don't take this as well." A soldier clipped her on the shoulder with his rifle butt and knocked her to the ground.

Other villagers, all women and elderly, stepped forward. The *kolkhoz* chairman put his hands up in a conciliatory gesture but quickly hid behind the lieutenant. The labour soldiers brandished their weapons, and the lieutenant fired his pistol into the air.

A warning shot, but a people who'd reached breaking point, who'd already seen the worst from the Germans, weren't about to take this from their own soldiers. Their supposed protectors.

Roza's senses came alive. She smelled the gunpowder, sweat, and earth. Danger fed her. Everything came into focus.

"Haven't they suffered enough already?" she asked, stepping in between the villagers and the soldiers.

"And where would you have us go, then?" asked the lieutenant. "To the next village? You don't think they've suffered as well?"

Roza had no easy answer. In every fibre of her being she wanted to fight back, as she'd always wanted to fight something. Fedka ran over in his new shoes to pull his aunt away. Roza remembered her vow to

Dmitriev; she needed to be a good little propaganda icon. She bit back a harsh response.

The sputtering, buzzing drone of an airplane engine made itself known. It soon grew loud enough to attract everyone's attention. Roza recognized the sound instantly as that of a little U-2 biplane, the Air Force's jack of all trades.

People rushed to the fence, eager to know who the visitor was. The plane banked and descended, landing in the field behind the cow's yard, pulling up to a stop very close to the street.

The pilot hopped out and shed his helmet and goggles. "That's quite a welcoming committee you've arranged for me," Stitches said.

Roza rushed over to intercept him as he walked toward the main street.

"Bet you weren't expecting me to be your ride back to base," Stitches said after they'd exchanged quick kisses on the cheeks.

After the initial excitement of the new arrival, the villagers and soldiers started to drift back to their confrontation. They barked at each other, their words growing heated.

"Want me to get you out of this place?" Stitches asked.

Roza quickly briefed him on the trouble. "We can't leave them like this," she said.

Stitches waded in immediately, hugging and kissing Nina and her mother. "Mama! *Babushka!* I've missed you so. Are these *makhras* your guests?" He turned to look at the labour battalion, prominently showing off his gold star.

"This is your family?" the lieutenant said.

"I don't recognize him," "Lenin" said, scratching his head.

"I've been away for so long—no wonder you don't recognize me, Comrade Chairman. I'm with the 74th Guards fighter regiment. You might have heard of us? We just recently had a visit from Vasily Stalin. He's very keen to look after our well-being and morale. I'd be very happy to report to him concerning your excellent conduct and compassionate treatment of my family and the villagers. After all the Nazis have done, it's much appreciated."

The lieutenant scrunched his eyes and shot Stitches a doubtful expression. But Stitches, with his new captain's stars and shoulder boards, clearly outranked him. The lieutenant sighed, shrugged, and ordered his men back onto the truck.

"What?" the *kolkhoz* chairman said, spluttering. "You can't just leave like that." He soon caught the stares of enough villagers to make him beat a path to the truck. "You think you're better than me?" he shouted as it drove away. "How many of you survived by helping the Germans?"

Mud kicked up in the truck's wake. Everyone remained quiet, staring until it disappeared over a ridge. They were relieved more than happy and barely acknowledged Stitches and Roza as they dispersed.

Fedka tugged on Roza's sleeve. "Are you going to leave us?"

"I have to."

Roza received a heartfelt goodbye hug from Nina. She couldn't bear the family's looks of gratitude. They would suffer worse now.

She and Stitches hurried to the U-2.

"The labour battalion will be back, and they'll probably lose the cow anyway in a few days," Roza said.

"Even if you lose, it's still worth the fight. It was nice to do something for a family. For once."

"After all they've suffered, they just couldn't take it anymore."

"I know what that's like."

As he helped her into the rear seat of the plane, he leaned in to kiss her on the lips, but Roza recoiled.

"Not here," she said. It didn't feel right. She just wanted to leave. She wasn't sure if it was the place, or a fear of thinking about the future. For whatever reason, Moscow had been different.

"You shouldn't feel guilty for experiencing joy while others suffer," said Stitches as he stood next to the plane. "Haven't we all suffered enough?"

Roza sighed, turning her head this way and that before finally looking at him. "Moscow was different, do you understand?"

"Of course." If he was hurt, he hid it well.

Roza kept going anyway. "I can't . . . it's just . . . some feelings don't have a place here. Maybe in the future."

Stitches leaned against the fuselage. "I think about that all the time —the future. Isn't that why you convinced Dmitriev to send you back here? For your vision of the future?"

Roza held out her hands and he clasped them. Everything in the look they shared spoke of what they couldn't tell others, what they could barely tell each other.

"I want a future with you," he said.

"And so do I, but we're here to fight. After the war."

"After the war." He pulled his hands away.

"Let's just leave this place," she said as he climbed into the front seat of the U-2. "I've been away from the front long enough."

He smiled. "You're right. Dema's been more insufferable than usual in your absence."

She just wanted to get back to fighting against an enemy that was easy to identify and destroy. There was a simple morality in combat that neither of them would ever find when contemplating what the arrests of their families had made them do. Or what this village had done to survive. And what the Red Army had to do to these villages. She was relieved to go back into a war zone. If she did her job, she would get what she wanted most: her family back together, and free from fear. But as Stitches started the plane, she realized that if she got that, she would have to leave him behind.

CHAPTER 13: HIDING IN PLAIN SIGHT

"Birch twigs are supple. You can give them a good twist, like so."

Aelya listened as the old peasant instructed her on intertwining leafy branches into the netting the village women had woven. She could only make out every other word over the rain pelting them in the open. She wished she had even half the cover they were giving to the planes. Couldn't they have done this somewhere under shelter?

"Makarova!"

At Red's shout, she stood to attention but gave off an air of misery for his benefit.

"What the hell are you doing out here?" Red asked. "The last thing I need is another sick pilot just as things are heating up."

"If you recall, Comrade Commander, you assigned me camouflage duty as my punishment." Only then did Aelya pick up on the implication that she was once more an active pilot.

Red ran a palm across his face, wiping away the dripping rain. "Troyanov didn't tell you? That damn wet noodle messed up again." Everyone agreed that was the most apt description for their new chief of staff. He was as in over his head as his predecessor had been comfortable in the role.

With a wave of his hand, Red signalled to the peasants that Aelya was done. They would continue the work they'd been drafted to do, disguising this airfield under camouflage netting, dummy buildings, and fake trees. Aelya plodded with the regiment's commander through a mucky dirt track toward the command post. On non-flying days, Red tended to walk rather than drive a jeep. He thought weathering the elements important for building one's character.

"How many planes are now undercover?" he asked.

"Twenty-one or twenty-two."

"I thought you'd be done by now."

"Everyone's trying their best, Comrade Commander." Then, worried he might assign her camouflage duty again to make up the shortfall, she added, "It's not like I had the right skill set to help out. I'm much more productive in a cockpit."

"Don't get smart, Makarova."

"Sorry. But am I back on active duty, then?"

"You're still in trouble for stealing the Yak trainer." He sighed. "But it's not like you were trying to desert."

Aelya swallowed, tentatively relieved they'd reached the end of the matter and she hadn't dragged anyone else down with her. When it had come time to explain herself, she'd made the theft seem like a solo enterprise. It wasn't convincing. She was sure Red could have punished Zina if he'd felt like it. As it was, he'd let the matter go.

There was the added annoyance that Petrushka's old navy unit had called about the theft of their liaison's plane and their missing pilot. All sides agreed to simply sweep it under the rug, because everyone liked Petrushka. His was the crime of an incorrigible scamp. Meanwhile, Aelya was treated like a neurotic. To excuse her behaviour, Dr. Krupenya had written her up for mental stress.

Maybe I *have* been dealing with a sickness, she thought. While on reserve, her anxiety had been nearly unbearable, a shadow looming over her. Arriving at the front had relieved much of it, though nightmares she could barely remember continued to plague her.

They walked past layers of trenches and sandbags, but there was little sense of urgency to this war zone. The sound of rain was calming, uninterrupted by the constant explosions that were among her first memories of Stalingrad.

Red shook his head as they moved around slit trenches and anti-aircraft pits, muttering, "Still not enough."

For Red, no amount of preparation would ever be enough. But during Aelya's stint on camouflage duty, she'd learned just how much the local peasants had been bled dry, first by the Nazis and now by their own liberators. She couldn't believe what they'd had to live through—those few who had survived.

"The people have no more to give," she said.

Red didn't reply as he held open the door of the command post for her. Inside the log and sandbag-lined bunker, set halfway below ground, the pace of the staff officers was much slower than it would be during the heat of battle. They were chatting instead of frantically yelling at each other. The adjutant, Legend, arranged a cup of tea for her to warm up.

Then Red sat her down on a crate next to the central map table while he stood facing her, leaning against the table with his arms crossed. "Tell me, Makarova, what do you think of all these defensive preparations?"

She sensed this was a test. "Well, it's much more extensive than anything we had at Stalingrad."

He stared at her in silence.

Perturbed, she continued, "So, it would seem we're going to stand and fight."

"Yes, it certainly appears that way. Our side got too cocky after Stalingrad and caught a bloody nose at Kharkov. We won't make the same mistake again. The supposed summer offensive is probably going to be a defensive operation instead."

He motioned for her to lean closer to the map while he waved his hand over a section marked up in coloured pencil. "Right here." Red pointed to a curve drawn in red denoting the battle front. Its arc radiated from a central point, the city of Kursk. "Can you see it?"

Aelya nodded. A fight was brewing, and it was going to be huge. Both sides were obviously building up. It wasn't clear who would strike first, but the where was obvious. The Germans were going to try to pinch off the bulge by attacking in a massive pincer movement and trap masses of Soviet soldiers, the same way they had again and again the past two summers.

"How do you feel about getting back into battle?" Red asked.

She itched at the prospect of fighting again for reasons she could barely understand. She was afraid, but the fear exhilarated her, the same way jumping out of a plane with a parachute did. She thought about the answer he'd want to hear. "I'm looking forward to killing Germans."

He laughed. "Then I truly admire the gutsy initiative you showed in your hurry to get back to that. That's the sort of attitude we're going to need."

She'd always been a little afraid of Red, but after his farewell speech, she saw him in a different light. And now that he seemed more open to her, she was going to take that initiative he'd praised.

"Well, sneaking back was probably the only way I was going to get into combat. You seemed pretty happy to fight without me."

Red shrugged. "Nazis are one thing. But there's not much you can do against VVS bureaucracy. I'm as shocked as you are about Boy Stalin's intervention."

There was little Red seemed afraid of. As his scarred face attested, he'd already been through some of the worst of the war. So his disrespectful attitude toward Stalin's son didn't surprise Aelya, but his reluctance to go against the bureaucracy did.

She said, "It seemed pretty easy for Lily, Honeybee, and Stone. No one asked any questions when they returned to this regiment."

"Get to your point."

Was there a point? Maybe she was just grousing. Jealous. But she remembered what was eating away at her. "You didn't select me for officers' training."

Red nodded slowly, so Aelya continued. "Instead, I had to ferry over new planes like some yellow-mouth. Legend said you had big things in mind for me. I shot down three planes over Stalingrad. I won a Red Star. And that's all you had for me?"

"Did Legend tell you that?" His jaw tightened. "Did he also say it was precisely because I think you're leadership material that I had you stay? I thought you'd be better off remaining on reserve with the regiment. You saw what it was like when all those hooligans were waiting, seeing no action. They needed a stabilizing influence."

"So you wanted me to be a nursemaid to the pilots?"

"You might not believe this, but you're respected by the men."

This echoed what Olga had said to her. She should have been grateful, but again the unfairness drove her to push back. "But not enough to be an officer."

"All pilots are going to be officers anyway. It's in the new regulations."

"Really?"

"Go see Legend after this and get your new shoulder boards. I'm promoting you all the way to full lieutenant. Guards lieutenant," he added.

He paused, perhaps waiting for some sign of gratitude, though he didn't look at her. Then he continued, "You're smart and dedicated, a good pilot. But I also wanted to see how you handled others when they needed guidance. The officers' course is just window dressing. I wasn't sure if the transfer was going to go through, so I thought you might as well get some practical experience. In spite of, or maybe *because* of your disciplinary issues, now I've seen what you're willing to risk to get what you want. You're the right type of daring. And the way you didn't reveal your co-conspirators? It's no wonder these people trust you. They'll risk themselves for you."

This was all a far cry from the stern lecture he'd given her about putting the needs of the regiment ahead of her friends. That was when he'd made her blame her squadron commander, "Auntie" Lara, for a botched mission.

"Or did you make me stay because you trust me to toe the line?" she asked.

His lips twisted as if to say she was pushing it.

Aelya clenched her fists, not willing to relent. "Am I right, Comrade Commander? What's the real reason you picked me to stay behind? Is it because you knew I wouldn't kick up a fuss the way the other women would have?"

Red placed his hands on the table and leaned forward but turned slightly in her direction, still not looking at her. "You know more than most when the greater good demands sacrifice."

She still wasn't sure if that made her strong or meek. Looking down at the map, she realized there was only one way to find out.

Battle.

CHAPTER 14: THROWING DOWN THE GAUNTLET

The door to the operations bunker flapped, but no one wanted to close it. The turn to warmer spring weather had made all the air base's half-buried facilities stifling, humid with sweat and mould.

As regimental navigator, Frost had convened a group of eight pilots near a wall map pinned with reconnaissance photos. Aelya had arrived with the rest of the pilots five minutes ago, but Frost still hadn't started. He was gossiping with Honeybee about the latest news from a recent trip to division headquarters. Apparently, General Platonov was keen to enforce the prohibition against gambling. Although she was frequently a big winner in the regiment's high-stakes card and domino games, Honeybee didn't miss a beat, continuing to smile and nod.

As they waited quietly by a sturdy wooden pillar holding up the bunker's roof, Sirin tapped Aelya on the shoulder. "I wish you hadn't gone through all that trouble to sneak back to the front," Sirin whispered. "If I'd known what you were going to do, I would have told you what was in the works."

Aelya raised her eyebrows. "You knew Vasily Stalin was going to rescind the order?"

Sirin smiled, her almond eyes sparkling. "So, what happened to those towering behemoths? What were their names?"

"Everest and Elbrus?" Aelya shrugged. She'd written a letter to Olga and Yulia explaining what had happened when she returned to the regiment but had heard nothing back. Military post being what it was, it was entirely possible they would only receive it at the end of the war. Or her message might have been censored beyond all recognition. Even if they'd received her letter, maybe they still didn't want to return.

Sirin whispered, "If only you'd let me know what you were up to."

Aelya wanted to say that she didn't know if Sirin could be trusted, but that seemed hurtful and stupid, considering they were about to fly a mission together.

Frost clapped his hands and called the pilots to attention. "I've brought you together from different squadrons for this mission because you're unfamiliar with our new Yak-1b model. You're also new to the area of operations. Before you can begin combat sorties, Red and I wanted you to get oriented. Stone, you have the floor."

The big peasant girl walked them through the flight plan. It would take them over enemy territory at high altitude, mainly to get familiar with the terrain. She droned on, unable to fake interest. Most of the male veterans had started flying combat missions, and Stone couldn't wait to get down to business. But due to the static nature of the front lines, combat mostly meant escorting deep bombing runs on transportation networks behind enemy lines. The frequently cloudy conditions, vast spaces, and number of potential targets kept aerial encounters to a minimum. Everyone knew, even hoped, it wouldn't last.

"Aelya, you'll be leading Sparrow Two flight, with Lily on your wing. Sirin and Offal will be your second pair." Stone had already discussed this with Aelya ahead of time, no doubt at Red's behest. Aelya and Honeybee were both guards lieutenants. Although Honeybee had seniority, she would be flying in Stone's group of four. This was clearly arranged to give Aelya a chance to make good on the promise Red had seen in her.

Leadership. Aelya wasn't prepared for the idea of people depending on her that way.

"Now, for you new guys, here are my ground rules." Stone gathered the four new pilots closer, Sirin among them.

Roza lingered at the back. She seemed a more subdued version of herself since returning from Moscow; she hadn't wanted to talk much about her time there. Aelya remembered the strange disappointment and stress that accompanied her own foray into the civilian world when she'd gone to the aircraft factory in Saratov to pick up the new Yaks. She couldn't imagine what it would have been like for Roza to see her family again, and she hadn't shared.

Honeybee sidled up to Aelya. "So, what do you want to call these new guys?"

"I thought we don't give them nicknames. They haven't passed the test." It was conventional wisdom that a pilot's first dozen combat missions were the most dangerous. If they survived that, then it was worth giving them names.

"The Germans are biding their time," Honeybee replied. "The ground's too wet. I reckon it will be at least another month before things heat up. Might as well get creative."

"Sirin already has her name. And both Petrushka and Stone called her wingman Offal. I think it's because he used to work in a butcher's shop."

"What do you think of the other two?"

Aelya shrugged. "That skinny blond guy has really gotten on my nerves." He was an annoyingly earnest diehard Communist who'd taken over from Aelya as Komsomol organizer. Aelya had officially given up that role as a result of the abortive transfer to the 586th. What did she know about the remaining pilot? She'd learned that he was Muslim at dinner. He wouldn't touch any of the suspicious meat the canteen served, not believing assurances from the cook that it didn't contain pork.

Stone closed the briefing. Everyone pretended to have been paying attention. Aelya realized ruefully that every pilot was depending on their immediate superior to know what was going on. They'd need to be sharper when the action heated up.

"Right, let's get to work," said Stone.

The sleek forms of eight new Yak-1b fighters cut across a rapidly yellowing afternoon sky. They moved in two groups separated by height and distance but able to help each other in case of trouble. Stone's four and Aelya's four scanned the sky constantly.

The wheat fields below had burst into green for spring. A flat, patchwork sameness stretched out to the horizon, broken up only by the familiar scars of battle below.

Aelya was tense about Roza's flying on her wing. They hadn't paired up since the early days at Stalingrad, when Roza had thrown herself headlong into battle, frequently butting up against or ignoring Aelya's instructions. Aelya wondered if she would do so again. Perhaps it was part of Red's test. At least this was supposed to be a non-combat mission, she thought.

"We're now over enemy territory," Sirin called out over the radio, noting the line of entrenchments they passed over, sure to be consecrated in blood and fire soon.

Sirin was a qualified navigator and had helped plot the route. She noted the landmarks as they approached the city of Orel. With only intermittent cloud cover, the snaking Oka River was easy to make out. Trying to pick out the military installations among the buildings was more difficult.

"Intelligence says there's a major airfield down there, probably disguised," Sirin said. "Designated Orel West."

Aelya looked down to her left, past the sparrow drawing she'd stuck just below the canopy. It was difficult to discern anything unusual among the industrial buildings outside Orel. But she thought she saw the telltale signs of pits dug for anti-aircraft emplacements. And a road that seemed to lead nowhere. Was it a disguised airstrip? "I think I see it," she said.

"The Green Hearts are supposed to be based there," Sirin responded. JG 54, known for the green hearts its pilots painted on the sides of their fighters, was one of the top Luftwaffe units in kills scored.

"Sounds like you want to take a look," said Aelya, half joking.

"I'm up for a fight if you are," said Roza, speaking for the first time in the flight.

"How are we doing for fuel?" Sirin asked with concern. The confidence she exuded on land now had abandoned her.

Aelya pressed home. "You stay in high cover, then."

"Shouldn't you check with Stone first?"

"Sparrow One-Zero, do you copy?" said Aelya. "Sparrow Two flight is going in for a closer look."

A garbled response from Stone. New radios—they always took a few tries to tune properly and had an annoying tendency to cut out at inopportune moments.

"Sounds like a yes to me," said Roza.

"Do you think the base is fully operational?" asked Aelya. She made note of the location for further reconnaissance.

"Maybe we should ask them," Roza said. "Should be right around dinnertime. You can find all the pilots in the canteen."

The Germans always liked their punctual meals. This was the perfect time for reconnaissance, with few enemy fighter patrols.

"Let's go, then." Aelya banked her plane to dive. She noticed that her hands were shaking. She wasn't sure if it was from fear or a thirst for action.

Roza followed on, matching her movements.

They rolled and dived steeply. The whine from Aelya's engine rose in pitch and reached a crescendo. G-forces pulled her forward. It was like the time she'd conducted reconnaissance with Auntie, grazing the tree-tops to scout out enemy armour positions. Only this time, she wouldn't forget to shoot.

On closer inspection, the arrogant Germans had barely bothered with camouflage. She could see supply dumps, gun emplacements, and equipment strewn around. Little dots of activity scurried among the buildings.

"I'm going in fast," she said. "When I pull up, I'm going to break hard right, give the anti-aircraft guns a more difficult target."

She knew Roza would scoff at such basic instructions, but she couldn't assume anything. Assumptions got people killed.

She lined up a path, trying to include as many structures or vehicles in her line of fire as she could.

Her descent continued. No sign of gunfire. She pulled in to level hard, feeling the dizzying effects of an impending red-out as the blood rushed to her head. Her eyes adjusted, and in that instant, seeing the enemy installations ahead of her, she fired her guns. The cannon and machine gun chewed up wood and sandbags and concrete.

A flame shot upward. She'd hit something sensitive.

"Roza, you still with me?"

"Right behind you."

She pulled up hard.

White tracers streaked past her canopy, but she rapidly escaped their range.

Glancing back, Aelya noticed the tracers were replaced by white puffs—explosions—as larger anti-aircraft guns opened up, all clearly visible from the new bubble-style canopy of the Yak-1b.

"I think they might be upset," said Roza.

Aelya kept peering behind her. Dark shapes moved on the airstrip, too far away to discern what. If they had any sense, the Germans were scrambling their fighters.

Looking herself over, Aelya saw that she'd wet her trousers and she burst into laughter. She'd actually missed this, she realized.

Back up high, Stone's flight had circled round to meet them. "I thought you were joking," said Honeybee to Aelya.

"Good job," said Stone. She'd never begrudge someone the chance to get in a few more hits on the enemy.

"That's all well and good for you," said Honeybee, "but I think you got them mad. I see possible vultures, bearing six-five high."

"Don't blame Mars," said Roza, referring to Aelya by her nickname. It came from her favourite book, *Aelita*, and its titular character, the queen of Mars. "They might be coming for me. I hear they're offering a bounty for the plane with the white rose painted on its side."

"Ha," said Honeybee. "How much is that? Fifty kopecks?"

"They use reichsmarks," said Roza.

Oh, how Aelya had missed them.

"We're low on fuel and carrying too many yellow-mouths," said Stone.

"We're ready," said Sirin.

"Not today," said Stone, radioing a thirty-three to their vectoring station; that was the code for returning to base. "Dive to pick up speed and get out."

With that order, Aelya's tension from strafing the enemy dissipated. Only a light giddiness remained. She laughed uncontrollably.

"Your transmitter's still on," said Honeybee. "Who are you and what have you done with Mars?"

CHAPTER 15: PARTNERS

Between the intermittent bad weather and both sides' reluctance to engage, Aelya's daily duties grew monotonous as the daylight hours lengthened. The desultory schedule of group exercises and routine patrols over the airfield was a far cry from the terror and death-filled days of Stalingrad, yet Aelya was more exhausted.

The last thing she wanted to do in the early evening was socialize in the pilots' club, pretending to understand the jokes of inebriated colleagues as they went through their stores of homebrew, long after they'd disposed of their vodka rations. Nevertheless, she dragged herself to the large building they'd converted into their social spot. Her eyes down, she trudged a few steps behind Baby and Vino, having finished the end-of-day briefing.

The door flew open and Honeybee bounded out purposefully.

"Not staying for a drink?" Baby asked.

"All they've got left is the liquor chassis," Honeybee said.

The two men looked sour and talked to each other in consternation. Distilled brake fluid was not what they were looking for.

Honeybee pulled Aelya to one side. "I've got my own ideas," she said quietly. She signalled for her to follow. "Come on, I need some help."

Help? The least Honeybee could have done was ask nicely, but that wasn't her style. Still looking impeccably glamorous after a long day, she dragged Aelya down the village's side street. When Baby asked where they were going, she just winked.

Nizhneye Chaynikovo's structures were all partly or wholly burned. Out of sight of the others, Honeybee stooped lower and skulked into the long shadow of a half-demolished house. Wading through the ruins, she knelt by the sooty hearth and pointed to a burlap sheet. "Look under there."

Gingerly, Aelya lifted the sheet, revealing a couple of dull silver square tins.

"Grab those and hide them under your shirt," Honeybee ordered.

Aelya tried not to stain her hands with charcoal as she picked up the tins by her fingertips. According to the labels, they contained military is-sue tea leaves, imported from China.

Honeybee was already out of the abandoned house and turning a corner.

Aelya stumbled awkwardly to catch up, the bulky tins not remotely discreet under her uniform. "Why do I need to be doing this?"

"Don't worry, it's nothing illegal. I just don't want anyone making a big deal of it."

But why am I doing it? Aelya wondered. But she knew. Looking awkward and bulky was just too undignified for her comrade.

At a two-storey house standing at the edge of the village, Honeybee stepped past the rickety fence into a yard overgrown with wild grass. Despite scorch marks, the walls looked mostly intact, and a plume of smoke from the chimney marked it as inhabited. Honeybee put two fin-gers in her mouth to whistle.

A moment later, a thickset woman with a green head scarf wrapped around her dirty blonde hair stomped out of the house. She wore a white nightdress and carried an oil lamp. The woman beckoned them to follow her inside. Beyond the door, they were met by a steamy wave of heat. A large pot bubbled over the wood stove that dominated the main room, lit by flickering candles on stout wooden furniture.

"Where is it?" Honeybee asked.

The woman signalled to the bulges under Aelya's field shirt. Honeybee nodded. Aelya revealed the tins, which the woman snatched up eagerly. She flicked her head toward a sturdy wooden table piled with cups, plates, and cutlery, as if it was waiting to be set for a large gathering.

Hands on her hips, Honeybee leaned to one side, her gaze falling to two clay jugs with cork stoppers, which sat beneath the table. She uncorked one of them, then grabbed a mug from the table and poured some of the contents out. She took a sip.

"Mmm. It's infused with elderberry. You should try some." She held out the mug to Aelya.

As Aelya sipped, the home-brewed vodka warmed the inside of her cheeks and burned as it went down her throat. She stifled a cough, tasting lingering sweetness. "Let me guess, you want me to carry these back to our quarters for you."

"No. Well, more than that. In fact, I have a larger proposition for you. I'd like you to be my partner."

"Doing what?"

"Lots of things. But first off, we need to build a bathhouse for this decrepit backwater. The Germans burned down the previous one."

Aelya's first thought was a positive one, but she remembered who she was talking to. "What are you playing at?" she asked.

"Don't you want to do something good for this village?" Honeybee turned to the other woman. "Honestly, some people can only think of themselves—am I right?"

The woman smiled wryly. She turned her focus to the pot, using a spoon to stir the contents.

Honeybee paced around Aelya. "We help the village recover from the occupation. Improve the general hygiene. Of course, members of the regiment will be able to use the bathhouse. For a fee. What else are they going to do with that money? Gamble it away? At least now, they'll smell good. But none of that can happen without your help."

Aelya rolled her eyes. "I don't know anything about construction."

"I don't need that. The boys in the support battalion owe me. I got them a hundred tins of British corned beef."

"I don't even want to know how you managed that."

"I just need your help obtaining materials."

Aelya gave her a skeptical look.

Honeybee waved her hand. "Seriously, you're the perfect person. You can talk to Cricket and Dr. Krupenya."

"You think they'll support this wild idea?"

"They will if you make it about a drive for better hygiene. Like one of your suggestions when you were Komsomol organizer."

Aelya eyed her suspiciously. Honeybee kept her mask of calm, the same one she used when playing cards. There was something more to this than what she was saying, Aelya suspected.

Honeybee clucked at her. "Come on, don't act like you're above this. I know you."

She guided Aelya to a dim corner of the room where the candles gave their faces a grotesque quality. She pulled Aelya's face close to hers. "That stunt you pulled on the enemy airfield . . ."

"What's that got to do with anything?" asked Aelya.

Honeybee crossed her arms. "I always thought you were a bit of a useless goody-goody, like Timur." That was the name they'd given the new Komsomol organizer, after an insufferably helpful children's book character. Aelya kept silent about her own love of the *Timur and His Team* stories.

Honeybee continued, "You came close to sabotaging your own chances for leadership."

Red couldn't truly punish her for buzzing the enemy airfield. After all, that's what they were supposed to do—shoot at the enemy. He'd simply berated her for going off plan, while over his shoulder, Cricket gave her a wink of approval.

"Do you think leadership is something I want?" Aelya asked.

"Maybe. I know your type—you're scared of responsibility. But that's only because you're not applying yourself in the right areas."

The gall of Honeybee, to probe into her thoughts like that. Worse, was she right? Could Aelya really be self-sabotaging? That was the behaviour of traitors. "And just how should I apply myself?"

"As my business partner. And don't tell me you wouldn't love using the bathhouse." Honeybee sighed. "I can't believe I survived Stalingrad without a good bath. You know my apartment in Moscow has its own bath?"

"Yes, I don't know how you've managed all this time," said Aelya in a mocking tone.

"Survival isn't just physical. Some who haven't had a scratch won't make it out of this war. You either embrace it or you shut yourself out and let it grind you into nothing. With this, you might actually come out ahead in the end."

Aelya wasn't sure she should be talking about profiteering in the open. She glanced at the villager.

Honeybee smiled. "It's all right. This woman is perfectly well compensated. Aren't you?"

The woman laughed. "You kill Germans, I'll help you with anything." She turned away and added something to the pot. Scars were visible on her back through the nightdress as she sweated.

Aelya could almost see Honeybee's point, but the scheme was un-Soviet and might land her in trouble—trouble that would conveniently fall on Aelya's head more likely than not. As with so many ambiguities she experienced on the ground, she wanted to avoid this, keep herself to the simple choices of air combat.

Aelya twisted her lips and considered the proposition. "You'd be better off with someone else. What about Sirin? She seems well connected."

Honeybee shook her head. "You really want to let this one pass?"

Aelya persisted. "I hear her father's NKVD."

Honeybee twisted and leaned against the wall. "I don't trust her. She has lies written all over her face."

"Sounds like a kindred spirit."

Honeybee laughed hard.

Aelya checked her watch. "I'd better turn in before curfew."

"So it's really a no?"

Aelya went to the door, but Honeybee reminded her to take the jugs of vodka. Aelya groaned.

"Hey, if you want an extra share . . ."

These non-combat lulls were difficult to take because they held back the daily vodka rations. She'd come to rely on the drink's soothing effects, as much as she hated the taste. The elderberry in the homebrew would certainly help it go down.

"That's a good girl," said Honeybee.

Aelya slapped away the condescending pat on the back. But Honeybee's abrasiveness was like a handrail she could hold on to when she questioned everything else in her life. She knew where she stood because of it.

Before she left, Aelya leaned her head back through the door frame. "Don't ever change, Honeybee."

CHAPTER 16: REDEMPTION

Today might finally be the day, thought Aelya. She had yet to meet the enemy in open combat since arriving here. Over the past month or so, the only aerial loss the regiment had suffered was a mid-air collision between two new pilots during training. Miraculously, one survived with several broken bones, while the other bailed out completely unscathed. Red duly signed both of them out of the regiment for not meeting his standards. Two technicians had also been killed after rolling over their jeep. Had Aelya become so callous that two deaths and a maiming seemed quiet?

But operations were increasing in pace, and after waiting an hour in readiness two, she and the three others in her flight got the call to intercept a small group of German bombers. Ground observers had spotted them late. With luck, though, Aelya would at least catch them on the way back.

"Anything?" Aelya asked.

Lucky, Vino, and Spam, all replied in the negative. After all the fuss over the latter's religious diet, Vino joked that his new wingman should stick to the Spam the Americans sent over because he could be sure there was no meat in it at all. And so another nickname was born.

After reaching two thousand metres, Aelya tensed when Lucky called in two silhouettes.

"Just the two?" Aelya said over the radio.

"Easy pickings," said Spam.

"Calm down, new guy."

They could be the enemy, or they could be Roza, whose pair had been sent free hunting earlier. "Osprey One-Two," she called out to Roza, "this is Sparrow Two-Zero. Is that you in Ivan One-Four, bearing southeast at height one-nine-zero-zero?"

"That would be me, Sparrow Two flight."

"Any luck?" Aelya asked.

"The fish aren't biting today. We're low on fuel, so we're going thirty-three. I hope you do better."

"Well, you wouldn't happen to have spotted a half dozen vultures? Vectoring station Giraffe last reported a sighting over Shura One-Five, bearing northward."

"If I had, they wouldn't still be in the air."

Aelya waggled her wings in salute as her foursome passed Roza's pair.

She continued her scan. This was going to be another disappointing scramble. Her mind drifted to Stalingrad, as it often did in the quiet space of the cockpit. Not any particular moment of the battle, but the sensations she'd experienced. The memories lingered like a shadow of some creature slavering over her shoulder, its jaws made of steel, ready to crush her as it made grinding and clanking noises she associated with bullets striking home.

"Contact," Lucky called out.

Aelya flinched, sweat dripping down her back.

"Two o'clock," Lucky continued. "I see five vultures, height one-two-zero-zero."

They were close enough that Aelya should have spotted them earlier. She cursed her wandering mind.

The enemy was lower than they were, and staying on course. Perhaps Aelya hadn't been spotted yet. When the telltale box frame in their midst came into focus, her heart leaped with excitement. A Rama. This type of unorthodox-looking German reconnaissance plane had eluded her and Auntie at Stalingrad, to her shame. It was high on the VVS list of priority targets. This one had four Messerschmitt Bf 109 fighters as escorts. She vowed not to let it get away.

Aelya reported in to Giraffe. "This is Sparrow Two-Zero, confirmed a Rama with four escorts over Ivan One-Five. Height one-two-zero-zero. Engaging."

"Need a hand, Sparrow Two-Zero?"

Aelya was momentarily confused by the intruding voice because she didn't expect it. Roza's high-pitched lilt was unmistakable.

"Aren't you low on fuel?" Aelya replied.

"Still got enough to help out."

Aelya grunted, then proceeded to lay out an attack plan. Roza and her wingman, Dema, would stay high, watching out for more vultures. Aelya and Lucky would split off and dive for the Rama first, then peel away to respond to the inevitable counter from its escorts. Vino and Spam would come at the Rama from a lower altitude, hopefully surprising it if they hadn't been spotted yet.

"Better get a move on," Roza called out. "More contacts."

Aelya continued circling, assessing the new threats.

"Looks like four of them, definitely heavies," said Roza, referring to German Focke-Wulf Fw 190 fighters. These were a new fighter type Aelya had learned about in classes at Astrakhan. *I guess time in reserve was good for something*, she thought.

"We're still going in," said Aelya. Eight fighters against their six was still fairly even. "Just keep the heavies off our backs."

There was no more time for deliberation. Aelya would show Red that she deserved his respect. She kept her flight split, increasing the separation between her pair and Vino's. The two pairs of Bf 109s had the Rama bracketed, ready to strike at anything coming from the left or right.

"We're going to hit the escorts directly on the right. That will give you a short window," she ordered Vino. "Strike the Rama from the same side with speed. Try to keep it between you and the other pair."

She was about to dive at the first pair of Messers when Lucky called out, "Mars, vultures on you at six!"

She glanced back and saw two fighters closing and ordered a break.

As she looped around, an Fw 190 came into view, approaching at an angle. She broke again, narrowly avoiding most of its tracer stream.

Metallic thunks shook her seat.

Dammit, she thought. The glare of flickering flames to her right caught her attention. Her wing was on fire.

"Lily, where are you?" she said in annoyance, but she got no response.

She scanned the sky but lost sight of the Rama. The Fw 190s that attacked her were looping around ahead of her. She tipped her Yak into a dive, letting the wind starve the flames of oxygen.

When she levelled out, she was lost. She searched for Lucky. She searched for anyone. Several dots moved around. She wiped sweat from her eyes, pulled her goggles down, then quickly pushed them up again. Sweat, combined with the distortion in the armoured canopy, impaired her visibility too much.

"Lucky," she called.

"Sorry, Mars. I lost you for a second." She saw him climbing to catch up from her left.

In the distance, two Yaks circled a hard-turning, boxy silhouette—the Rama wildly trying to shake its pursuers.

"Stay on the Rama, Vino. Anticipate the turn. I'll get the escorts."

"Hurry up, then," said Vino. "I can't get through."

Aelya shivered with the realization that she'd misunderstood what was happening. She looked around and saw yet another pair of Yaks tangling with two Messers. Were these Vino and Spam? Where were the

Fw 190s? What the hell was going on? The fight was getting out of hand, and doubt crept into her mind.

"I got the Rama!" Roza said.

The square-framed plane dropped like a rock. Aelya slammed her hand on the dashboard, wanting to curse Roza for confusing everything. But she spotted more vultures diving at her. She pulled into a tight turn, expecting a chase, but looking back, saw the enemy make an about-face. Having failed to protect the Rama, the German fighters saw no point in sticking around, even to defend the downed crew. They hightailed it out of the area.

"We're low on fuel," Roza reported, "so we have to thirty-three. If you're pursuing, you're on your own, Sparrow Two flight."

Aelya looked at the torn fabric in her wing. She called out to Vino. Spam responded that Vino's radio seemed to be out and that his own engine coolant was showing low.

"I'm still good to go," said Lucky, who finally reformed on her wing. But they were in no shape to carry on the fight. Aelya should have been happy they'd gotten the German reconnaissance plane, but she questioned Roza's recklessness in going for the Rama and failing to keep the heavies away. Was that because Aelya was in the right, or was she just jealous?

She bit her lip, then said over the radio that her flight was returning to base.

CHAPTER 17: MARRIED TO THE CAUSE

A cool spring breeze swept over Roza at the threshold to her revetment. During another uneventful mission escorting bombers to soften up enemy troop positions, her main challenge had been staying alert. They had got in and out before any response from enemy fighters came. Sensible, if a little disappointing. Her excitement from downing the Rama had worn off days ago.

Roza turned her head toward loud voices from the revetment sheltering Stitches's plane. She went to check on the commotion. Stitches talked rapidly in the Special Department man's face. This special officer was so quiet normally, she couldn't even remember if he was the same man who'd searched for imaginary traitors at Stalingrad. Two blue-capped NKVD guards held Stitches's armourer, Ulanova, by the arms, while his crew chief, Nemchinov, clasped his hands, pleading and on the verge of tears.

Everyone knew that this odd pair of technicians were lovers. Roza remembered their rare display of affection when they'd been rescued from another regiment that had drafted them into their ranks during a transportation mishap. The cheeky pilots of that regiment had propositioned Roza, Honeybee, and Olga while they retrieved the mechanics. For that, Roza had orchestrated the theft of a water truck to supply their showers.

The officer said, "No matter Comrade Ulanova's sterling service record, she is of questionable stock—she comes from a people whose loyalty is suspect." Ulanova was a Kalmyk, from the Caucasus region.

Stitches backed off, his hands up in conciliation. He used Stalin's own words: "'The sins of the father are not visited on their sons.' Or their daughters."

"And look how that generosity has been rewarded," the special officer replied. "Time and again, the Kalmyks have betrayed the Soviet Union, yet each time they have been dealt with using a light hand. Kalmyk villages, including Sergeant Ulanova's hometown, have collaborated with the Nazis. They've given false legitimacy to the German invasion and helped to kill good Soviets. Better ten innocents be locked up than let a guilty one go free to kill ten more."

Ulanova, for the first time since Roza had met her, looked cowed. Roza knew well that once people fell under suspicion, there was no going back. The Kalmyk people had been labelled unreliable. It would only get harder for Ulanova.

Nemchinov, Ulanova's lover, spoke up. "This is ridiculous. You can't possibly accuse her of treason. Look at her awards for loyal service and technical excellence. She's a true socialist."

"All traitors appear like good citizens to the unobservant."

Roza snapped at the officer. "It was a pretty clever disguise, pretending to be such an outstanding servicewoman. Making sure her pilot's weapons were in top shape so he could shoot down so many Fascists. By the way, how many Germans have *you* killed?"

The officer's eyes narrowed and his cheek twitched.

Stitches spoke in even tones. "What more can Comrade Ulanova do to show her loyalty? Everyone here knows that her love for her country is matched only by her love of Comrade Nemchinov."

Roza thought, with some unease, of what future lay in store for these two lovers. Did the nebulous promise of "after the war" keep them going the way it did Stitches? Maybe that could be used to their advantage. She turned to Nemchinov. "Do you love her?"

"With all my heart." The crew chief removed his *pilotka* cap and pressed it tightly to his chest.

"Don't you want to marry her? I mean that's the point, right?"

Nemchinov looked flustered, but Stitches caught Roza's look and nodded. "Yes, of course," he said. "In all this commotion, I'd forgotten they were secretly engaged. Weren't you two just waiting for the right moment to marry?"

Roza and Stitches both knew the shadowy men had inconsistent interpretations of marriage. If guilt could be transferred to a spouse, so too could innocence. Roza had heard stories during the Great Terror that some ethnically suspect women were spared by marrying upstanding citizens. Ulanova may have been Kalmyk, but she could become Russian by marriage.

Stitches prodded his crew chief in the ribs. Nemchinov took Ulanova's hands in his and said, "Duya Yagurovna, will you take your vows with me now?"

Ulanova put her hands over her mouth and nodded solemnly.

The special officer grimaced.

In the command post, Ulanova and Nemchinov, still in their mechanic's coveralls, stood before Cricket, who acted in his capacity as organizer for the Party. Roza was shocked at how supportive the *zampolit* had been of the wedding plan. Red approved as well—anything to keep his excellent ground crew together.

It was an impromptu affair, performed in the midst of the day's duties, right after Roza and her flight finished their debriefing.

The staff looked over with occasional curiosity but were discouraged by the presence of the special officer and mostly kept their noses in their work. One clerk wiped tears from her face. Red made himself scarce during the ceremony, loudly proclaiming his need to finish paperwork. That left just Roza and Stitches acting as witnesses, their respective wingmen completing the wedding party. It would have been cozy except for the unfortunate attendance of the special officer, who was there to make sure everything was above board.

Cricket spouted generic platitudes about the importance of marriage and family to the Soviet people. "I wish you both a long and productive life together, contributing to the furtherance of the Soviet Union, and hopefully bringing many future good Soviets into the world." He chuckled but was met with silence.

Clearing his throat, he signalled to Legend, who brought over a tray with glasses of vodka. As the happy couple and their witnesses took their glasses, Cricket raised his own. "To Comrade Stalin, without whom our happiness wouldn't be possible."

"To Comrade Stalin," Roza muttered, downing her glass with the others. Stalin had been toasted at Aunt Yelena and Uncle Nikolai's wedding. What Stalin had to do with the happiness of any of these marriages, she had no idea.

Stitches's and Roza's wingmen, Starik and Dema, joined hands by the door to form an arch. Ulanova and Nemchinov walked under them on their way out of the command post. Roza couldn't help but notice the sad expression on Ulanova's face.

Outside, a crowd of technicians gathered, as many as could be excused from their regular duties. Ulanova beamed among the women and looked back at her new husband, her eyes aglow.

The newlyweds kissed to raucous applause, prompting Stitches to look at Roza. He leaned over to whisper, "I was thinking about reading some poetry."

"Which piece?"

"It doesn't matter now. I think it would just ruin the moment."

"With you reading, it would." She smiled.

His hand, hanging relaxed at his side, brushed against hers. An electric tingle moved across her skin. Her body remembered clinging to him, naked, lying on the narrow bed in the spare room of her aunt's apartment. For the first time since Moscow, she welcomed the desire to be with him. Still, something in her mind rebelled against it. Something she feared, lurking in the shadows of her memory.

He clasped her hands and faced her. "I can't help but be moved in my soul."

"You're too soft-hearted. Are you sure you belong in the Air Force?"

He came close and they touched foreheads. "Sorry, I'm out of jokes to respond with."

She kissed him, then looked around to see if they'd been spotted. There was nothing to be ashamed of, yet she was afraid, as if being seen would make it real and cross some invisible barrier. The others were still congratulating the newlyweds.

Stitches said, "You know, couples fighting side by side are very much a trend. The Boykos even bought a tank together."

The husband-and-wife team, a tank commander and her driver, had been celebrated in the news as exemplars of familial devotion to the motherland.

Roza said, "Are you suggesting we buy a fighter together? There'd only be space for one."

"Then I'll sit in your lap," Stitches said. "Anything to stay close to you."

Roza laughed grimly. "Then I guess we'd die together."

"Morbid and romantic at the same time." Stitches manoeuvred himself so she was forced to look at him. Another caustic joke died on her tongue. He had a way of breaking down her careful defences.

After a pause, she said, "I don't know if I could take that. After the war, remember? We have to stick to that."

He pulled away for a moment, pacing in front of her, looking as if an outburst was coming. But the cool reactions that served him so well in the air stayed with him on the ground.

"Yes. After the war." His eyes sparkled with genuine happiness. "I'll just have to fight so hard, we'll be done by the new year."

She almost pitied his optimism. It was too beautiful for this war. Too beautiful for this country. She wanted to love him so much. She looked over her shoulder at the special officer. He stood stone-faced by the entrance to the command post, watching Ulanova as if warning that he would keep an eye on her. Roza felt a sense of doom creeping up on them all. It would hang over Ulanova, just as it hung over Roza.

CHAPTER 18: VICTORY ROLL

"What do you think, Lily?" asked Stone.

Flying at two thousand metres, Roza flicked the transmitter to reply. "Either the spotters aren't doing their job or Fritz is up to something. Either way, I'd expect fighters to show up." They were both skeptical of the report that ten medium German bombers, probably Ju 88s, were incoming without escorts. "We still better hit the bombers early, just in case."

Along with their wingmen, they had been ordered to intercept yet another probing attack by the Luftwaffe. For once, they'd gotten in the air ahead of the strike and had a good chance of intercepting it.

Given their heading, the bombers were possibly searching for a Soviet airfield. Better to break up the enemy bombers and force a retreat before they got a good look at the area. Even if that failed, Roza hoped their camouflage would hold up. Unlike the Germans, the VVS had made airfield camouflage and deception tactics into an art form. *Maskirovka*, they called it. From the air, their base looked like a farm, an extension of the whole village, complete with wooden livestock. Not satisfied with mere hiding, they had created at least two fake airfields in the vicinity.

It wasn't long before Roza spotted them: ten Junkers Ju 88s. "No sign of escorts." She searched the patches of cloud.

"All right, Lily," Stone said. "You hunt them down, and I'll stay in cover. It never pays to be complacent."

Roza couldn't help smiling as she acknowledged and plotted a course to take the enemy bombers high, from the direction of the sun. She and Dema had flown together long enough that they didn't need words. They dived into attack in unison while Stone and her wingman stayed up high in an extended figure eight.

The angle of attack was well chosen, and the enemy gunners barely had time to react before Roza laced the leading bomber with cannon fire. Bits of debris struck her canopy with a satisfying patter. Trailing smoke, the lead Junkers released its bombs early. The remaining bombers followed suit, then banked in formation to retreat rather than scatter. The bomber crews who'd made those types of mistakes had already been wiped out earlier in the war, so it would be harder to do now, but Roza still wanted that ninth kill. One step closer to the magic number that would get her gold star. One step closer to her family's salvation.

"Stone, any signs of enemy fighters?"

"Negative."

Even if some were hiding in the intermittent clouds, she should have enough visibility to react in time. Roza needed no further words; she had Stone's permission to pursue.

After the report of approaching bombers interrupted their debriefing, Red took Aelya on a breakneck, bumpy jeep ride beyond the line of anti-aircraft pits protecting their base. She gripped the sides of her seat as tightly as she would her control column during combat. Lucky tagged along, unsure if Red meant for him to follow, holding on to Aelya just as tightly.

Amid a copse of tall aspens and oaks lay an observation platform that looked like a sturdy children's tree house, but with many more levels. Rickety wooden ladders zigzagged up to a wide enclosed platform where the observation crew sheltered their water, snacks, and other essentials from the sun. Aelya could smell urine from the corner where the spotters, unable to leave their posts, must have relieved themselves.

They climbed one last ladder to the roof, above the treetops. There was barely enough space for two people to operate freely. Aelya and Lucky squeezed behind Red. The two spotters assigned to this station, both women, backed up to give way, scowling.

Red swivelled a large pair of range-finding binoculars mounted on a pole to one side. He beckoned Aelya to take a look and said, "Always take every opportunity to observe. You might learn something."

Bombs dropped far away, near a decoy site. Above, a pair of Yaks spit tracers into a formation of Junkers. Was that Roza? The aggressive style matched. The bombers didn't linger, which was typical of the half-hearted strikes they'd been seeing from the Luftwaffe, but it didn't make it any easier to watch from the sidelines. Aelya would much rather be in the fight, but as she often told the young, impetuous new pilots, there would be plenty of fights to go around.

Roza's pair chased after the fleeing bombers, while Stone's pair stayed high, observing smartly. Aelya's eyes sharpened with that awareness that always kept her on edge in combat. She perceived a new pair of dots in the distance that seemed to stalk Stone's pair of Yaks. Aelya silently willed Stone to spot the interlopers, but that was unnecessary; Stone moved her pair to intercept. We're not so thick, Aelya thought. But something didn't look right about the enemy's movements. It took a fraction of a second for her to register that yet another pair of dots had appeared out of the clouds.

The Junkers had maintained their unit integrity. Their damaged leader managed to stay with the pack. Forty turrets kept up a withering wall of machine-gun fire, keeping Roza at bay.

Unwilling to give up, she looped around high to one side, picking out a new target at the extreme right of the enemy formation. Time was running out. They were getting closer to enemy territory and farther from her patrol area. She'd already lost visual contact with Stone.

"Dema, you go first this time. Come in high, behind, and to the right of the target."

Her wingman complied without question. While he began his attack run, she dived rapidly, dropping below the level of the Junkers just as Dema fired a short burst and pulled away.

"Sorry, Lily, I took a few hits. Couldn't get a good line," he said, just as Roza closed below and to the left of the bomber. Its ventral turret swivelled over, but not before Roza sent a tracer stream to shatter it. As she pulled away, her cannon and machine gun peppered the bomber's engine, setting it alight.

She and Dema climbed again, regrouping safely. She saw with satisfaction that the stricken Ju 88 began to lose altitude. Now for the finish.

Aelya watched, paralyzed in impotence as the new pair of Fw 190s streaked down toward Stone. Her wingman tipped hard to the right as his Yak caught fire, then dropped rapidly. The heavies climbed for another attack run. The original pair Stone had been chasing now turned as well. Stone was on her own against four enemy fighters.

A radio call from Stone's wingman that he was bailing out was the first Roza heard of the trouble her flight leader was facing.

"Stone, do you need a hand?"

"Negative." Stone was straining to speak. "You're too far away. Stay on the bombers."

Roza quickly put her comrade's plight out of her mind and focused on lining up the ailing Junkers.

Aelya watched the developing dogfight with concern. While Stone kept one pair at bay with turning manoeuvres, the other pair kept climbing and diving, looking for an opening.

"She's close enough to us," Aelya said. "Can't we help her out with anti-aircraft fire? Scare the enemy away?"

"No," replied Red. "I don't want anti-air to open up unless there's a close, direct threat. They still don't know where we're located, and I prefer to keep it that way. Stone knows how to handle this."

Even with the binoculars, it was hard to track what was happening. After a stretch of uncertainty, the control tower barked over the radio that the enemy had disengaged. But there was no word from Stone. Aelya swivelled the binoculars and locked onto a Yak coming down for a landing.

She let go of the binoculars and slid down the ladders and ran clear of the trees for a naked-eye look, as if she could somehow guide Stone's plane down.

There it was. But it was going too fast, descending too steeply. It veered off course and dipped below view behind a line of airfield structures. Aelya winced even before she heard the crash. Ground crew rushed to the wreck, apparently somewhere near the maintenance shelters and marked by a plume of smoke.

She ran to the jeep. Red and Lucky were already getting in. They drove toward the site of the crash, but had to stop at a line of slit trenches marking the sandbagged supply dumps of the maintenance area.

Stone's plane had plowed into the side of a chemical dump, scattering steel drums across the dirt. Orange flames from the wreckage licked the remains of the installation, but the situation was far from unsalvageable—the aircraft was still in one piece.

Aelya ran to the nearest technician and shouted, "What can I do to help?"

The mechanic waved his arms to stop her. "Get back!"

Someone called out, "Vulture!"

Aelya lost sight of Red and Lucky as she scrambled away, diving into a nearby trench. The buzz of an enemy fighter pierced the air above the roar of the flames. She peeked over the top of her trench to see the silhouette of a single Fw 190 diving rapidly.

Someone shouted a warning to man the guns.

An elbow nudged her; Petrushka had also taken shelter in this trench. "He's on his own," he remarked. "What cheek." His voice held admiration for the brash Luftwaffe pilot.

Aelya stood up, transfixed, affronted by this invasion of their home. Others in the line of fire scrambled for cover, including civilian labourers. Instantly, her mind went back to that time she'd strafed the enemy airfield. Had she killed anyone? What if the Germans had used Soviet civilians? Had she hit them too? Were they collaborators, or just unfortunates pressed into working for the detested invaders? The ugly possibility that she had harmed innocent Soviets she pushed to the back of her mind, and worked to keep it hidden away.

The enemy fighter levelled out, then executed a perfect victory roll, right over their airstrip. She saw the insignia of the Green Hearts, plus another marking: an enormous black bird. The Fw 190 pulled away just as the anti-aircraft gunners opened fire, but their efforts were to no avail. It power climbed and rapidly shrank from view.

The ground crew quickly returned to their shovels. The technicians surrounded the plane, but they weren't trying to get its pilot out. They were shovelling dirt over the stricken Yak.

"What are you doing?" Aelya asked, emerging from the trench.

Zina appeared at her side and grabbed her shoulder. "This is a chemical store. We need to get the fire out or everything could blow. We're lucky the ammo hasn't cooked off yet." She pushed Aelya away from the fire.

"What about Stone?"

Zina shook her head and turned to direct the fire control once more. "Come on, I need a pair of shovels over on that side. Let's move!"

A scream caught Aelya's attention. Katya, Stone's crew chief, rushed toward the fire. Behind her, Stone's dog Volkov yapped, perhaps smelling the fear brewing in everyone. Aelya took hold of Katya's arm as she stormed past. A lean girl, Katya was a head taller than her, and they both toppled into the dirt from her momentum. Katya pleaded for the crew to stop, cursing them.

Aelya struggled to get an arm around Katya. "We need to let them put out the fire. If we don't, the chemicals could blow."

Katya shook her loose. She reached out and pulled Aelya's pistol out of its holster. She pointed it at the nearest technician with a shovel. "Stop right now. I don't care what you're doing—stop right now. She's still alive."

Whether the noise from the fire drowned out Katya's voice or the crew were too aware of their priorities, no one paid attention to her threat.

Aelya and Katya both glanced over at the cockpit. No signs of movement. They didn't know for sure, but left unsaid was that Stone, if alive, might as well be dead.

Red shouted to Katya from behind Aelya. "Comrade technician, stand down!" He firmly guided Aelya away from the line of fire.

Katya faced her regimental commander. Her grip on the pistol wavered.

He stalked past her and grabbed a shovel. "Better one pilot than the whole regiment. You want to kill me, kill me, but I'm not letting this fire spread."

Zina approached slowly from the side with her hands up. "Katyusha."

Katya's eyes softened and she lowered the gun as Zina approached.

Zina reached out and gently stroked Katya on the cheek. "You know Stone wouldn't want you doing this for her. And you know I wouldn't lie to you. We have to do this."

Katya nodded, handing over the pistol. She sobbed quietly as Zina gave her a quick hug. Then Zina gave the pistol back to Aelya, nodding at her.

Aelya took Katya's arm gently and pulled her away so Zina could get back to fighting the fire. If Katya wasn't helping, she needed to stay out of the way. There was no sense hanging around if the chemicals caught fire.

Katya turned and buried her face on Aelya's shoulder, her short dark hair prickly against Aelya's ear. Aelya put her arms around her and watched as their friend was interred, her cockpit becoming her coffin.

Volkov howled somewhere in the distance.

CHAPTER 19: GROUND LEVEL

The truck bucked with every bump and pilots were jostled in the open cargo bed. Aelya was amazed there were no injuries so far. It was one thing to traverse the rutted, dusty roads that connected all the little villages in the area, but now they were crossing uneven grassy fields, winding carefully around hidden entrenchments.

The overcast sky that threatened rain kept holding off. Through the clouds the sun shone brighter each day, drying the famous black earth of the region into yellowish dust. A choking haze kicked up as they drove, forcing the passengers to cover their faces with their sleeves.

Red thought it would be a great idea for the pilots to observe the lay of the land from ground level. Thanks to heavy clouds cancelling flights, it had been easy to find the time to do this. This "scenic" ride wasn't Aelya's ideal way to spend a day off, but it beat trying to keep her eyes open in a humid, stuffy bunker as she listened to political lectures.

The truck passed seemingly endless entrenchments. Massive gangs of labourers, from bent-backed elders to schoolgirls, toiled with shovels and picks. Some sang cheerful songs. Others, large groups of men more Asian in appearance, were empty-eyed and sullen.

The entire landscape had transformed into one massive fortification. The people and villages were no longer part of the geography; the land itself was what mattered, the people were to be used and disposed of. How many of them had disappeared over the past two years, either ground into the earth by the German invaders or taken away as slaves?

A lump caught in Aelya's throat as she thought of these peasants' fates. Between morose silences and outbursts of rage, Stone had occasionally reminisced about village life among peasants just like these. Of her big Ukrainian family, Stone and one brother in the Red Army had been the only survivors after the Germans massacred their home village. Now she was gone too.

And what was left of Aelya's hometown? The Soviet winter counter-offensive had stopped mere kilometres short of Smolensk. Her family and everyone she knew had been evacuated to Kuybyshev, along with the aircraft plant. The city had burned before her eyes. Was it even a hometown if there was nothing left?

As they left the more populated areas of the defensive works, it became easier to focus on other things.

"Who knows when this sector will heat up?" Roza said. "Let's have nice things while we can." They'd been debating how much of a proper celebration to have for Nemchinov and Ulanova's wedding. That rushed ceremony for the benefit of the special officer was deeply unsatisfying for everyone.

"We haven't had a real bash in a long time," said Honeybee. "It'll be like Kupala Night last year. Too bad you weren't there." She elbowed Sirin gently.

"I love a good party, but I don't think Ulanova wants one," Sirin replied.

Roza shrugged. "She seemed all right with it."

Aelya watched her face, looking for any semblance of worry or sadness, any sign that she'd been affected by Stone's death. But Roza was focused on frivolity. That was probably for the best, Aelya reminded herself. Better to distract herself from death. Soon there'd be little time to avoid it.

Honeybee shrugged. "We should do one anyway."

Normally cheery, Sirin cinched her lips and paused before saying, "She might say yes, only to not hurt Nemchinov's feelings. But how much can she truly celebrate without her parents?"

"Nemchinov's aren't here either," said Aelya.

"It's different for the bride." Sirin spoke condescendingly, as if there was a huge gap in age between them. "And it can't be easy for her parents, being Kalmyk."

"And what about your parents?" Honeybee asked, glancing sidelong at Sirin. "Maybe one of them might be what some would term 'unreliable.'" She nodded toward the many labourers the truck passed.

Honeybee and Sirin looked each other up and down. Kalmyks. Tartars. Koreans. Word had been flying around of betrayals by numerous Asian peoples who were against the cause. Despite Sirin's Georgian surname, Honeybee was clearly implying something about her ancestry.

"I could say the same about you," Sirin said, staring right back at Honeybee's almond-shaped eyes.

Looking at the two of them, Aelya realized that where Honeybee used her appearance to hint at exoticism, for Sirin it was different. There was a shadow over her, a hidden danger.

Honeybee retorted, "I just have a touch of that blood." She stared at Sirin for a moment, then broke into quiet laughter while the other shrugged.

Aelya wasn't sure if Honeybee had taken up her suggestion of partnering with Sirin, but the bathhouse was fully operational and Honeybee was charging fees, so something must have happened.

The line of trucks screeched to a halt and a liaison officer called for all the pilots to disembark. They found themselves in something resembling a massive construction site. Aelya wondered if there had been this many people building the great pyramids of Egypt.

They were in a semicircular fortification of reinforced earthworks and trenches. Multiple lines of trenches connected the emplacement with other strongpoints that dotted the landscape from one horizon to the other. Aelya quickly oriented herself and saw that they all faced northward, toward a flat stretch of open grass, bounded by dark green patches of forest in the distance.

"Do not stray beyond the last line of trenches just north of this strongpoint," called out the liaison officer. "You'll be walking into minefields."

From the air, the battlefield appeared so vast, it seemed fruitless to predict where the enemy might go. It was much clearer now. Looking at the way the forest contours created a funnel from the north into the open plain. Aelya realized that this was where the battle would take place. If it was obvious to her, it was also obvious to the Germans. Surely one side or the other should be hitting the enemy while they were getting ready. Well, that was what the commanders were supposed to figure out. She was happy to concern herself with simpler matters of flying.

In all her contemplation, she'd missed the droning introduction by an artillery officer who was in charge here. "This is where the Fascists will be hurled back. Where the superiority of our socialist system is on full display. Productive labour. Talent and merit rising to the occasion, regardless of birth . . ."

He was just a political organizer. This was supposed to be a battlefield orientation but now they were getting a propaganda screed. Roza rolled her eyes and slid away from the cluster of pilots. She flashed an inviting smile at Aelya, who discreetly made her way over.

"Do you think Ulanova would prefer to wait? Maybe celebrate after the war?" Roza asked. "Then she could have a storybook ending," she added with a hint of envy.

After the war. Surely, Aelya told herself, all these security measures and expediencies that were unfairly targeting their comrades would end after the war. The truth would come out. Looking at Roza, remembering her comrade's own hidden past, Aelya wondered how much would really change.

"Who knows what will happen?" Aelya said. "A wedding is a good idea. They have to seize the moment, I guess."

Aelya thought about her own desires. Where once she'd thought she was in love with Stitches, she had come to think of everyone as brothers and sisters. It was better, she decided. Opening her heart any more than that would just leave her vulnerable to more pain.

Roza's expression soured. "Do you ever wonder, if we could just go away anywhere, where you'd want to be? I mean, does anything we do here matter?"

Surprised, Aelya took hold of Roza's arm. At least she didn't pull away. She took a guess as to what was really bothering Roza. "I know what happened to Stone was . . . Look, you have to stop thinking like that. Yes, we all thought Stone was indestructible. That's how we fighter pilots feel about ourselves. Well, guess what? We are, until proven otherwise."

Roza shook her head but broke into a slight smile. "You sound like Red."

"And what did Red say about chasing down those Junkers instead of staying with Stone?"

"That it was the right thing to do. The smart thing." She still didn't sound convinced of it.

This unsettled Aelya. Roza was her rock. Always so reliably aggressive. Always prickly. Lively, not gloomy. Never running from a fight. What was this almost timid side she was showing?

Aelya leaned closer to Roza. "You had to go for the kill. That's what makes you you. You have to stick with that."

Roza seemed embarrassed. "Never mind."

The political talk was over. Stitches and the other squadron commanders paced with the artillery commander, observing the view from an anti-tank gun emplacement while other pilots milled around, chatting with the *makhras*.

Stitches waved them over. "If you skip over their *zampolit*'s platitudes, there's some useful information to be had here," he said quietly. "This is the second time they've tried to dig this emplacement. Some German artillery spotter in a balloon got the measure of the last location and they got pounded until they moved."

"A balloon?" Roza said. "Why don't we just take it out?"

"A bunch of people have tried," Petrushka chimed in, "but Fritz always spots our fighters and reels it in. Apparently it's based in a forest with tree cover and a ton of anti-aircraft guns around it."

"Sounds like a challenge," Aelya said, looking at Roza, who arched an eyebrow.

Stitches said, "Let's not get carried away. We need a plan first. If it's a good one, then we can bring it to Red."

Roza stared into the open space behind Aelya. She wasn't the same girl anymore, the one who in training had an opinion on everything and constantly sought something to fight. Aelya was conflicted about pushing Roza into risky actions, but she needed the old Roza back. "Look, I don't know how to say this."

"What?"

"You need to get over Stone."

"I need to? Or you need me to?"

Aelya swallowed. Somewhere deep down, that creeping fear gnawed at the pit of her stomach. Was Roza right? Was this about her?

Roza held up her hands. "I've got my own war to fight right now. Whatever you need to deal with, get it sorted without me."

Aelya backed away, looking to hide somewhere in the whirlwind of activity. She wandered forward, close to the last line of trenches they had been warned about. She watched as a woman in uniform supervised soldiers placing mines in the vast open space before the entrenchment.

The woman directing the mine laying called a break, and her men gathered around as she ladled water from a bucket. There was an easy warmth among them. The woman's uniform was so dusty and worn compared to Aelya's crisp number.

She looked at Aelya and they exchanged the slightest of nods, a silent acknowledgement of the connection between this combat engineer on the ground, and the women tasked with protecting her men from the air. Once the battle began in earnest, so many of these *makhras* would die. They looked up to the Air Force for protection. Aelya realized clearly that she had a responsibility that went beyond her fellow flyers. It was something she'd always known, but now it felt real.

CHAPTER 20: THE NIGHT RAVEN

"Escorts at two o'clock," Petrushka reported. "Height, one-eight-zero-zero, maybe one-nine. They're trying to use the sun."

Roza squinted in that direction, trying to make out the enemy composition. The dots coming into view definitely outnumbered the eight Yaks of Stitches's squadron. That was on top of the formation of Heinkel bombers they'd already spotted.

She flexed her gloves, itching with sweat as she adjusted her grip on the control column. Aelya's words danced around her mind. She needed this. Her heart pounded with the anticipation of diving in.

"Looks like we'll finally have a good fight on our hands," said Stitches. "KV, take your pair and descend to gain speed to intercept the bombers. Petrushka and I will stay level with our pairs and put ourselves between you and the fighters." They were well rehearsed with these tactics.

"Lily," he called, "take high cover."

Roza swallowed. She was being ordered to gain a height advantage and stay out of the thick of fighting, only picking her spots when opportunity or urgency dictated. It was precisely how she'd been operating these past weeks and was the safest way to get her award and get out of here. She'd had enough of that.

"Negative, Stitches," There was a staticky pause, so she pressed on. "If you want someone to hang out there as bait, Dema and I will do it, right Dema?"

"I'm good with being bait." Her wingman had a fighter pilot's healthy paranoia. The way Dema saw things, the safer an option sounded, the more dangerous it always ended up being.

Roza took control. "We'll switch with KV's pair. Stitches, you and Petrushka keep your four up high and get ready to hammer them with numbers." Before she received any response, she banked and dived toward a gap between the enemy bombers and fighters, with Dema following faithfully.

"All right," Stitches said, "we'll do it your way."

KV took his pair high, while Roza and Dema threatened the twin-engine Heinkels from below, forcing several pairs of enemy escorts down to catch them. Stitches and Petrushka's pairs moved to intercept. Most of the Fw 190 fighters peeled off to meet them, leaving four heavies to speed toward Roza unimpeded.

"Four on your tail, Lily," Stitches called. "I don't think I can reach them."

"Don't try," she said. "We've got them handled." Glancing back every half second, she said to Dema over the radio, "Time to brush off an old favourite. You ready, Dema?" That was the signal to use a tactic that they'd worked out many times in exercises.

Looking back constantly, Roza counted down. Three . . . two . . . one. She pulled hard on the stick and rolled, her body whipping against the side of the cockpit. She knew without looking that Dema was breaking in the other direction. The blocky profile of an Fw 190 crossed her view as it overshot her. The German realized his mistake and tried to escape with a hard climb, but Roza had already anticipated the move, lining up the empty space ahead of him.

Closer . . . closer . . . fire!

Roza sat with the rest of Stitches's squadron on the grass surrounding the airstrip. Sleeves rolled up, uniform unbuttoned, she tried to let the sweat evaporate as she baked in the sun. The others must have already been thinking of their vodka ration. With the sun going down, they'd finished their last sortie of the day, and Roza looked forward to speeding through the debriefing and just getting some rest.

Petrushka punched her on the arm. "Damn, that was some trick you pulled on that heavy. I got to say, I've missed seeing that."

He knelt down as Volkov bounded happily toward him. He had taken to caring for the dog since Stone's death.

It had been a feast. KV and Stitches each had a kill. Two others had probables. But Roza was the star of the moment. After she had taken down one Fw 190 on the initial pass, the enemy fighters became disorganized and scattered, allowing Roza to chase down and destroy a Heinkel that had retreated.

"I don't know why everyone keeps talking about these Green Hearts," said Petrushka. "They don't seem so tough." They'd been on the lookout for black bird markings on the fighters but were disappointed. Roza began to doubt this daring enemy pilot even existed.

"They're probably using us to get rid of all their new and useless pilots first," said Dema.

A truck drove up the side of the runway, stopping nearby and dropping its rear gate. The squadron wearily rose to board.

Stitches put a hand on Roza's arm. "Can I talk to you first?"

She nodded.

"We'll walk," he said to Petrushka.

"You'll be late. Troyanov won't like that."

"Troyanov's always late himself." Yet another reason they couldn't stand their new chief of staff.

Petrushka made kissing noises. "You guys going to swing by the bathhouse before the briefing?"

Roza laughed and turned to Stitches. "Maybe we should. I'd hate to disappoint." The bathhouse had rapidly developed a reputation for lurid escapades, which ensured maximum profit for Honeybee.

Stitches stammered, "No. Well, I mean—" Roza touched his arm to put him at ease.

She wanted to play with him like this. It reminded her of Moscow, as if she could recapture that time. She could see there were more pressing concerns, though. "All right, you wanted to talk to me about something?" she asked.

"I'm concerned about you taking unnecessary risks."

"Come on. It's just like Stalingrad. You've been away from real action too long." Had he already forgotten what that battle was like? She'd challenged and occasionally disobeyed his orders. He'd always end up going along, if only to keep the squadron together. And inevitably, she'd be proven right.

"It was a good plan, but dangerous," he said. "You didn't see it, but another heavy nearly caught you because you lost too much energy turning after those bombers. Next time, get back to cover like I ask?"

"I like getting into dogfights. I'm good at it. And the Germans are squeamish about fighting close-turning battles."

"You know they have a reward out for the White Lily?"

"How many reichsmarks is it up to?"

She laughed, but he reacted with a serious look, saying, "You're falling into their trap."

"No, they're afraid of me." Roza put her hands on her hips and tilted her head. "Are you trying to protect me? Preserve me for after the war?"

"I'm a squadron commander trying to preserve his best pilot."

While she'd been calmly parrying his arguments, he'd grown agitated. He was breathing heavily. And the way he looked at her . . . They drew close. She wanted to kiss him so badly.

"There's no need to prove anything . . ." he said.

Her brows furrowed

". . . like you did anything wrong when Stone went down."

She wanted to snap back, say that she knew she hadn't made any mistakes. But now that he'd brought it up, she realized it had been preying on her mind. Had she been too eager to get her kills? If these latest two were confirmed, Dmitriev would have what he wanted and she could go back to her mother. Her "after the war" would begin. Could she really leave, just like that?

"Oh, you beautiful idiot. I'm not worried about that," she lied.

"What is it, then?"

In the light of the setting sun, she felt overwhelmingly alone. "Hold me. Just hold me."

What mattered to Roza was the here and now. There would be no future unless they made it through. And they held each other as time and everything around them seemed to slip away. No war. No past. Just them.

The drone of the Li-2 transport bearing Dmitriev reverberated through the pilots' clubhouse as it landed. With practised obliviousness, Roza pretended not to notice, sipping home-brewed vodka and berry compote as she awaited her visitor and decompressed after low clouds had cancelled that afternoon's sorties.

Colonel Dmitriev appeared at the door. Pilots who'd known the former commissar eyed him suspiciously and muttered to each other.

"Put down the drink, Kulik." He motioned for Roza to leave and she complied, though slowly, and only after a sigh.

Before exiting, he tapped a piece of scrap metal next to the doorway; it displayed the names of all the regiment's pilots, their victories were tallied in chalk.

"I see that you're close," Dmitriev said as she exited the club. "Honestly, I thought you'd be past that by now."

"I will be, once ground confirmation comes in. And besides, if the VVS rules weren't so stringent, I'd have been long past that point. Can't you do the same thing as when you made me a 'fighter ace' at four victories?" When a news crew from *Red Star* had interviewed her at Stalingrad, Dmitriev had ordered an extra victory star painted on the side of her plane to imply she was already an ace.

"It's one thing to exaggerate like that for the news, but we're talking about an award to be conferred on you by Kalinin himself. Just keep up the good work. And don't get killed."

"How is my family? I haven't received any letters." She wasn't sure if this was due to the poor state of the postal service or her family's negligence. She certainly hadn't expected correspondence from Zhora or her aunt. As for her mother, perhaps she didn't know what to say. That was how Roza felt; she hadn't written anything beyond a perfunctory note acknowledging her arrival back with her unit.

Dmitriev said, "I've lined up an apartment for your mother. But I'm not trusting her with it until she starts her new job at the metro. For now, she's staying at a communal apartment for workers. The housing committee chair is keeping tabs on her for me, but she's well on her way to becoming a model citizen once more. Of course, that's all contingent on you becoming a bona fide Hero of the Soviet Union."

Stitches emerged from the command post after his squadron leaders' debriefing. He struggled out of his flight gear. Legend, always on the ball, had already retrieved Stitches's clean uniform to change into. The diligent adjutant held one out for Roza as well. She took the clothes and found a supply shed to hide behind for privacy as she changed.

Dmitriev continued speaking with her from the other side. "If you do your part, your past will no longer exist. But for your present, just be a good girl, please. Stay quiet around this foreign reporter and let me handle everything. And look feminine. We can't have the Brits thinking our womankind are all haggard and manly."

"Much better than a grubby sniper or a squat tank driver," Roza said, emerging from behind the shed with a smarmy twirl.

"Exactly."

Dmitriev manoeuvred Stitches next to her and adjusted the latter's officers' cap. "Beautiful," he said. He motioned for them to follow and jogged toward the transport plane.

Meeting a foreigner. This was a rare change from the usual propaganda duties. It was one of the few times Roza was genuinely interested in what Dmitriev had cooked up.

They caught up to the colonel at the steps of the Li-2, where several dignitaries waited.

Roza wasn't sure how to greet an Englishman. She relied on her imagination and the few stories she'd heard about King Arthur and, more recently, about Edward VIII. The English all seemed connected to royalty. This had been reinforced when the current king sent gold watches to two of her former comrades in the 586th who'd fought off forty-two enemy bombers in one mission. Perhaps this man was a royal. Should she curtsy?

She dispelled her foolishness and shook the man's hand as instructed by Dmitriev. His name was Jack, from what she gathered. They were all called Jack, weren't they?

The British correspondent had clothes finer than any she'd ever seen. Did they all have gold watches, or just the nobility who oppressed the masses?

It occurred to her why it was important for Dmitriev that she behave. It was not just for Roza's sake, but to limit what this foreigner heard. The troubles people like Roza had gone through were not for outsiders to hear. Well, she thought, while the Soviet people had their own problems, they were trying, weren't they? In spite of all her family had been subjected to, she felt a defensive sort of pride in her country in the presence of this outsider.

Dmitriev put his arms around Roza and Stitches. "We have our own royalty," he said, then snapped at the translator, "Wait, don't use that! Try this. 'No one is born special. But here in the Soviet Union, our leading lights are not nobles but those most willing to contribute to our cause, be they man or woman.'"

Stitches stood next to her after being introduced, shaking the correspondent's hand.

"Dmitriev seems to think we're an ongoing story," she said out of the side of her mouth.

He turned to lock eyes with her as they posed like a golden couple. "Let's give them what they want."

It was what she wanted too, wasn't it? But it would only be playing at happiness. She knew if she gave Dmitriev what he wanted, what she needed to do to get her family back together, then he would make her leave the front. And that meant casting Stitches aside.

The reporter asked Stitches, through the translator, what it was like to fly with such beautiful women, and Stitches, blushing, composed himself. "In the air, facing the enemy, we're all brothers."

Dmitriev frowned at that and whispered something to the translator. Roza was sure he was playing up something else entirely.

"What happens when the girl is in danger?" asked the reporter.

"I can take care of myself," Roza said.

"She certainly can," Dmitriev said, beaming. "The Fascists are scared of her. They've even posted a bounty for shooting down the famous White Lily."

The reporter looked intrigued.

"In fact," Dmitriev continued, "the Germans have sent one of their top aces specifically to target her. They call him the Night Raven."

That was the first Roza had heard of this.

"They mentioned it in our briefing," Stitches whispered. "*Hauptmann* Schreck, a *staffelkapitän* in JG 54. He made a name hunting our aces up north on the Leningrad front. They say he has over a hundred kills."

"I'm flattered," Roza said.

"What if the Night Raven threatens your girl?" asked the reporter.

"I'll kill him before that happens," said Stitches.

Roza leaned in, "Not if I get him first."

That elicited a laugh from the reporter, who seemed besotted with her. Dmitriev was very happy and decided to cut things off while the going was good and hustled the reporter back up into the plane.

Dmitriev put a hand on Roza's shoulder. "That would really be something, if you destroyed this Night Raven. Why, I might even allow myself to imagine a foreign tour, like that sniper, Pavlichenko, did."

Roza smiled. "Only I'll be better behaved."

Dmitriev positively bounced up the steps of the Li-2, bound for the next stop on his tour with the British correspondent.

"How much do you want to bet that I kill the Night Raven before you do?" Roza said as she and Stitches backed away from the airstrip.

"Gambling? Really, Lily, I'm shocked." He smiled. "So what sort of stakes are we talking about? A kiss, perhaps?" He looked at her without leaning closer, as if he expected some retort.

"I don't think you need to go to those lengths for a kiss."

And she kissed him on the lips. And it felt right.

CHAPTER 21: OPPORTUNITY

Four Yak fighters cut through the air over lines of German entrenchments. Aelya, Lucky, Vino, and Spam were almost home free. The bombers they had escorted dropped their payload unopposed over the right stretch of road and were already nearing their own lines once more.

Aelya was supposed to be in charge, but she didn't feel like it. She knew that somewhere high above them, hiding in the intermittent clouds, Roza and Dema were stalking her. It was Red's plan, if not exactly his idea. She remembered walking into the command post as he slammed down the telephone receiver and let out a stream of curses about cigar-smoking generals in their cushy headquarters. Dmitriev's visit had stoked interest in this Night Raven, and suddenly the regiment was ordered to prioritize hunting the Luftwaffe ace.

Squadrons led by Baby and Tractor, an Air Force veteran at least a decade older than most of the others, were to continue escorting air strikes and intercepting enemy bombers. But Stitches's squadron, the free hunters, were to hover over different sectors of the battlefield, waiting to converge on any reports of enemy fighters. That meant Aelya was bait. She didn't like it.

The Peshka bombers they'd escorted were now free and clear. Aelya signalled to Vino and Spam to continue escorting them home while she and Lucky circled back over no man's land. Perhaps the Night Raven would find two lone fighters too tempting and they could get this all over with.

She twitched, looking in every direction with heightened alertness. A shape on the ground caught her eye. The two fighters continued their wide, loping turn, allowing her to take a closer look at irregular shadows cast by a line of trees, as if some had been chopped down.

"Is something hidden there?" Aelya asked Lucky.

"I see it!" he exclaimed. "It's that balloon everyone's been talking about."

Aelya kept watch while carefully continuing on a path away from the shape protruding oddly from the trees. It was round and painted green and brown to blend in with the trees, but it was floating too high above its neighbours. There was no sign of movement, though she thought she saw disturbances in the earth marking anti-aircraft pits. She might not have been spotted yet.

"Mars, what was that about a balloon?" It was Roza.

Aelya called in the location.

"So, do you think you have a shot?" Roza asked.

Was she asking what she thought she was asking? Aelya checked her fuel. There was still time. This was her opportunity. She could do it. Do what no one else had been able to do. A shiver of excitement rippled through her.

"I'm going to take a run at it," she said. She ordered Lucky to stay high and look out for vultures.

"Hit them from the northwest, behind them," advised Roza. "Most of their anti-aircraft fire will be trained forward. We'll watch your back too."

Aelya flexed her hands, adjusting her grip on the control column. She was too jittery, so she bit her lower lip to stay focused.

She gave the balloon a wide berth, then pulled her Yak into a tight turn, pitching it into a shallow dive. She'd probably have only one shot at this. The greenish dot on the landscape grew into a fuzzy patch, then into individual trees. There was the balloon. It seemed lower than before. They'd spotted her and were reeling it in. Only seconds now. Lines of bluish-white appeared beside her. The anti-aircraft fire looked like streaks of horizontal lightning, laced with metal trying to tear her to shreds.

She needed to stay on course, but her body wouldn't obey. She unleashed a burst from her cannon and machine gun even as she pulled on the stick to escape the storm of fire. A violent impact ripped through the plane. She slipped her safety belt and struck her head against the canopy. It was all she could do to stay in control and guide the plane back up, chased all the way by more tracers.

A quick look back. The balloon continued its controlled descent. She had lost her nerve and missed. She let out a primal scream.

"I got it!" Roza yelled over the radio.

Aelya glanced back once more. The balloon was on fire, dropping into the trees. Roza's Yak swept upward and away, on a path perpendicular to Aelya's. Blue-white tracer fire, spreading wildly, chased after it.

"You used me as a distraction," Aelya said, still struggling against the sluggish controls. Her engine wasn't performing, even if all the gauges read normal.

"I had to get in there," said Roza. "You had your chance."

"Lily! Vultures on your six!" Dema shouted.

Aelya checked behind her. Two dark shapes streaked down toward Roza. She dodged them nimbly, climbing and rolling out of the way, but two more shapes appeared. They soon mingled together into indistinct shadows in the distance. Aelya banked and pleaded with her plane to turn around and help.

Roza's Yak came into view. Part of the fuselage was torn and flapping in the wind.

"Lily," Aelya called out. "Regroup on me. Lucky, pair up with Dema and stay high."

Roza waggled her wing to acknowledge. Her radio must have been out.

Aelya kept a wary eye on the enemy fighters, who were circling high, getting ready for another attack run. Something warm and wet coated the inside of her helmet and trickled down her forehead. She led Roza on a climb, back toward friendly airspace. Despite what damage Roza had suffered, her Yak rapidly caught up. But Aelya's plane seemed the worse for wear. She searched frantically for the others.

"More vultures!" called Dema.

Black dots peppered the sky above. Aelya hoped that somewhere up there, Lucky and Dema were keeping the enemy at bay. Two dots grew larger and hurtled at them. Their chunky profiles matched Fw 190s.

Roza waggled again, signalling a manoeuvre. Aelya kept watch closely, constantly glancing behind her. If it were up to her, she'd have started evasion already, but Roza was going to push things to the limit. Another half second, then Roza pitched forward and Aelya followed. Having once been her wingman, Aelya could read Roza's intentions. She could tell Roza was inverting her plane into a split S. The enemy planes overshot them as she and Roza levelled out at a much lower height, full of speed and in the opposite direction.

Aelya glanced back, then saw Roza turning and instinctively followed. The enemy tried to circle back on them, but they kept guessing wrong as Roza continued a swerving path. Soon a wide enough gap opened between them and the vultures that Aelya could call in a return to base. Two other Yaks appeared in the distance to follow them, and she breathed a little easier as Lucky and Dema drew near.

"That was wild, Lily. I'm supposed to die first, remember?" said Dema.

In the pause that followed, Aelya could hear Dema clearing his throat, as if expecting a retort from his wingman.

The enemy fighters grew more distant, pulling back toward their own lines. Even so, Aelya didn't let up her guard for one second. She kept diligently scanning the sky, checking the instruments, listening to radio signals. She barely allowed herself the chance to wipe blood away from her eyes. Only when their home airfield came into view did Aelya realize she'd been biting down on her lip the whole time. The metallic taste of blood trickled over her tongue.

As her plane was struggling the most, Aelya landed first. She rolled onto the taxiway. Zina climbed the wing to slide open the canopy before the plane even stopped moving. "I saw the hits to your plane, so . . . my God, Mars, are you hurt badly?"

For a moment, Aelya had forgotten her injury. She wiped more blood from her face. "I just banged my head a bit."

The growing buzz from a Yak passing overhead soon made it difficult to talk. The fighter came down hard on its belly, its landing gear not deployed. It scraped the ground so loudly, Aelya was amazed the plane didn't break up as it slid along the runway. A white rose was painted on its fuselage.

As other technicians came to stow her plane, Aelya hopped onto the ground, ignoring Zina. She ran down the airstrip toward Roza's stricken fighter. Crew already rushed in, throwing dirt to tamp down smoke rising from the engine. Roza's crew chief was on top of the engine cowling, frantically trying to open the canopy. Someone passed the woman a hammer, and as she banged at the latch Aelya slid it open.

Splashes of red were everywhere inside the cockpit. Roza's left leg was completely soaked in blood. As Aelya leaned over to see if she could find the wound, Roza said softly, "Sorry, I had to take my shot."

Then her eyes rolled back into her head and closed.

PART III:

Before the Storm

CHAPTER 22: ANOTHER WAR

Aelya grunted as she heaved Roza onto the back seat of the black Packard sedan. Even light-headed from painkillers, her friend grimaced as Aelya laid the injured leg along the length of the seat.

Satisfied, Aelya shut the door and navigated the edge of the bustling sidewalk outside of Kursky Station. She took a seat in the front of the car, next to the blank-faced Air Force driver sent by Dmitriev. The moment Roza had been discharged from the field hospital, the colonel had routed her straight to her mother's apartment in Moscow. Aelya assumed it was to allow him to keep a closer eye on his prized asset as much as it was to help her recover.

"Do you know the way?" she asked the driver.

"Colonel Dmitriev was very clear with his instructions."

Aelya chafed at having to play nursemaid to Roza. Dr. Krupenya had stitched up her forehead on base. There was no reason to keep her from active duty. She also wasn't feeling positive toward Roza. She'd felt manipulated into being a decoy in their last engagement. It wasn't about getting credit. The regiment heaped praise on both of them for destroying the balloon. But she wanted badly to get back in the air and prove that she deserved the accolades.

Red thought it best for her to have some time off active duty. This short leave, ostensibly to help Roza get home to recuperate from her leg injury, was considered a gift. Before Aelya returned to the front, she was also to stop at Zhukovsky Air Force Academy to write her officer's exam. A mere formality, she'd been assured by her commander.

She supposed she should be grateful but sniffed at the idea that any of this was a reward. Instead of Moscow, she would have preferred going to Kuybyshev, to the family she hadn't seen in nearly two years. Oh, why hadn't she taken that chance to see them a year ago when Roza told her to? But as much as she longed for it, the thought of a reunion also filled her with trepidation. Deep down, she wasn't sure she really wanted to see them.

On top of that, she was overwhelmingly anxious that a big fight was about to start and she would miss it all. She hated the idea of others doing her job, her friends and comrades putting their lives on the line without her. It lingered like an itch she had no way of scratching.

As the car merged into traffic along the Garden Ring, the sights outside the window were both familiar and different. The bright sun cast a glow on the city's landmarks. Gone were the panicked refugees, the aimless fear she'd seen in October 1941. No matter how ragged the civilians, they all seemed busy, moving purposefully. A cheery optimism filled the soldiers heading westward out of the city. They looked so young. Aelya realized many might be the same age as her, perhaps even younger.

Life was coming back. Cafés were open. Shops sold flowers. Cinemas showed British and American movies. It was alien to her. Astrakhan had been a respite but still felt like a part of the war. In Moscow, it was as if they were fighting a different war from the one she knew, where every village had suffered a massacre, where survivors were crushed under the demands of Red Army labour battalions. The city didn't match her reality.

Moving off the Ring into the narrow streets of Tagansky District, they passed a public park where teenagers drilled for the home guard, wooden sticks standing in for rifles that were more badly needed at the front. They smiled and laughed as they did so. In the courtyards of apartment blocks, women tended plots of dirt planted for the war effort. Here and there, the gardens sprouted vegetables.

The car stopped at a whitewashed modern residential building on Vorontsovsky Street, probably recently built during one of Stalin's Five Year Plans for rapid industrialization. Aelya had to nudge Roza awake as the driver carried their suitcases out of the trunk. Placing an arm over her shoulders, she pulled Roza from the car. The driver gave Roza her wooden crutch, then hefted their suitcases. Together, they entered the building and climbed the stairs, making their way to the third-floor landing in fits and starts.

At Aelya's knock on the door, there was a shuffling from within, then a brief silence, as if someone hesitated to answer. Dmitriev had sent a message ahead, and Roza's mother must have known they had arrived.

When the door finally opened, Aelya was startled by the initial resemblance between Roza and her mother. Roza's mother was short like her daughter and had the same eyes and freckled cheeks. But her hair was darker and thinner, her face lined and marked by discolouration. She looked much older than she probably was.

The woman's eyes fell on Roza's crutch, and she covered her mouth with her hands, uttering only a clipped "Rozita!"

"Mama, I'm all right," Roza said weakly.

The driver cleared his throat, and Aelya nodded as he put the suitcases down on the landing and left in a hurry. Aelya helped Roza through the foyer as her mother pulled out a chair in the adjoining kitchen.

"Actually, I think she needs to lie down," said Aelya.

"Of course. She can use my bed."

As Roza's mother opened the door to the bedroom and fussed over the sheets on the bed, she introduced herself as Darya. When Aelya gave her name, Darya insisted on calling her Comrade Makarova.

Aelya was surprised by the apartment's spaciousness. It wasn't the cramped the way Legend had told her to expect of Moscow. It also felt new. The bedroom was sparsely furnished, with a conspicuous lack of family photos.

As they helped Roza lie down, Darya knelt by her side and clasped her daughter's hand, wiping away tears.

"I'm all right. Just a bit feverish," Roza said. She closed her eyes.

Aelya unpacked Roza's suitcase. She playfully pulled out a nightdress that Stitches had bought from a telephone clerk at division headquarters. A parting gift for his beloved. The way they looked at each other, their relationship was obvious. It was good for Roza, she decided. It coincided with the return of the determined fighter she knew. Now she wondered how Stitches would fare without her.

Aelya withdrew the bottle of painkillers Dr. Krupenya had prescribed. "She needs to take one of these every twelve hours," she said, "and an extra pill if the pain flares up in her leg. But no more than four in one day."

Roza opened her eyes and asked, "Where's Zhora?"

Darya swallowed. "I haven't seen him for a while." She leaned in close, embracing her daughter with both arms, laying her head down to kiss her on the cheek.

"I've been managing on my own," Darya continued. "I'm working. They found me a job at the metro, with Yelena. There's lots to do there. Did you know they're still expanding, even with the war on? And this apartment . . ." She straightened out and gestured around her. "We have our own bathroom and kitchen!"

Roza certainly seemed to have done well for herself, Aelya thought.

"That's good, Mother," Roza mumbled as she drifted off to sleep.

"Get some rest, Lily," Aelya said. "I'll try to see you tomorrow."

"Wait," Darya stood up. "Where are you staying?"

"I'm supposed to write an exam at the Air Force Academy. I'll arrange something at the barracks there."

"Nonsense, Comrade Makarova. I insist you stay with us. We have a second bedroom, you know. You can sleep there. It's not like my son will be coming home anytime soon."

"Where will you sleep?"

"We have benches in the kitchen. I can put some blankets and pillows out there."

"No, absolutely not. Let me take the bench."

After a bit of back and forth, Darya deferred the matter by saying, "Please let me make you some dinner. It's the least I can offer you for bringing my Rozita back safely."

Aelya didn't think she'd had much to do with it but let the matter rest. She offered to help prepare the meal, but after Darya made her a cup of tea she insisted Aelya sit down and talk while she prepared the food, even pushing her into the chair with two wiry hands.

Darya opened a cupboard and measured out meagre portions of bread, onions, and potato from the bare shelves.

"No," Aelya said, "it's not right for me to be eating your rations." She wondered what the alternatives were. She'd been fed by the Air Force for so long, she had no idea how civilian ration cards worked. The system had probably changed multiple times since the war began. "I do have my own money. I can find a market and get something."

"The *kolkhoz* markets? The farmers send their surplus to the front. There's nothing to be had. Besides, my son . . . he spends his time at the factory and gets food from their commissary. We have all we need here. Comrade Stalin looks after the families of those fighting for our country."

Aelya sat fidgeting. She thought about the other errands she'd promised to do: deliver letters to Honeybee's and Sirin's parents. It was too late in the day to get started. Already dreading the trip across town to Zhukovsky Academy, she decided she would take Darya up on her hospitality. After all, they seemed to be doing quite well for themselves. Comrade Stalin looked after his heroes.

"This is a very nice apartment," she said to fill the silence.

"I know. A bedroom for each of us. Who would have dreamed? Perhaps after the war, it will be like this for us all. Of course, when Rozita returns, she'll have to share a room with Zhora. At least until she's married."

Darya stopped chopping the potatoes. She shakily put the knife down and sniffled. She wiped her face, sobbing. "I'm sorry, I don't know what's making me feel this way."

Aelya wanted to give Darya a hug but stayed rooted in her chair. Everything about this visit seemed like an intrusion, a peek into the life Roza had so diligently kept hidden. All she could say was "There's no shame in it. I'm sure this is very emotional for you."

Aelya wondered how much Darya's outburst had to do with the persecution Roza had hinted at. She realized everything Darya had experienced was completely alien to Aelya, who had her own very different memories of life before the war.

"My poor Rozita," Darya muttered. "My poor Rozita."

"Please, Darya Klimentovna, you needn't worry about Roza," Aelya reassured her. "She's gotten all the best medical care. The Air Force sees to everything—she's one of their brightest stars."

Darya buried her face in her hands. "Can they leave my Rozita alone now? She's done enough. I couldn't bear it if she . . ."

"We all love Roza. We'll always look out for her." Aelya couldn't reassure her more than this. What was she going to do? Lie and say they could protect Roza?

"I'll be all alone."

"But . . . what about your son?" Aelya immediately regretted asking that. She sensed she was opening a wound.

"He's been . . ." Darya sighed. "Things have been hard for him." She reached into the back of a cupboard and brought out a bottle of vodka and two glasses. She gestured at Aelya with one of the glasses.

Aelya often needed vodka to calm her nerves now, so she readily accepted as Darya took a seat opposite her.

"How is your family?" the older woman said, pouring the vodka into both glasses. Darya quickly downed hers while Aelya took a small sip.

"Fine. They're in Kuybyshev." Aelya grimaced on the inside. She kept pushing her family out of her thoughts. It was as if she didn't want them to be part of her life right now. Could Roza's brother be doing the same? She'd rather talk about him.

"Roza will be thrilled to see Zhora," Aelya said. "She loves talking about him." Roza never shared more than superficial information about Zhora, if she mentioned him at all, but still, it sounded believable. They were brother and sister, after all.

"We'll see." Darya refilled and drained her glass, her periodic gulps slicing through the silence. She plunked the glass on the table with a sharp intake of breath.

"It's my fault, you understand?" She let that hang for a moment. "I divorced my husband. They said he was a traitor. So that's what I had to do. He was a traitor." She said the right words, but it was clear she didn't believe them. She slapped both hands on the table, shaking, until Aelya reached out and patted an arm to soothe her.

Darya's voice cracked. "My boy thinks I'm a traitor for marrying Slava in the first place. But aren't I also a traitor to my vows for turning my back on him? I'm a traitor either way."

Aelya thought about what Ulanova had to do to survive, how she had to marry even as people in her hometown were branded traitors. At least she had Nemchinov. And Darya had Roza, for now. Eventually, her daughter would head back to the front. This son, Zhora—he needed to be here. Whatever responsibilities he owed the war effort, surely he was needed here more.

In her mind, she heard echoes of what her sister Vasya had written in a letter early in the war. She seemed to think Aelya risking her life with the Air Force was some sort of holiday. But Aelya now understood the kind of anguish her decision to join up had caused her parents. What did that say about her?

She put a hand over Darya's glass as she was about to pour herself another drink. "I'll speak to Zhora tomorrow," Aelya said. "Let me do that for you."

Darya moved her hand away but looked at the glass, then screwed the top back onto the vodka bottle. "I'd better get started on the soup."

CHAPTER 23: SINS OF THE FATHER

Dust drifted through the open ceiling of the factory manager's office, a windowless room situated on the floor of the vast ZiS plant. Its walls reached only a third of the factory's height, and the noise, particle-clogged fumes, and smell of grease freely entered.

Aelya wrinkled her nose as she remained standing, even as the manager leaned back in his chair behind the desk.

Behind her, the door was flung open. A tall, skinny teenager with a mop of blond hair parted down the middle stopped to attention next to Aelya. Though Zhora was taller than she was, he looked so much younger than she expected, based on the way Roza and Darya talked about him. He was still a boy. His eyes assessed her coldly.

The manager spoke. "Comrade Kulik, this is—"

"You with the Air Force?" Zhora asked.

"Yes, I'm a friend of your sister's. I've accompanied her to Moscow so she can convalesce."

His response was immediate. "I was told she was returning. How is she?"

"You should ask her yourself."

"I'll look in when I get the chance. Where is she staying?"

Roza had hardly mentioned her brother these past months, and now Aelya could see why. He had no warmth that she could detect. She grasped for a response, imagining what sort of awkward reunion would take place at the apartment, knowing how he viewed his mother.

Zhora saw through her. His face contorted, as if he was holding himself back from saying terrible things in the presence of his manager. "I see. Well, thank you for your help and for your service." He turned back to his manager. "Is that all? I should be back on the floor. We're just in the middle of morning calisthenics."

Aelya looked at the manager, her eyes boring into him.

He cleared his throat. "Hold on, Kulik. Being courteous for a few more minutes won't affect your productivity. Comrade, er . . ."

"Makarova."

"Comrade Makarova is a war hero, just like your sister."

Such praise made Aelya slightly nauseous.

"I have a message from your sister," she lied.

Zhora relented. "Yes?"

"She would dearly love to see you. She's eager to return to the fight, so she won't be staying in Moscow long."

"There's not much I can do. I can't jeopardize my productivity."

"Surely you can take some of your off-shift hours to visit? She's not far from here."

"I spend all of my spare hours helping the war effort. It's more than just making parts. We plan improvements every day."

"Yes," the manager chimed in. "Comrade Kulik has been an exemplar. We have our own heroes, you know."

Zhora added, "In any case, I need to rest before my next shift."

Aelya snapped. "Your sister almost died. It's because of her your mother has a place to live. The place where you should be. Is it too much to ask that her family be whole again, just for one hour? Before your sister has to go into battle again?"

The manager looked between the two of them, then stared at his hands, drumming them on his desk. "Well, now that you put it that way, yes, surely that would be all right. Comrade Kulik, you've worked many extra hours. There's no need to stay late tonight."

Zhora glared at Aelya, then sighed. "I suppose I can make some time."

Aelya reached for his arm. "I don't know what's come between you. Maybe sometime—somehow—your mother and your sister wronged you. I can't guess what you've been through."

He stared icily at her while moving slightly toward the door.

Aelya kept close, talking softly. "Just know that when you care for people, you do what you have to do to keep them safe. And sometimes, it might even seem like you're hurting them."

He glanced warily at his manager.

Aelya leaned into his ear. "Don't let this opportunity slip from your grasp."

Zhora said nothing, but he looked contemplative as he turned to leave the room.

Roza leaned on the cushions lining the bench at the side of the dining area. She'd insisted on coming out for this meal. How long had it been since the family had sat together like this? Her injured leg stretched out along the length of the seat, leaving only a small space for Aelya. Zhora reached across the table to pass his sister a bowl of borscht. She savoured the smell before she took a spoonful, letting the warmth flow through her even as its heat burned.

The other residents of the block, on hearing the "famous hero" had come home, insisted on digging up all the beets in the apartment garden for them. Darya and Aelya had taken turns mixing ingredients for a large pot of soup, and Darya promised to share the leftovers with the neighbours.

Aelya had been supposed to run some errands for Honeybee and Sirin, but in the afternoon she'd burst in to inform Roza and her mother that Zhora would be visiting. Then she went back to the factory to make sure he did.

He'd hugged Roza when he arrived and asked about her injury, but it was all an act. Whatever his true feelings, it didn't matter to their mother. She'd broken down into tears, hugging him and begging forgiveness, and that seemed to soften his demeanour.

"This is a wonderful place to live," Zhora remarked, obviously not having seen the apartment before.

Roza could barely believe her good fortune. When had they ever had their own bathroom and their own dining area, even before her father's troubles? For that matter, when was the last time neighbours had done anything nice for them?

Some borscht caught in Roza's throat and she coughed. Zhora passed her a cup of water and he smiled slightly, or did a reasonable approximation of a smile. He was doing his best to be civil.

He turned to his mother. "I never would have thought you could match the ideal socialist matron, but you've done well, Mama. This borscht is very good."

"Just like how you remember it?" Roza said, irked by his detached way of addressing their mother. He didn't respond.

Aelya kept looking back and forth between them like an eager puppy, as if willing them to come together as a family. Roza loved Aelya. She couldn't fathom how much the amiable girl from Smolensk had done for her. So long as Aelya was by her side, she had someone to look out for her.

Darya put down her soup spoon and sighed. "I remember the garden of your grandfather's house in Fryanovo." Roza tensed, as did her brother. That was their father's side of the family. "The summers were so dry there, I had to make a dozen trips every day from the well to water the beets. You were so little then, Zhora, I had to carry you on my back in a sling. And you, little Rozita, kept begging me for the same ride. You didn't understand you were too big by then. I had to swat you away. Your Papa used to—" She stopped short uncomfortably and took another spoonful of soup.

"We shouldn't dwell on stories of the past," Zhora said. "It's to the future we need to look."

Roza snorted.

He twitched but continued, "The future of our nation looks brighter than ever now that the Fascists are on the verge of defeat."

"I think that's a very good attitude," said Aelya.

Roza's stomach churned. Nothing seemed to get through to Zhora. He probably only believed in their mother's goodness because the State had said she was now reformed. To him, this apartment wasn't a sign of a new, improved life; it only mattered as proof of their mother's rehabilitation. She quelled an angry outburst rising within her. Instead, she tried to nudge him in the right direction.

"Speaking of the future," Roza said, "have you thought about continuing your education?"

He waved the question off. "The factory is what matters now."

Aelya spoke before Roza could respond. "It was very interesting to see all the different things the ZiS plant is producing for the war effort. And how many different people contribute to it. It reminded me of the Yak plant in Saratov. After Stalingrad, I had to fly there to pick up new fighter planes. I got a tour, and even met a boy who had helped us pick out our lucky planes when we first joined the fighter regiment. Do you remember him, Lily?"

The painkillers were wearing off and Roza closed her mind to the ache in her leg. She thought back to that first factory visit, remembering all the women who had started in the 586th with her. They'd been so eager to choose their new fighters fresh from the factory floor. How many of them were already dead?

Aelya continued, "With a little, um, creative documentation, the boy was old enough to try enlisting. He was so eager to see what it was like at the front. He thought he could contribute much more by fighting than by making planes. But I pointed out the engineers to him. One worker who does a good job on a plane might save one life. But an engineer who designs the planes could save a thousand lives. 'If you're going to leave, go back to school,' I told him. 'Be an engineer.' I couldn't bear to think of him taking all that potential and dying in a ditch somewhere."

"And what did he do?" said Roza. She shifted in her seat but couldn't find any comfort.

"I don't know."

Zhora rebuked Aelya. "That's a bit rich coming from you."

"Georgiy Vyacheslavovich!" his mother scolded.

Zhora continued, "You could be in school yourself, studying."

"Don't throw that guilt on her," Roza snapped.

Aelya put a hand on her shoulder and said calmly, "We made the choice to fight and . . . maybe later we can have the chance again to go to school. But you have it now."

Zhora looked at Roza. "No, I don't. Even if I'm back at school, I can't do much with that. They won't let me into the Komsomol."

Roza almost dropped her spoon. Everyone tensed, and even Aelya knew they'd crossed into some new territory. Zhora had never been allowed into any of the Communist youth organizations. He hadn't been able to lie or bluff his way in as Roza had. Bad luck and an unsympathetic teacher had made his forged papers useless. Everything her brother had done since their father's arrest, Roza thought, was a desperate bid for the State's approval, but to little avail. But she had something better than forged documents now. She had a colonel in SovInformBuro.

"That can be overcome. I know someone who can give you a recommendation." Roza strained to speak through her pain, but she pressed on. "Fighting the Germans isn't the only way to make a name for yourself.

You can make a name for yourself with academics—more than I ever could. Maybe you could be a famous inventor. I want that so much for you."

Zhora shifted uncomfortably, then looked at her empty bowl. "Would you like some more? No? I'll go clear the dishes, then."

As he took the empty bowls toward the kitchen sink, her mother leaned in to Aelya and whispered, "Thank you, for everything."

There was a knock at the door. Zhora went to answer. Roza heard a familiar voice and she shuffled down the bench with Aelya's help to take a look. At the door, a woman with dark hair neatly tied in a bun held a bouquet of flowers.

"It's all right," Roza said. "She works for Colonel Dmitriev."

The woman strode in officiously, heels clacking. Her eyes took in the spacious apartment. She set the flowers down on the dinner table.

"I'm here to offer congratulations personally from the colonel. He says your tenth, eleventh, and twelfth aerial victories have all been confirmed." She looked Roza over. "Your roots are showing. We'll have to have another peroxide session."

As Roza examined the flowers on the table, she found a note from Dmitriev. It told her that confirmation of her Hero of the Soviet Union award was merely a matter of time and hoped she was enjoying her stay in Moscow. "Have I not done well for you?" Dmitriev seemed to ask. He'd already done all these things for her family: gotten them this apartment, found employment for her mother, expunged their records. The note ended with encouragement for her to take as much time as she needed to recover and to stay safe and to await further instructions. She had discharged her duties well, and he foresaw a great future in Moscow and beyond.

The woman dipped her finger in the pot of soup for a taste, then left.

Aelya looked the note over. "What is this? You're leaving us?"

"Is that true?" Darya asked, her eyes bright. "So you're not going back?"

Aelya leaned against the kitchen wall. "Of course. It makes sense."

Roza wanted to tell her something, but what exactly? That she was going to disobey Dmitriev and return to the fight? And break her mother's heart? Or that she was leaving her comrades at the front? Nothing she could say felt any better. An intense pain pulsed through her body and she felt faint.

Zhora helped her stand. "Let's get you into bed."

Aelya looked out the window. "It's still light. I should be able to get to the academy before curfew. Thank you so much for your hospitality, all of you."

"Please stay," said Darya. Roza concurred but was too weak to say so as Zhora guided her into her room.

"I can't impose anymore. It'll be too crowded," said Aelya. "Zhora, surely you can stay here now." She walked into Roza's room, her eyes welling with tears. "This is good. It's everything you wanted."

Roza lifted her arm. Zhora got in the way, reaching over to her suitcase for the painkillers. A combination of pain and fatigue nailed her to the bed. She looked past her brother for Aelya, but she heard only a suitcase fastening, and a moment later the front door opened and shut.

CHAPTER 24: SHADOWY MEN

The apartment building in front of Aelya was set in a row of identical structures, all faced with reddish ornamental masonry. They felt like part of an alternate universe within the city, and not simply because they dated from before the revolution. The neighbourhood showed no signs of air raid warnings, shelters, sandbags, barrage balloons, or trenches. The only hints of wartime expediency were the whitewashed footpaths to help pedestrians navigate blackout conditions.

Aelya was troubled by the way she'd left Roza. She should have been happy for her comrade's good fortune. It wasn't as if Roza was abandoning her duties. She'd done more than her fair share of fighting. Aelya's first impulse on hearing the news had been a selfish one; she'd been terrified to go back to the front without her friend. Thinking of it had cast a gloom over her whole day.

But in the back of her mind, a suspicion lingered that Roza had been trophy hunting at the front—that everything she'd done had been aimed at being pulled from duty quicker. It forced Aelya to reconsider why Roza had chased down that Rama, and to acknowledge that she'd used her as a diversion for the artillery balloon.

The pull of family was strong when it was within reach. Would Aelya have done the same in those circumstances as Roza had? She didn't want to think about it. Still waiting for her officers' course to begin, she took leave of the academy and threw herself into carrying out her errands for her friends.

She found the right address and passed through an archway into an entrance hall. A wrought iron chandelier fitted with electric lights hung low overhead. She went down a hall to the right, past a stairwell with an ornate wooden banister. After she knocked on the door of a ground-floor apartment, a grey-haired woman in a plain black jacket and skirt greeted her. There was a refined look about her. She eyed Aelya with an arched eyebrow.

"Maria Nikolayevna?" Aelya asked.

"My mistress isn't at home."

So this was one of Honeybee's servants. Now that Aelya thought of it, this woman was too plain to match the picture of exotic beauty Honeybee had painted of her mother. When Honeybee had mentioned servants, Aelya thought she had meant before the war. Such things weren't supposed to exist amid all the hardship now, surely.

"Do you know where I might find the Gorbatys? I'm a comrade of their daughter's."

The woman gasped and put a hand to her mouth. She looked weak-kneed and Aelya moved to help her stand. A bearded man, also grey-haired, appeared from a door at the other end of the foyer and guided the woman to a bench next to a coat rack.

"This girl is a friend of our little Ninochka's," the woman said.

"Oh no, what's happened?" the man asked with trembling lips.

It took a moment for Aelya to register that the woman had used the diminutive for Honeybee's given name of Antonina, as for so long she had she been using nicknames and radio call signs.

"No, nothing's wrong. I'm sorry to give you a fright. I'm merely paying a visit. She wanted me to look in on her parents. And to deliver this letter."

She handed the man a folded piece of paper from her pocket. It occurred to her that this pair had been fearful for Honeybee as if she were their own child, not their employers'.

"Forgive the emotion," the old man said. "We've looked after little Ninochka her whole life, and we worry about her so. This is Nadezhda Semyonovna, the housekeeper, and I'm Ivan Pavlovich, the driver."

If he was the family driver, he was noticeably older than the man who had driven Honeybee to the aeroclub that fateful day when Aelya met her. How many people did Honeybee's family have working for them?

Ivan and Nadezhda warmly smiled and motioned for her to come in. The decor seemed modest enough, with mostly modern furniture. Even so, this apartment, left over from the days when nobles and the bourgeoisie kept homes of convenience in the city, was probably twice the size of Roza's.

"The Gorbatys are away at their *dacha*," said Ivan.

"Are they due back anytime soon?"

"We don't know. They've been away since the evacuation. Though Savvit Grigorovich returns occasionally on business. That's Ninochka's father."

Aelya chuckled. Seeing their quizzical look, she explained, "Everyone calls her Honeybee."

"Oh, Honeybee!" Nadezhda said, gushing. "That's so perfect for her. She's such a sweet darling."

"Yes, she, uh, certainly is something."

"Yes, so brave," Ivan said.

If their masters had been away since the evacuation, that was a year and a half that the servants had stayed here without their employers. Doing what job, exactly? Aelya wondered. As if reading her mind, Ivan glanced over at the front corner of the foyer, where a battered old helmet lay next to a pair of well-worn padded jackets and a first aid kit—the same sort of kit worn by volunteer fire brigades she'd seen in Moscow when she'd first joined the Air Force. He was too aged and frail-looking to be anywhere near combat. Aelya avoided his eyes for a moment. What right did she have to judge him?

The couple wanted her to stay to eat, but she demurred. Then they offered every imaginable luxury to take back with her: teacups, perfumes, cutlery. What would she do with all that? She ultimately accepted a package of soap bars from Central Universal Store; Honeybee was so fond of using and parcelling out the bars as bribes.

"Please," Nadezhda said, handing her the soap, "for you and all your comrades. You're so brave. True heroes."

"Are you sure you won't stay for a while?" Ivan asked.

Aelya politely refused again. To be honest, their fawning air of servitude bothered her.

"Well, safe travels back to the front," Ivan said, casually adding, "May you kill many Germans."

The Arbat neighbourhood also wasn't what Aelya had expected. When her father had taken her to Moscow on Aviation Day, they hadn't had a chance to visit the area, though he had shared fond memories of it. He spoke of lively crowds at all hours, the cafés and restaurants full of noise, and a sense of being at the epicentre of their great revolution as intellectuals debated how they would change the world. His words had also been tinged with sadness, as he noted that was all in the past. Things had changed, even before the war.

Now there were just shuttered storefronts and identical black cars parked along the street. A bland sameness characterized the buildings, and as she walked Aelya frequently glanced at the address numbers to compare them to the scribbling on the front of Sirin's letter. She tried not to feel self-conscious as men in suits stood watch while trying to remain inconspicuous.

It was disconcerting, though it made sense. If Sirin's father was NKVD, then he would work and live in an NKVD compound. They appeared to have taken over the whole neighbourhood. In time of war, the security commissariat would naturally be suspicious of everyone.

She wondered at these shadowy men. She dimly remembered waking up to stomping on the stairs outside her apartment, the motors of black vans still running outside. Her mother had warned her and her sister to stay in bed, reassuring them that the good guys were here to take away criminals. Aelya had rarely questioned that, until she met Roza and so many others who opened her eyes to how widespread and indiscriminate the arrests had been.

"Are you lost?" The words were more of a statement than a question, coming from a man in a trench coat at the corner of the intersection. Before she could say anything, he added, "What are you looking for?"

The man's forceful attitude unnerved her. For all the world she just wanted to say she'd made a mistake and turn around. She'd promised Sirin she would do this errand and wouldn't dishonour that promise just because she was uncomfortable. What was this man compared to a Luftwaffe ace? She slowly said, "I'm here to see Davit Dolidze."

The man tensed immediately, his eyes narrowing as he approached her. His face loomed close to hers. "I'll need to search that." He grabbed the package of soap, a box wrapped in brown paper tied with string.

"No. What business is this of yours?" Aelya said as she yanked it away.

The man grabbed her arms and nodded toward another man in an identical trench coat crossing the street toward them. The second man ripped the package out of her hands, undid the string, and tore the wrapping. On opening the box and finding the soap, he said. "What's this?

Very nice." He drew out one soap bar and sniffed it. "Looks like you're hoarding."

"I'm not hoarding—it's a gift."

The two men shared a smirk.

Aelya scowled. "You leave that alone. I'm just here to deliver a letter from Davit Dolidze's daughter."

The two men's expressions grew serious and they looked at each other. The first man reached toward the letter in Aelya's hand. She held on tightly.

"I'll deliver it to him," he said.

"I would still like to see him and his wife."

"I'm sorry, but they're busy. Comrade Dolidze has very important work for the State to conduct. You can't just waltz in here and think you can knock on every door." He snatched the letter away. He slipped a finger under the flap, then thinking better of it, crammed the folded piece of paper into the pocket of his trench coat.

Down the street, a car door slammed. She looked over her right shoulder, her automatic response to any sudden noise.

Someone tapped her other shoulder and she turned to face the second man, who handed back the package of soap. From their officious demeanour, their looks of suspicion and contempt, she knew these were the shadowy men who took people away in the middle of the night. She wanted to call them out as bullies for besmirching the honour of her former squadron commander, Auntie. For terrorizing heroes like Roza. For painting loyal workers like Ulanova as traitors. What had these men been doing while Stalingrad burned? But she bit it all back.

Doing her best to stop her hand from shaking, Aelya took the soap and hurried away toward the tram stop while other men in black suits and black cars followed with their eyes.

She was sick of men like that. Sick of Moscow. The arrogant NKVD men lording it over everyone. The rich, off hiding away in their *dachas*. The sense of vibrant life continuing as normal, as if the war were a world away. It burned her inside. She felt as if she needed to wear a mask of calm while walking through the city, while everything inside her wanted to scream.

She just wanted to go back to the front, to the only thing that felt real to her. But she would be going back without Roza. She needed to make peace with that.

CHAPTER 25: SISTERS

Aelya trudged down Vorontsovsky Street and entered the courtyard of Roza's apartment. Her eyes adjusted to long shadows cast by the late-afternoon sun. The garden was teeming with old women among rows of newly sprouting lettuce and cauliflower. To one side, Zhora dug holes in a soil bed for summer planting, while Roza sat on a chair, her legs extended, crutch on the ground next to her.

"Mars!" Roza attempted to rise but stumbled as Zhora turned to catch her with his dirt-stained arms. As Aelya rushed over, she couldn't believe how small and vulnerable Roza looked—diminished somehow.

After helping Roza to her chair, she stood in awkward silence for a moment. "What are you planting?" she finally asked, using that old trick about ignoring whatever topic was causing trouble—an old reliable in the Air Force.

"Spinach," said Zhora. A *babushka* with a bent back beckoned him over to help.

Aelya and Roza watched him zip around the courtyard for a while. There was always another old woman who needed his strong hands to help with something. Roza pointed at the package under Aelya's arm. "What's that?"

"Soap. The nice stuff from Central Universal Store. It's a gift to take back to the front from Honeybee's parents. Sort of."

She set down the package and carefully unfolded the damaged brown wrapping. She handed one bar to Roza, who sniffed it demonstratively.

"Honeybee would want you to have one," Aelya said.

"No, she wouldn't. But thanks for taking the liberty."

Aelya knelt next to her and threw her arms around her. "I . . . I don't know what you might have . . ."

"I know what you're trying to say," Roza said. "Maybe my priorities haven't always been straight."

Aelya cleared her throat. "Well, you do what you have to for your family, understand?"

"But you're my family too now," Roza said.

Tears flowed down both their faces as they hugged.

"I'll miss you," said Aelya.

"Don't. I'll come back. I'll say a proper goodbye to the regiment." Roza pulled back, still holding Aelya's arms. "I don't want to be out of the fighting. It's just . . ." She looked at Zhora. Another old woman was patting him on the back as he carried a piece of lumber to hem in a new soil bed.

"There's nothing to explain," Aelya said.

"I'll come back. I need to explain it to Stitches."

"He'd be the one happiest for you. I'll talk to him."

"Well, that's reassuring. You're so famously poetic with your words."

"I guess I'll need to be so I can talk some fool into taking Dema on as a wingman."

They shared a laugh, and then Roza shook her head softly. "He may be about as much fun as a Dostoevsky hero, but the man knows how to cover." Then Roza patted her shoulder. "I will go back. I'll tell Stitches myself. I promise."

"Dmitriev won't want to risk his prize. We'll look after Stitches. Keep him intact until . . ." Some force compelled her not to acknowledge an "after the war." She shook her head. "Twelve victories. You're going to be a Hero of the Soviet Union. The gold star. Just like Marina Raskova. You'll have bigger things to do than visit us." Aelya brightened and gushed, "Maybe they'll send you to America and you can finally get them to start their second front."

Roza leaned back in the chair, staring off into the distance, taking in the implications. "I'll find time," she said. "I've never let the people in charge stop me before."

They hugged again tightly. Roza cried out in pain, wincing as Aelya gingerly released her from her grip. "It's all right, I'm still a little tender," she said.

Zhora rushed over. "You've been out too long. You need more rest."

Roza waved off any help, retrieved her crutch, and rose. She looked as thought she was about to say something. Aelya felt the need to speak too, but she couldn't find the words. No words would be good enough anyway, because . . . She could barely let the thought creep into her head. *This could be the last time they saw each other.*

Roza just smiled, then made her way to the apartment entrance. Aelya and Zhora went after her, but Roza waved them off as she took one step up at time. She looked at Aelya one more time, her mouth opening slightly but not saying anything. Aelya blew her a kiss, and she exchanged the favour before heading up the steps.

Back outside, Zhora said, "I shouldn't forget how strong my sister can be." His eyes were lined with worry. "I used to spend so much time fighting her."

"It's just the same for me and my sister."

He sighed. "Seeing her laid out like that, weak, wounded. It . . . I guess I wasn't prepared for that. It's good to see her on her feet again." He straightened up. "I'm sorry, that was overly sentimental. She's only doing her duty."

"I think it's a very good sign. You still care for her."

He blushed. "You were right. Thank you for convincing me to come home. I should never have been angry with Roza. Comrade Stalin says that the sins of the father are not visited on the sons. Or the daughters. And my mother . . . I shouldn't have . . ." He seemed on the verge of tears, then composed himself.

Aelya patted him on the back, but he turned away and stood up tall. Towering over her, looking determined in profile, he hardly seemed a boy. Wanting to keep him talking, she asked, "Have you changed to a late shift at the factory?"

"No, I've stopped altogether. I've been admitted to the Komsomol."

"That's wonderful."

"That was my sister's doing, wasn't it?"

"Whatever the cause, this is the chance I was talking about."

He nodded. "I'll be meeting with them later to plan out summer activities, before starting school in the fall." He extended his hand. "Thank you. For what you did for her. For all of us."

Aelya looked down as she took his hand, feeling that accepting any gratitude would be unseemly.

"I wish I was old enough to fight alongside you," Zhora said. "Don't get me wrong—I know the war isn't all glory and the danger is real. But, well . . . it's important to fight for our way of life."

Aelya frowned but didn't want to totally disabuse him of his notions. "Fighting for our country isn't just about shooting at the enemy. There's so much other work to be done here."

They watched the old women working the garden. Zhora asked, "So, do you think you'll keep flying? After the war, I mean."

She couldn't conceive of an "after the war." It was an unknowable blank space. "I don't really let myself think that far ahead."

"The war's going to end someday. I thought about what you said. I think I'd like to be an engineer, maybe on aircraft."

"That's good," Aelya said. "It's good to have dreams. I've forgotten how to."

She put a smile on her face, remembering what she used to dream about when she was Zhora's age. She patted the breast pocket of her uniform, feeling for the book she'd kept with her since leaving home. Some urge made her hand it to him.

"'*Aelita*, by Aleksey Tolstoy,'" he read off the cover.

"This used to be everything to me. It might mean more to you now. My mother is an aircraft engineer. She used this book to inspire me." Aelya traced the embossed image of Mars on the cover. "Have you read it?"

"I saw the movie."

"The book is better." She finally let go of it. "Don't forget to dream. It's so precious, but you'll never realize it until you can't do it anymore."

CHAPTER 26: THE ROAD BACK

The town where Aelya arrived existed mostly to serve the railhead, the last stop on the line. The tracks continued northward where, another fifteen or twenty kilometres on, the Germans lay waiting. The railway yard was so crowded with carriages, she was forced to alight when the train lurched to a halt several hundred metres from the station platform.

The atmosphere of dust, earth, and sweat overwhelmed her after weeks in antiseptic classrooms and barracks in Moscow. A human vortex of fresh troops, civilians, labour gangs, and the wounded knocked her around as they jostled on and off the train.

She escaped the suffocating press to the outskirts of town, toward buildings where the Red Army had set up their administration. The scale of destruction was obvious up close. There were barely any streets or buildings, just an obstacle course of rubble and craters. Bullet holes and scorch marks on the remaining walls marked the fight the Germans had waged before fleeing. The fact that a rudimentary train station had been restored was testament to the efforts of the labourers.

Another testament to their efforts: huge stretches of earthworks, sandbag walls, and camouflaged gun pits that bristled from the perimeter in the same sort of defensive arrangement she'd seen on her visit to the front line. It seemed there was little space left for more fortifications, which was probably why so many labourers were moving on to the next place in the line.

She squeezed past another cluster of workers. These ones were thin, wearing tattered clothing, and looking ahead vacantly as blue-capped NKVD guards trudged alongside with carelessly held submachine guns.

A familiar face stood to the side. A female Air Force officer always drew Aelya's attention, and one with an Asian appearance even more so. They locked eyes momentarily, and then the woman ducked out of view behind a house. But Aelya was sure it was Sirin.

The urge to cling to something familiar spurred her on, and she cut through the crowds to round the corner. Running, she called out to Sirin, who walked down a side road.

Sirin stopped and turned, then smiled, donning a cheerful mask. "Mars, you're back."

"I'm so glad to find you. I wasn't fancying lining up at the transport coordinator's office to get out of here."

"Huh?"

"How are you getting back to base? You are going, aren't you?"

"Yes, that's right. I'm on an errand." Sirin shifted uncomfortably, then beamed like a cherub. "But I'm done with that now. I brought the U-2. Landed it in the next village over. We still have time to make it back to base before last light." She elbowed Aelya in the ribs. "Bet you thought you'd have to hitchhike out of here."

"Let's go, then."

They diverged from the village's main street onto a connecting road leading eastward. Away from the rail line, civilians and soldiers still cluttered the road. Some *makhras* butchered a dead horse in the shade of an elm.

Roaring bombers crossing the sky caught Aelya's attention. She immediately assessed their silhouettes, determining they were friendly. No one else seemed much bothered by them; most people were aware but kept to their business. Seeing them must have been a common occurrence here.

Sirin chattered amiably about the past month. "Apparently, intelligence thinks the big push by Fritz is imminent. They've been saying this for the whole month. We've been getting an alert every day—every few hours, actually. If it's daytime, we scramble one squadron while the rest of us hide in trenches. If it's nighttime, we *all* hide. But whatever happens, it's never a real attack. No one ever finds anything when we scramble. I mean, what's Fritz waiting for? Surely they won't survive another of our winters."

She paused briefly, then slapped Aelya on the back. "This is all boring. How was Moscow?"

"Unfortunately, I didn't manage to see your parents, but I dropped your letter off."

"Oh. Yes, thank you. And other than that?"

"Good," Aelya lied.

As the road cleared of crowds, the air grew thick with dust, carried by a hot wind that offered no relief from the late-afternoon sun. Aelya had almost lost hold of the package of soap under her arm when Sirin offered to take it off her hands.

"Thanks. One of those is for you. They're from Honeybee's parents."

"Well, I'd thank her, but she owes me for a ream of paper, of all things, that I had to find for her." So Honeybee had taken Aelya's suggestion and Sirin was receptive to a "business" partnership.

They plodded along a path marked by crashed, broken trees, the occasional crater, and an abandoned vehicle, stripped to the bone. In the distance, to both the north and the south, were unmistakable scars in the terrain where the Red Army had set defensive positions.

Sirin asked about Roza, and Aelya only offered generic assurances she was on the mend. It didn't seem right for Aelya to speak about Roza's imminent departure from the unit, at least not right now. Stitches needed to hear about it first.

More questions came about what movies were playing, which restaurants were open, and what food they were serving. But Aelya hadn't seen any movies or dined in any restaurants. If she had, she wondered, would it have been harder to come back?

As they neared the next settlement along the road, also bustling with the activity of soldiers, they skirted it toward a clump of trees. Following the tire marks made when she'd rolled the U-2 to its hiding spot, Sirin picked up the pace.

"Oh no. No, no, no, no, no!" She ran and Aelya followed briefly before slowing down. Someone had stolen the U-2.

Sirin swore loudly. "I mean, who goes and does that?" she said, shooting Aelya a look.

Aelya couldn't suppress a laugh.

"Not funny," Sirin said, deflated. She stomped toward the village to ask questions. Most villagers and *makhras* were completely oblivious about what had happened to the plane. Finally, a bored-looking elderly man said he'd seen a pair of uniformed men rolling it out of the woods and taking off in it. He provided no further description of the men.

"Face it, it's gone," said Aelya. "It'll probably turn up some day at the nearest reserve base."

"What am I going to do?"

"Look, it's not your fault. You were here on orders and you did your best to secure it. Let's just report it and find alternate transport. We may need to stay here overnight, though."

As Aelya turned back toward the railhead, Sirin grabbed her. "No, we can't report it until we get back to base."

"Why not?"

"Look, let's just sort out a ride first. I'd feel much better then."

Back in town, they accosted the driver of every rolling vehicle they could find. It was only then that Aelya learned the regiment had relocated. The old base had gotten too much attention from the Luftwaffe.

"Kind of them to let me know," Aelya said dryly, though it didn't surprise her. Typical VVS bureaucracy. She could have been circling around different transport hubs for hours, even days, trying to figure out where to go, all to get to a place that had already been abandoned. She was doubly grateful now to have run into Sirin.

It was nightfall by the time they managed to find a truck full of *makhras* resting in the back and its driver about to sleep inside the cab. In the morning, they could hitch a ride on the running boards all the way to a crossroads about ten kilometres from Rogachevsk. From there, they could either try to hitch another ride or, in a pinch, walk the rest of the way.

"Rogachevsk?" Aelya felt her heart lurch upon hearing the name.

"Yeah, it's a place built from scratch. It's so new, there's no name on the map, so we named it after one of your former comrades, I believe."

That was Auntie Lara, officially a disgraced former comrade.

"And Cricket was all right with that?"

"Sure. He was all for it."

Despite her misgivings, Aelya couldn't help but feel gratitude toward the *zampolit*.

Starving, she bargained away her own bar of soap for stew cooked from the horse they'd seen earlier. Sirin offered her own bar of soap back to Aelya, but she declined.

As they sat away from the *makhras,* Sirin spoke quietly. "Listen, when we get back, you can say you ran into me at the crossroads. I was at Zolo-tukhino when the plane was stolen, all right?"

Aelya glanced at her with narrowed eyes. "Care to elaborate?"

"No."

"So it's like that, then." Obviously, Sirin had taken a detour for one of Honeybee's schemes. Even though Aelya had refused Honeybee's offer, she still felt as if she had a right to know what had happened. "You know," she said, "I was the one who told Honeybee you'd make a good business partner."

Sirin laughed. "I'm sorry. It's just that you're so straight. What would you know?"

Aelya was indignant. "I stole that plane, remember?"

"Yes, but that was so you could return to duty." Sirin patted her on the back. "It's not a bad thing. Having such narrow interests keeps you out of trouble."

"So you like being troublemaker?"

Sirin gave her a wry smile. "It's hard to get into trouble when everyone's afraid of your father."

They both stared, uncomfortable in the silence.

Sirin spoke first. "He's not really my father. But he took me as his own after he married my mother. My real father . . . had to leave when I was very young."

Aelya's *babushka* had often gossiped disparagingly about the broken families around their neighbourhood. Too many women were working, she'd said, and too many men were moving to the cities in search of jobs. In school, Aelya heard rumours that her classmate Zoya Kamenskaya's father had abandoned a previous family in Belarus to take a job at Smolensk's aircraft plant. She wondered how Sirin felt about her biological father.

"So, getting involved in Honeybee's nonsense . . . is that something to do with your stepfather?"

"I'd love it if it pissed him off." Sirin laughed. "But I doubt he'd even take notice. Don't get me wrong—he's always treated me well. But things haven't been the same since my mother told me he wasn't my real father. I guess I've always known. I mean, look at me." She gestured to her face.

She continued, "I think now he loved the *idea* of having a daughter more than he loved me. He liked having me as a doll, an ornament. He never wanted me to live my own life. I had to fight every step of the way. To fly. To join the Air Force."

"He's probably worried for you. It shows he loves you."

"Not really."

Aelya did have to wonder. If her father had the power Sirin's step-father had, she was sure he'd thwart her risk-taking ambitions at every turn. But whatever the protestations, Sirin had still been allowed to fly fighters—on the front lines, no less.

"What about intervening with Vasily Stalin?" Aelya asked. "Didn't your stepfather help with that?"

Sirin smiled, leaning toward Aelya to whisper. "That was me. I faked an official letter using my father's name. A few years ago, he helped falsify Vasily's school records to get him into the Air Force Academy. I'm sure as soon as Stalin the younger saw my father's name, he moved heaven and earth to do whatever the letter asked."

Sirin rubbed her hands and huddled close to Aelya as the evening cooled under cloudless skies. "I was really hoping you'd get to meet my father in Moscow. I told him what I'd done in that letter. I wanted you to tell me how he reacted."

Aelya liked the way Sirin seemed to trust her. She realized she'd been unfair to the newcomer. It must have been hard, growing up surrounded by the same shadowy men Aelya had encountered in Moscow. No won-der people like Petrushka spread nasty rumours about Sirin. Aelya could never be sure of the whole truth, but she decided this was a person she could trust in the air. That mattered more than Sirin's background, or anything she had done.

They caught the sleep that only soldiers could, in the most uncom-fortable of places and positions. By first light, they were ready to move out. Later, after bidding farewell to their transport, they ended up getting lucky and catching a supply truck to take them the rest of the way to Rogachevsk.

As the sun rose over the battle-scarred land, Aelya felt an odd sort of contentment about heading back to the front. It was a mood she wished she could express to her parents. The bland pleasantries she dashed off in letter after letter did nothing to convey her certainty that this was where she was meant to be. She rarely wanted to write at all. But everyone was doing it; she felt pressured by the other pilots. She might have once wanted to ask Vasya, her sister, about love. But that was meaningless now. Better that she made small talk in her letters and asked her family about life in Kuybyshev. How could they ever understand her anyway?

They arrived to the peal of an alarm bell and an enlisted woman waving the truck off the road toward some trees. "Air raid alert. You pilots?" the woman said.

"Yes," answered Aelya.

"Better go find your squadrons."

Aelya and Sirin reunited with their respective squadrons, which were holed up in different slit trenches not far from the airstrip itself.

Honeybee greeted her loudly as Aelya stumbled into a trench with her squadron. "Your timing is impeccable." She turned to a junior lieutenant with peach fuzz on his chin. "Myshkin, I don't need you anymore. Get the hell back to First Squadron."

The young man slowly rose into a stooped position.

"Go on! This is Second Squadron. Move!" She turned to Aelya. "What a relief—I thought I was actually going to have to fly with that yellow-mouth. Genius, you're back with me."

Genius, blond haired and rosy cheeked, and one of the newer pilots Aelya recognized, dropped into their trench. He'd been a chess champion and was exempted from service for his talent. The others derisively called him Genius because he'd chosen to fight anyway.

Honeybee gave him a stern look. "You're still pretty new, so I'm going to use you as bait. I hope you're up to scratch with belly landings.

Because once you get hit, you better bring that Yak home—it's more valuable than you are. And if you're dead, just keep your hands on the stick. Rigor mortis will do the rest."

Genius paled. "Yes, Comrade Commander."

Aelya blew a raspberry and told him, "The old hands will try to scare you. It's just how they relieve tension. Remember your training and you'll be fine."

Honeybee said, "Don't be contradicting your squadron commander, Mars."

"I go away for a month and now you're in charge?" Aelya said.

"Only temporarily," said Spam.

Honeybee shot him a withering look. "Yes, I'm acting squadron commander. Baby was injured in the line of duty while, uh, dictating supply orders to a clerk in the maintenance battalion. Tragic. It really burns, I hear." Honeybee scratched her crotch in an exaggerated fashion.

"Baby has a field wife?" Aelya said with little surprise.

"I wouldn't call her a wife," said Honeybee. "She's not exactly the marrying kind. Isn't that right, Vino?"

"Don't ask me. I didn't have enough rubles for her."

Aelya frowned at the thought of these men, her brothers, engaging in prostitution. She wanted to hate that woman, but she knew enough of the realities women had to deal with.

"I'd say that was money well saved," said Honeybee. She dismissed an oncoming retort with a wave. "Enough about your disgusting predilections," she said to Vino, then turned to Aelya. "So tell me, how was Moscow? Did you see my parents?"

"No, but I met Ivan and Nadezhda."

"Who're they?" Lucky asked.

"Her servants."

"Servants? Can you imagine?" He seemed in genuine awe, not disapproving. His lack of guile was endearing. She remembered the boyish wonder Lucky had shown while walking the floor of the aircraft factory in Saratov, the largest building he'd ever been inside.

"What else did you see in Moscow?" Lucky said. He rattled off a list of questions, as if she had been a tourist checking off Red Square, Gorky Park, the Bolshoi Ballet, and other destinations. He leaned closer and closer to Aelya, eventually sniffing her khaki field shirt shamelessly. Vino, Honeybee, and soon all the others followed suit.

"Smells like home," said Vino.

Aelya couldn't help laughing. "It's been a long time since anyone found my smell tolerable." She reached over her suitcase and retrieved the hastily re-wrapped parcel of soap, handing out a bar to each. She'd originally intended to save them for the women pilots, but this was her squadron. They were her brothers and sister. She held back one bar for Zina and her crew, though.

Frost appeared at the lip of the trench. "Second Squadron, move to readiness one!"

The lazy, tired, jokey expressions of the eight pilots in the trench were all replaced by the determined looks of professionals. They clambered up and walked with purpose toward the camouflage shelters where their fighters were ready for action.

Overhead, a squadron of fighters came down in pairs to land. By the time Aelya reached her plane, Stitches had emerged from his fighter, stowed away nearby.

"Mars," he called out. "Welcome back. How's our Lily?"

Not now. She wanted more time. "She's fine. Getting better."

He was about to ask more, but Lucky hurried into her shelter, holding out his pistol. This was what they did before every sortie. She took the pistol, chambered a round, then loaded an extra bullet into the magazine. When the ritual was done, Aelya had lost sight of Stitches. Climbing into her cockpit, she wondered if he knew about Dmitriev's plans for Roza. Would he approve of her trophy hunting?

She looked over the side of the plane, expecting to see Zina handing over the pre-flight checklist, but it was Katya, Stone's former crew chief, who held the clipboard.

"I'm just filling in," the statuesque technician said. "Zina's writing her engineer's exam."

"Is that so?"

"Yeah. Next time you see her, she'll be squadron engineer." Katya beamed with pride.

Aelya was happy for her friend. If Zina made squadron engineer, she'd be an officer as well. But her crew, the same one that had served Aelya throughout her Air Force career, would be broken up. As it was, Zina was already doubling up in her duties since the previous engineer had been promoted and transferred to the mobile maintenance unit.

Aelya swallowed, trying to suppress her annoyance. She suddenly had an irrational fear that something would be wrong with her plane. Katya surely wasn't familiar with Aelya's preferences. Something would have been missed.

She held her hand to stop it from shaking. She looked around the shelter and saw the familiar faces of the other members of her crew: Raya, her mechanic; Inga, her armourer. Stop it, she told herself.

After a deep breath, the call came over the radio, cancelling the alert.

Emerging from the cockpit, she found herself wobbly and tired, though it was still mid-morning. She shoved aside some spare parts, laid on a blanket, and went to sleep.

CHAPTER 27: TROPHIES

The grand facade of Gorky Park's pavilion dominated Roza's view. Towering letters many metres high announced the EXHIBITION OF TROPHY ARTIFACTS. She could see row upon row of captured German vehicles beyond the gates, parked along the wide avenues of the park. She hesitated in the pavilion's shadow. Zhora cracked a slight smile. At least his smiles seemed less forced these days.

As children, they had weaved through clowns and vendors hawking candied apples, and had raced to the rides. Her favourite was the helter-skelter. Sliding down its spiral ramp on an old carpet, she'd feel her heart press against her rib cage, the butterflies in her stomach only adding to the thrilling sensation of flying. Long before she could dream of joining an aeroclub, she'd already developed a taste for flight. She remembered little Zhora stamping the ground in a tantrum when their parents said he was too little to follow his sister on the ride. She couldn't believe how much she missed that now.

She returned Zhora's smile and hesitantly offered her arm. She could limp without her crutch or painkillers now, but she liked to let him support her. Gorgeous summer skies brought out visitors in the hundreds, many of them in uniform. Zhora was one of only a few minors.

Moscow had been a bubble of escape for Roza these last few weeks. She'd been happily cooped up in her mother's apartment, occasionally helping the neighbours by watering the vegetable garden and picking away pests. Dmitriev hadn't bothered visiting but had regularly sent his secretary to check on Roza's progress, complaining that the awards process was tied up in bureaucracy. All the while, her leg grew stronger, though she still favoured one side. The limp lingered, which she took as a reminder of past mistakes.

She'd considered wearing a summer dress instead of a uniform but couldn't bear letting the ugly leg injury and burns on her forearm show in public. She hadn't wanted to go out, but after weeks of quiet, tentative coexistence, Zhora's enthusiasm to see this exhibition was welcome. He sought to occupy his time before joining his Komsomol group outside the city to harvest summer crops. There were only so many tasks he could perform for the old women of the apartment block, and if not for those, he might well have decided to return to the factory out of boredom. Roza couldn't allow that; it was as if, with one slip, she might never get him back.

Past the entrance pillars, the park was transformed. Every patch of green grass and every section of pavement was covered in captured German tanks, vehicles, and artillery. Down a walkway toward the river, more unusual vehicles were parked: mine-clearing tanks, bridge layers, and other heavy engineering equipment. On the banks of the river, Red Army engineers demonstrated pontoons and rubber dinghies used by German sappers in their crossings.

Zhora grew animated as he pointed out the section displaying captured enemy aircraft. He ran down the footpath, occasionally stopping to let her catch up. Men in Air Force uniforms stood near the planes, explaining to curious onlookers various aspects of the Luftwaffe's machinery. People laughed, smiled, and pointed out holes and burn marks in the planes.

Where once they held dead and dying men, these objects were novelties to hordes of visitors, who were curious about them as if they were wares at a market to be tasted. Roza wasn't sure how she felt about this condensed, sanitized slice of the war.

She spotted a few visible injuries among the Air Force guides. One man was missing an arm. Another wore an eye patch. Perhaps they were all injured, but some wounds can't be seen.

Zhora ducked under a Heinkel, crouching to face the ventral turret. It was in reasonably good condition with no signs of damage from gunfire. Perhaps it had been captured on the ground at Stalingrad. He emerged, a smile plastered on his face. She couldn't help laughing a little in relief. Her little brother was still there, the one who had marvelled at the carousel and the Ferris wheel. He asked the Air Force officer on duty if he could climb in.

"I'm afraid not. And who is this young lady?"

Roza and the officer sized each other up. They wore matching Orders of the Red Banner, and her limp was balanced by his gnarled hand, which he kept curled in a fist close to his side.

"That's my sister," Zhora said proudly.

Roza and the other pilot shared a quiet nod. As much as she liked having her family together, they would always be alien to her in a way her comrades, even this pilot, wouldn't. It was because of what she and her comrades had been through. It had been wrenching since Aelya left. She missed her. She missed Stitches. She felt alone.

Dmitriev had asked her to help open the exhibition a week before, on the second anniversary of the invasion, but she'd declined on the basis of her health. She'd been feeling quite well, but the idea of being put on display, to be trotted out like a prize, made her sick. Or worse, to have everyone somehow treating her like a hero. She'd fought in one major battle and was now slinking away as her comrades continued to put their lives on the line. Only Zhora's childlike interest in the planes kept her from fleeing the park.

"Where are the fighters?" Zhora asked.

The officer pointed and he rushed off in that direction, towing Roza behind him.

"I know those ones," he said, approaching a row of fighters. "One of the boys at the factory lent me his copies of *Murzilka*. I read all about enemy aircraft. Messerschmitt Bf 109, an E type. And there's the Focke-Wulf 190. BMW 801 engine. It does over fifteen hundred horsepower."

As they neared, he began to imagine flying against the plane, making shooting noises and imitating the diving drone of an engine, almost bumping into a pilot holding hands with a civilian woman. Roza shrugged sheepishly, but the couple smiled.

"Yes, I always go to children's magazines for the latest technical details," Roza said as she caught up to her brother.

"It's not for children. Anyway, which one is tougher, the Messer or the Focke-Wulf?"

"Depends on the pilot."

He whistled, looking at a 20 mm cannon poking from the wing of the Fw 190. Roza watched, rooted to the spot, staring down the dark depths of the cannon's barrel. Goosebumps rose on her flesh. Her body shivered with the chill of recognition, her heart thumping, thoughts coalescing around something familiar, something she'd missed all this time in Moscow. She wondered if she could just climb into the cockpit and fly away. Involuntarily, thoughts crept into her brain of sweeping over the city, shooting something, anything.

Zhora broke the spell. "And how do you think our planes compare? They're much tougher, aren't they?" For years, he'd been nurtured by the toughness and resilience of the Soviet people and, by extension, their technology.

"My Yak is mostly made of plywood and fabric. I told you—it's not the plane, it's the pilot."

She heard a woman call to Zhora. The pilot and his sweetheart waved him over to take their photo. They posed with a kiss. Imagining how the photo would turn out, she thought about the life that she wanted with Stitches. She wondered if Aelya had told him. Roza should have said something already, written a letter. She'd wanted to, but something always held her back.

If only he were here. She thought about returning to the front. It would be painful. Out there, she would long to be close to him, seeking to steal moments alone together that might be their last. But at least he would be near.

No, that time was over. Still, she needed to go back, but only to say goodbye. No, not just that. She needed to check on him. Dmitriev had given a few updates on the regiment, but she didn't trust him. Yes, I'll go back, she told herself.

Wanting desperately to run away from the park, she found it hard to breathe. She had to lean against the fuselage of a fallen fighter and noticed the green heart painted on it.

She looked around the other side of the fighter and saw a civilian man and woman playing with their little girl and boy. Together. Happy.

She looked behind her. Zhora was gawking at the next plane, painted with an even more colourful insignia. She didn't like the way he seemed to be glorifying the war, but he was interested in what she had done. She felt the stirrings of a real connection, early steps in putting her family back together. But other people needed her. And she had unfinished business with the one who'd killed Stone, the Night Raven. She lightly banged a fist against the green heart, eliciting a hollow metallic thump. A thought crystallized in her mind.

"Zhora. I'll be going soon."

"What?"

"Just for a visit to the front. It's part of a propaganda tour."

"I—I was hoping we'd have the whole summer."

"I'll be back right away. I just need you to keep an eye on Mama."

He grimaced. "I found another bottle under her bed."

"Yes, I know." She put her hands on his arms. "I trust you to take care of her. You're the man of the house, you know? And anyway, it's just for a little bit. I'll be back."

He nodded. She let him go and he turned to look at the next fighter plane, but slowly now, without a word. She let him wander a bit more as she stood by the Fw 190, looking at the green heart.

"Just for a visit," she said to herself, too quiet for anyone to hear.

PART IV:

The Battle of Kursk

CHAPTER 28: NIGHTMARE OF STEEL

Rogachevsk, July 5, 1943

The din of clanging metal woke Aelya. She froze, her drowsy mind trying to reconcile the open air tent with memories of the barracks at the Engels Higher Aviation School, where Marina Raskova used to get them up in the middle of the night for alert drills, banging spoons against helmets. This was a bell, its ring a harsh, jarring peal of metal striking metal, unnervingly close to the crack of guns firing.

She stumbled in the darkness to a slit trench outside her tent, still dressed in the standard issue male underwear of a singlet and linen shorts. She landed, dripping in sweat, and squeezed between Petrushka and Vino, her back scraping the rough dirt sides of the narrow ditch.

"You've gotten soft from your time in Moscow," Petrushka said, pushing her away. "I think you must have put on ten kilos."

Aelya swore at him.

There was a silence in the trench, even as the alarm continued. It was too dark to make out Petrushka's expression and whether he was shocked at Aelya's uncharacteristic language; she certainly was.

Dirt trickled down as someone scrabbled around at the top of the trench, their shadow blocking the moonlit sky.

"Midnight treat, anyone?" Stitches extended his hand down. He held a dozen individually wrapped candies, marked by the distinctive artwork of the Babaevsky factory.

"I thought they stopped making candies for the war?" Aelya said.

"How old are those, exactly?" said Vino.

"Beware of Tartars bearing gifts," said Petrushka.

"Well, don't look a gift Tartar in the mouth," Stitches said, loudly chewing his own candy. "Seriously, it's so sticky, I can barely open my mouth."

Aelya snapped one up and popped the little caramel into her mouth. Stitches's glibness calmed her. Like Roza, he was a rock on which she could steady itself.

She flipped the candy wrapper in her hand. "Where did you get these?"

"Platonov's driver always brings a few from the general's secret stash when she drives him over here to see Red."

"You hiding another field wife?" Petrushka smirked. "Better not tell Lily."

Stitches cleared his throat. "I hear she only likes bad boys. More your speed, Petrushka."

"Careful what you say," Petrushka warned. "There are ladies present. This one might snap your head off."

"Mars? Never."

Stitches dropped into the trench, crouching to face them with his feet planted between Petrushka's and Aelya's.

Muffled explosions cracked in the distance, too far away for them to care. Perhaps the bombs were intended for them, perhaps not. Night bombing was notoriously inaccurate. And while Aelya and the others might long to get up in the air and punish the enemy, it was liable to be more dangerous for them than staying put. None of them had night-fighting experience.

"How long do you think Lily will stay in Moscow?" Stitches asked.

Aelya had talked only a little about her time there, sticking to the topic of Roza's health. Satisfied that she was on the mend, Stitches had left it at that, although he'd been calling on Legend frequently for up-dates. There had been no official word about Roza being taken out of combat entirely. Maybe things had changed? No—Aelya had put off telling Stitches for too long.

"I'm sure it will be a while," she said. "Dmitriev's got all sorts of plans to use her for propaganda, especially now that she's up for a gold star. She might never come back." She wasn't sure why her last statement came out so caustically. Thinking of her time in Moscow left her with a lingering bad taste. She sucked on the caramel more.

"Good," Stitches said.

She watched in the dim starlight for some flicker of emotion. How could he be so accepting of Roza's departure, even from a strictly milit-ary standpoint? "Don't you want the best pilot in your squadron?"

Petrushka coughed. "Best?"

Stitches ignored him. "I'd wish the same for any of you. You've done your duty. Far beyond what was asked of you. If any of you get that chance, then good. Have a long life for the rest of us."

"I don't know if she likes Moscow," said Aelya "I hated it. I felt out of sorts all the time. It was . . . I don't know . . . scary."

"It's strange going back into the world of civilians," Stitches reflec-ted. "The spring of '42, when the regiment was refitting with Yak-1s, I was given four days' liberty in Tambov. I would wake up in the hostel be-fore the first sun, frightened, paralyzed in bed, with no one to tell me what I should do."

"The Air Force takes the agony of choice away from you," Pet-rushka said.

Aelya agreed. "Maybe that's why I keep trying to get out of being a flight leader. I can't make those choices."

"Did I ever tell you about my first day of the war?" asked Stitches. Everyone remembered that first day. Everyone had a story.

"You got evacuated right before the German bombers hit your airfield, didn't you?" Aelya said.

He nodded. "But that's not the whole story. Our regiment commander had taken a squadron into action while the rest of us awaited orders. There were only five of us. It was a Sunday, remember, so it had been hard getting people back from leave. We had no idea who was still on their way, or who'd been killed by German bombs while trying to get to our airfield. We had only a skeleton crew. Then we received two phone calls in quick succession. The first, from a regimental commander in our division, told us to regroup with the other units at a reserve airfield. The other, from a neighbouring divisional commander, said to get our planes up and patrol our airfield. When we tried to call back for clarification, the lines had gone dead. Bear in mind, this was before we had radios in our planes, so we had no idea what our commander's situation was. The Germans were really getting close, and they'd already bombed the airfield that morning.

"So it was just me and four younger pilots with even less experience. We could either stay put, patrolling our airfield and hope our comrades would return, or we could relocate to another base, as the first order said. All I knew was, if we did nothing we'd be lost. So I decided to go with the first message and we took off for the new base."

"Do you think it was the right choice?"

"Who knows? We may have sacrificed our comrades by rebasing."

He wouldn't say "retreating." If he had used that word the first day, it might have meant a bullet to the head. He'd probably convinced himself it wasn't a retreat since then.

"It turns out, our comrades had already been lost. The entire squadron had been wiped out in an aerial engagement. And if we'd stayed, we all would have been killed. The field was bombed to oblivion later that day."

"So it was the right choice."

"That was just luck. Based on the information I had, there was no way to know what was best. Someone just needed to make a decision. It could have been right, it could have been wrong. I made a choice and I gave up on our comrades. But I've learned to live with it, as I have a lot of other decisions, in the belief that somehow, at the end of all of this, it will have been worth it. You won't know. You just have to do it."

"If only there were some mathematical formula that would give an easy answer every time," Aelya said.

"Focus on what's at hand. It'll be fine." He patted her on the shoulder. "I have faith in you."

The alarm had stopped. It might have stopped a while ago; Aelya hadn't noticed.

"Is it all clear?" someone shouted from another trench.

Aelya and the others stood and stretched.

Petrushka yawned. "Damn these alerts. I was having the most wonderful dream and now I can't remember it. Hopefully, I can get back into it."

But Legend, running up to their trench, quickly quashed that notion. "All squadron and flight leaders to the command post."

They went out in the grey pre-dawn light. They flew in tight, large formations at twenty-five hundred metres. Since none of them were used to flying in such dark conditions, this would help, the rationale went. Easy targets, Aelya thought.

At this altitude, with the sun barely above the horizon, the early-morning coolness overwhelmed Aelya's cockpit. She briefly regretted not putting extra layers over her summer field uniform, but there would be time enough for things to heat up. Time for the sun to rise, and time for the intense action and terror of battle to turn the atmosphere into the familiar stew of sweat, urine, vomit, and oil. But right now, this was beautiful. This was flying.

All around her—to the right of her, to the left, some above, some below—hundreds of planes floated, locked in serene formations against the endless sky. Like steps up to heaven. Aelya was grateful for the radio silence that allowed them to pass over the ugly, scarred battle lines below without any distressing sounds to mar the view from the air.

This was it, and everyone knew it. The battle on the ground had already started. Radio chatter farther south indicated an immense fight in the air that had started before sunrise. Wild rumours circulated the base. The Germans had broken through. The Red Army was counterattacking. The south was all a decoy, and the real battle was going to happen here.

In the back of her mind, Aelya knew all about the mission. Similar ones were given to individual flights among every fighter regiment. There were too many targets to strike, but they would try to hit everything and protect everything regardless. On leaving the briefing, Red had wished her good luck. She'd been surprised and wanted to say something, but he turned away, as if embarrassed by his uncharacteristic show of sentiment. From the briefing, she could only vaguely recall the order in which her four fighters were to escort a wave of Peshkas, but that didn't seem important right now.

What mattered was remembering this beauty.

The sun's rays pierced the sky in glorious red and orange hues. It was radiant, as it had been that morning in Stalingrad. Again she thought, What better way to start my last day?

The battle front was easy to spot. Masses of vehicles, smoke, and fire. Streaks of tracers criss-crossed the steppe, already torn up by tank tracks and craters. Here and there, sparks flowered when shells and bullets struck metal.

Aelya's mind returned to the responsibility of leadership as she signalled with her wings for Vino's pair to space themselves properly. Dots appeared on the rising sun. Vultures. She called them out. First a few, then so many that, as they grew closer, they threatened to blot out the daylight.

At that moment, she was at peace with the likelihood of dying, that shadowy presence over her shoulder comforting her like an old friend.

She gave a signal to bank and climb. Lucky matched her, with Vino and Spam following closely, hoping to get enough height to gain an advantage on the nearest enemy formation. She saw the silver bodies of their planes glinting in the sunlight. And it was breathtaking.

CHAPTER 29: COLLISION COURSE

Roza limped toward her plane, the pain still there in her left leg despite Dr. Krupenya's medication. She didn't want to take anything stronger, in case it affected her reflexes.

"You know, we're making quite the exception for you," said Stitches, walking alongside her. "We usually have a trial period before we let new pilots into action . . ." And for pilots returning from injury, but he left that unsaid. His humour was forced. All around them, the tension of battle pervaded the atmosphere.

"I'm serious," he added. "This isn't like anything you've seen before. You need to ease yourself back."

She told herself she didn't have that luxury. "You've already been fighting for days. I'm fresh."

He smiled grimly, shaking his head.

When she'd arrived at Rogachevsk, the situation was frantic and the pace relentless. Legend barely showed surprise at her presence before filling her in. They were in a constant cycle of escort and intercept missions. Tangling with the enemy was expected on virtually every sortie. There was no more nonsense about hunting the Night Raven. Roza regretted not taking him down when she had the chance, but with flying five or six sorties a day, a rematch would only be a matter of time. It was scarcely comprehensible that four sorties a day during the short daylight hours over Stalingrad had seemed too much. They were long past that now.

The regiment was dying for replacements, having lost a half dozen pilots in the first day of battle, including Wolf, one of their aces, and Offal, Sirin's wingman. Their sister regiment, the 466th, was also hit hard in an airfield strike on the first day. The ranks that had been built up and trained carefully over the past five months were decimated in a matter of hours. As soon as Roza said she was ready to fight, Red threw her in without asking questions.

Stitches followed Roza to her plane's shelter and a technician helped her with a parachute. Their wingmen, Starik and Dema, carried on toward their fighters. Another flight of four roared down the runway. Soon, another flight would land, and then it would be their turn.

"I thought you were supposed to be on some sort of propaganda tour," he said.

"What better propaganda is there than shooting down more Nazis?"

He narrowed his eyes.

"Come on," she said. "What's with the sour face? You're as bad as Dema now." At least her wingman hadn't been surprised by her return. He firmly believed that death had already marked them all, so Roza's return to the front merely conformed to fate. At times like this, his blunt pessimism was almost enjoyable.

Two pairs of Yaks descended toward the airstrip. Aelya's flight.

"We've got to get moving," Roza said.

But Stitches wouldn't let the matter go. "Mars made it sound like you weren't coming back."

"You should be happy, then. Don't you want me back here? I thought we make a great team."

"We do, but I want you far away from all of this. You've already done your part."

"While you still do yours? No, I can't live with that."

He looked torn with emotion, but he suppressed any further objections. She grabbed him and kissed him. And the world fell away, for just a few seconds. When she released him from her embrace, Stitches grinned, but his eyes didn't play along.

Dema hurried over from his shelter. "Come on, you lovebirds. I'd rather not die unless my wingman goes down with me," he said to Roza.

She shook her head playfully. "Dema, when will you learn—"

"I know. 'There's no such thing as fate,'" he said, mimicking her voice. He was actually smiling, happy to be joining the action after having been relegated to duties in the command post during much of Roza's absence.

As Stitches left, he passed Aelya, heading to debrief. She and Roza locked eyes for a moment. Aelya stared blankly. She looked hollowed out. Weak. But to Roza, it was energizing. Here was tangible proof that her friend was still with them, at least for the moment. Aelya bent over and spewed a mouthful onto the ground. Behind her, Vino, Lucky, and Spam trudged along in a daze. Then she turned and followed them.

"Just like old times," Roza shouted out to Stitches.

He turned and shouted back, "Just like old times."

Roza had missed the air. Her back pressed against the sweltering leather of the seat. Her pulse throbbed, her skin prickled. She felt good back in the cockpit. It meant she was fully alive and in control. There wasn't the uncertainty of home or questions about after the war. She would just do her job and kill the enemy.

When the first silhouettes appeared, her breath caught with excitement. Stitches called in the contact at that exact moment. "Those are the Stukas. Looks like they have four escorts."

They'd been lucky enough to make this interception early, while still over the German side of the line—or where it had been an hour ago. The situation on the ground was fluid, with tens of thousands of soldiers and vehicles hurling themselves at each other, the space between them filled with shells, bullets, fire, and smoke. Up above, planes occupied every sector of the sky, and they had to trust their vectoring station that they were in the right place, fighting the right enemy.

"Wait," Dema said over the radio. "I see four more vultures, ten o'clock high. They're trying to hide in the sun."

"Starik and I will hit the Stukas and try to dodge their escorts," Stitches said. "Lily and Dema, stay in high cover and pick off those new vultures if they try to follow us."

Without delay, Stitches took his pair in a wide turn, trying to put the Stukas between him and the escorts. The four Fw 190s guarding the Stukas didn't wait around. As soon as Stitches began his dive, they split up, one pair throttling forward to put themselves in front of their bombers, the other pair aiming to intercept Stitches's attack path.

Stitches swore as he had to break from his dive and engage in a turning fight against the heavies. The Germans were learning from past mistakes and taking this escort seriously. No more "knights of the air" nonsense; they were no longer content to let their bombers get picked apart while waiting to duel enemy fighters.

Roza split her attention between the dogfight below, the four remaining Fw 190s up high, and watching for danger from everywhere else in the sky. Stitches and Starik rolled and turned beautifully, their classes in Lyubertsy paying off. Unable to line up a target, the Fw 190s chasing them broke off to regroup. But they'd done their job and pulled the battle far away from the Stukas.

"Let's get in on the action," Roza said to Dema.

They dived at the Stukas, which had descended for an attack run. The four Fw 190s which had stayed out of the fight now shadowed Roza. But she could read the enemy planes' intentions, noticing tiny movements and course corrections, interpreting them with her finely honed instinct. When the first pair dived at them, she anticipated where they were going and adjusted her angle and throttle to catch the enemy at their most vulnerable when they closed. But this enemy pair was too experienced; they broke and climbed away before they could be caught.

Immediately, Roza spotted the next pair moving to attack and banked hard, gritting her teeth and trying to ignore the pain shooting up her injured leg as she put pressure on the rudder. The plane resisted violently, vibrations hammering at her eyeballs as she swung around tightly. She came face to face with her stalkers. The thick profile of the Fw 190 bristled with its cannon, earning its nickname of "heavy" in every way. Roza and Dema would be outgunned. Only nerves would save them.

The enemy broke away first, but Roza didn't get the shot off in time and sliced the air with tracers the colour of lightning. She shook her head, exhaled, then pulled to gain height again, just as another pair of Fw 190s came into view on her right. She had to break to avoid their tracer streams, losing sight of Dema. An Fw 190 zipped by her field of view. Green heart. Black raven.

She was in the thick of it now. With every manoeuvre she made, she barely stayed ahead of the enemy. The Night Raven would appear, she would evade, and then he'd pull away while another Fw 190 would intercept her, preventing her from chasing.

"Dema, where the hell are you?"

"Sorry, Lily, I've got my hands full."

"So do I, damn it! Stitches, you better be hitting those Stukas. These heavies are riding us hard."

She rolled and turned, first one way, then another, trying to get clear. Her mouth went dry. Sweat poured down from the lining of her helmet, forcing her to squint. She didn't dare take a hand away from the controls to wipe her forehead. This wasn't just normal combat fear—this was something unfamiliar. The enemy was slowly gaining an edge on her. There were no mission goals. No tactical assessment. This was pure survival.

And then, there was the Night Raven in front of her, chasing another Yak. She angled her fighter to get below, in his blind spot. She checked for her own pursuers.

That tiny pause was enough for the Night Raven to avert danger. He broke off, banking and climbing, using his more powerful engine to pull away.

Now where was Dema?

Roza flew a snaking path, looping around, trying to reorient herself to shadows that kept moving across a crowded sky.

"Get back onto my wing, Dema."

"You don't think I'm trying?"

Streams of tracers flew across her canopy. From the corner of her eye, she saw an Fw 190 whip past. Its left wing broke apart, flames trailing as it spun out. She glanced back. A Yak was above and behind. The Fw 190's wingman jinked hard, frantically diving away from the Yak's line of fire.

"Dema, it's about time."

She climbed fast, finally able to take a full breath. She now saw not one but two Yaks following her and could read their bort numbers: Stitches and Starik.

"Giraffe," Stitches reported, "this is Osprey One-Zero. We managed to get one Stuka, but the rest delivered their bombs to target. The enemy is breaking off and going home. Permission to thirty-three."

Giraffe relayed permission to head home.

Roza shook her head. "Hurry and form up, Dema. We have to do better than that."

She scanned the sky as they gained altitude. There were just the three Yaks, including Roza.

"Dema? Stitches, Starik, did you see Dema?"

"Negative."

She called out several more times, but the only response was Giraffe telling her to keep the airwaves clear.

CHAPTER 30: PAINFUL REMINDERS

Sauna-like humidity prickled Aelya's skin. The women pilots had established their sleeping quarters under a camouflaged open air tent by a copse of trees at the edge of Rogachevsk. It was exposed to the elements and the noise of guns and bombs pounding away with regularity in the distance. But it was the heat that kept Aelya awake. She struggled vainly to reach a state of dreaming. She needed the rest, even if some shadowy creature of grinding metal lay waiting in the recesses of her mind. Only in the air, in that domain of fire and steel where death seemed imminent, could she feel at peace.

She fell out of bed.

"Ha!" Sirin exclaimed from the next cot over. "I'm glad someone else can't sleep."

Aelya brushed the dirt off her skivvies. "It's too hot."

"Tell me about it." Sirin sighed. "I can't stop my mind from turning."

"That's what the vodka is for."

"There's not enough of it."

"Well, would you rather be hungover or tired?"

Aelya was parched and reached for the water flask at the foot of Sirin's bed. She took a swig, trying to ignore the tang of diesel. In the relentless summer heat, Dr. Krupenya had been on their backs to stay hydrated. Water had to be trucked in, filling whole cargo beds with steel drums once used for fuel. Between the thirsty planes and the crew, there was no water for washing. But no one wanted to wash. That would have taken time away from precious sleep. No amount of breeze could clear the odour that permeated everything in their quarters. Aelya had thought it was something she would get used to, but she was wrong.

She lay back on her cot without a blanket, closing her eyes, her skin itching from heat rash. In the blackness, she envisioned the same torrent of enemy planes, buffeting her like a hail storm. Echoes of the endless procession she'd seen since that first morning, each encounter blurring into the next.

She had the feeling Sirin was still on her side, looking at her.

"What's bothering you?" Aelya asked.

After a moment's silence, Sirin said, "You know I had three different pilots fly on my wing today. It's hard to relax when you don't know who's got your back."

Aelya sensed the trouble: guilt. She'd seen that look from Sirin for a while, ever since her wingman, Offal, had been shot down on the first day of the battle.

Whatever cheery confidence Sirin had possessed was wiped away by her first combat. Where once she'd found her manner annoying, Aelya missed it and could only sympathize. "You know that's how it is. Your wingman died to protect you. That's his job."

"But I'm not doing mine. When we got into the air that first day, the sky was so full of . . . everything. I just didn't know what to do. I mean, I went through the motions, but it was all so difficult. I was thinking so slowly, like my brain was picking its way through a muddy swamp. The whole time, with everything happening—all the bullets and shells, tracers, smoke and fire, planes, smashing, exploding—it was like one huge . . . thing surrounding me. Do you know that feeling? Like some . . . force was behind it all. Watching me, creeping up on me. Waiting to get me. What I mean is, I froze."

"But you kept flying anyway. You're still alive. You must be doing something right." The casualties among pilots who'd joined after Stalingrad was worse than for the veterans. Sirin stood out as one of the few who were still around.

"Yeah, I keep flying. But I'm afraid."

Aelya wondered what it was about her that made people want to share their troubles with her. Yulia and Olga had tried to make her understand their problems, but she had failed them. Despite her brain telling her it was too much bother, she had the urge to listen to Sirin.

"That's how you're supposed to feel," Aelya said.

"I'm not afraid for myself. Well, not so much. I'm afraid I'm going to let everyone down." Sirin sat up on her cot. "It's like this weight I can never escape. It's strange. It's like . . . you know what it's like being different? I mean, looking so different when growing up?"

"Didn't your stepfather protect you?"

"No one can protect you from feeling like you don't belong. I always had to put up a false front. I thought I could keep it up my whole life, but I can't anymore. This is too much. I'm just lost."

Aelya looked at Roza, thinking of her own battle with the past. She was still happily asleep, her face soft and unworried, despite the trauma of losing her own wingman.

"Feeling lost is also totally normal," Aelya said, as if to convince herself. "I've been worried too. All this responsibility is being shoved on me at a time when I feel like I'm losing my connection with this world." She grasped for something reassuring. When was the last time she'd felt lost? She remembered Stitches's story about the first day of the war and told it, repeating his advice. "Who knows if our choices are the right ones? But doing the wrong thing is better than doing nothing at all."

"But I'm still terrified of doing something wrong," Sirin said.

"I'm scared out of my wits too." Aelya counted her lucky stars that she had yet to lose anyone under her command. It had been a close call when Vino bailed out the day before, but he'd been rescued by some *makhras*. She'd been lucky to survive herself. When she returned from that same mission, her entire tail section had been perforated.

Her concerns weren't restricted to the air. Since Stone's crash, Katya had only been able to draw work as a swing mechanic. The pilots hadn't said it, but they didn't trust her after she'd pulled her pistol on others. Aelya was sure a man who'd done the same wouldn't have been blacklisted like that. After repeated pleading from Zina, Aelya had taken Katya on as crew chief. But integrating a new team had been rife with teething issues. Every sortie, she took off in fear her crew had missed something.

"Everyone's scared," said Roza, her eyes still closed. Aelya and Sirin turned, and she continued, "You can't let fear control you."

"Have you been awake this whole time?" Aelya asked. She looked over at Honeybee, who snored lightly in her decidedly non-regulation nightgown. In their open tent quarters, she was daring Red, Troyanov, or Cricket to do something about it, but even the most officious sticklers on the staff had more important things to worry about.

"You can't let it control you," Roza repeated. She wrung her hands.

Aelya couldn't quite allow her mind to accept it, but Roza seemed unsure. Roza, the most confident person she'd ever met. But Roza had never lost a wingman before.

"You can't blame yourself for Dema," Aelya said, sitting up in her bed.

Roza sat up too. "I can. The Green Hearts had the edge on me the whole time. If Stitches hadn't come when he did . . ."

Aelya's empty stomach twisted into knots. No. Doubting herself wasn't something that could happen to Roza.

"That's to be expected," Sirin said. "The Luftwaffe's targeting you. I read some radio intercepts. They're trying to hunt down the White Lily."

"Yes, that's right." Aelya remembered. "No one can stand up against that alone."

Roza shook her head. "But I should have held out longer. Maybe it would have given Stitches enough time to get to Dema."

"He did the right thing," Aelya said. "You're the senior pilot, the priority. You're too valuable to the rest of us."

"I hate being valuable." Roza groaned, flopping back down noisily. "We're thinking too much."

"We'd better make some more vodka compote tomorrow," Aelya said. But underneath, she was afraid. She didn't like a doubt-filled Roza. And she wondered if Stitches was affected too. If their best two pilots were cracking, what hope did the rest of them have?

"What we need is a game," Sirin said. "The activity will help wear us out."

"How about twenty questions?" Aelya suggested.

"I just told you we're thinking too much," said Roza.

"I know," said Sirin, suddenly inspired. "I've seen Petrushka and Vino doing this in the clubhouse."

Aelya didn't like the sound of that. Those two were the biggest hooligans among the pilots. "What?"

"Here, I'll show you."

Roza came to sit close to them as Sirin explained. The point was for two people to place their hands on top of each other's. Then they would try to be the first to slap the other person with both hands. It was a test of reflexes, a point of pride among the pilots.

Roza leaned close to Sirin's face. "You know, I wasn't sure about you when I heard all this talk about your father being high up with the NKVD."

Sirin swallowed. She might not know Roza's experience, but surely Sirin had encountered more than a few victims of the shadowy men. Aelya said, "It's not like that at all."

"I know it's all a front you put on," Roza continued. "Honeybee thinks you're okay, and she'd have no time for you if you were connected that way. But it doesn't matter. Sins of the father and all." She smiled and clapped Sirin on the shoulder. "Besides, this game's a brilliant idea."

"It's asinine is what it is," said Aelya.

"Got any better ideas?" asked Sirin.

And so they proceeded, agreeing to a best-two-out-of-three format. First Roza and Sirin. Sirin twitched and Roza struck first, clapping Sirin's cheeks with a loud *thwap* that sounded enough like gunfire that Aelya flinched.

"Hey, no fair, I wasn't ready," said Sirin, rubbing her face.

"That's the point of the game, isn't it?" said Roza. "All right, I'll give you a do-over, just so I can slap you an extra time."

Sirin made the most of the opportunity, using her arms to block Roza while giving as hard as she'd gotten. Roza only smiled. They went twice more, with Roza winning both times. Since Sirin was the loser, she'd have to go against Aelya. Her face might have been red and throbbing, but in the light of the moon and stars, Aelya could only make out the white of Sirin's toothy grin.

Aelya lost two in a row and was glad it had been over so quickly. Her face stung badly. "The object of this is to test your reflexes, not your strength," she complained, to Roza and Sirin's laughter. Honeybee slept through it all.

"I guess that makes me grand champion," Roza declared.

"No way," said Sirin. "You and Mars only did it once."

"Yeah, but I got slapped as many times as you did," said Aelya.

"You're forgetting the practice slap. I'm not letting either of you sleep until the two of you go a round."

Reluctantly, Aelya went against Roza and promptly lost two to one, though she was enraged enough to slap hard on her one win. Roza laughed it off, and Aelya had to laugh too, even though she was hurting badly.

Sirin said, "See, you're so focused on the pain, you've forgotten everything else and can go to sleep now."

It was a stupid game, but Aelya was glad Sirin had suggested it. They could always rely on each other, she, Roza, and Sirin. And yes, even Honeybee. She would go through fire for her. For all of them. She knew they'd do the same for her. It might not be enough, but it was the best they had.

CHAPTER 31: A ROUGH RECEPTION

Muggy air clung to Roza and covered her in a sheen of sweat, sapping her energy as if it were in league with the enemy. She sat on the dusty ground next to her plane while it was serviced. The canteen waitress carried a canister of soup, gesturing to her to have some. Hot soup? On a day like this? Roza waved her off.

She simply couldn't stay put. Braving the merciless sun, she crossed the grass to the next camouflage shelter, where Stitches napped under the shade of his wing. She lay down next to him and he put an arm around her. If she'd woken him, he didn't seem to mind.

She sighed.

"Stop thinking about it," he said. His eyes were still closed.

"Have you ever lost a wingman?"

"No, though I tried to get rid of Petrushka for a year."

"Shut up."

Try as she might to laugh, she thought back to Dema—not him as a person, but what her actions had meant for him.

"Tell me you couldn't have saved Dema," she said. "That you didn't have a choice."

"You already heard it in the debriefing."

Her leg throbbed. She raised and lowered it, flexed and unflexed it, trying to make the pain go away.

Now Stitches opened his eyes. "Honestly, I have no idea. I couldn't figure out where Dema was. I just said I was too far away so I could get

Troyanov off my back about the after-action report. You know what it's like. It's impossible to know what's going on most of the time."

She sat up and shook her head. There was only one way to erase the doubts. She clenched her fists. "When are they going to be done with my ride? I need to get up there."

"Relax. If anything, you should—" He wanted to say more, but he knew he'd never talk her out of flying.

"Come on, out with it. I don't like you bottling things up."

"If it were up to me, I'd want you to rest until you're a hundred percent." Even if she wanted to, she wouldn't be allowed to. The whole regiment was being pushed to the limit. The line for Dr. Krupenya's office every evening was growing with stress- and fatigue-related ailments. The orders were clear: anyone with two legs, two arms, and two eyes had to fly. They were making five or six sorties a day, vomiting between each one. The gaunt, drawn faces, the wobbly limbs—that was the norm.

Roza smiled wryly. "Didn't you tell me once that I was twice as good as most pilots? Even at fifty percent, I should be good enough."

Stitches laughed. "That's called an empty compliment."

She hit him on the arm. He pretended it hurt, then cradled her, hugging her from behind as she shifted closer. "Anyway, yes, the fact is, you *are* twice as good," he said. "So be smart—don't try to do too much just yet."

"It's not fair to the others."

"When has this war ever been about fairness?"

Roza glanced up at Stitches. He'd lost that cherubic fullness to his appearance. His wasted look made her feel more affection for him, to want him more. But desire was just a concept in her mind; her body could barely feel anything beyond the motions needed for combat. Still, she knew that she wanted to hold him.

Stitches whispered in her ear, "In spite of how things are going, it's okay to let yourself think about the future."

"My future consists of making if through the next mission." But she knew she was lying to herself; it was about more than this. Dema's death made her wonder what she might be costing her family by forcing her way back to the front.

"Here's what I think," Stitches said. "We're either going to die in this war or we'll live. If we live, great, and if we die, well, how sad would it be that we never allowed ourselves to have the happiness that's right in front of us?"

"Isn't that happiness an illusion, when everything could be taken away, just like that?"

He said, "I used to think I needed to outrun my past. I thought everything I did now would in some way help to erase what I'd done before. But that's not true happiness. Happiness is believing in the illusion, especially when it might be taken away. Because in the future, there's always a chance for happiness."

And in some way, she thought he understood her. She had every opportunity to ensure a good life after the war. But she wanted a life with him.

"Just focus on your job and trust in that," Stitches said.

Everything will be better after the war, she told herself. Just keep on believing that.

She held on to him fiercely. It was all a confusing mess, and she felt the need to cling to him, and he to her. They alone understood how the other one felt, needing to free themselves from the past and endure the uncertain present.

"Love will get us through this war," he said.

A message blasted out over the radio. It was time.

This particular battleground had become painfully familiar; they'd visited it eleven times over the past three days. There, the train tracks. There, the smouldering ruins of a village church. There, the semicircular patch of trees completely denuded by artillery blasts. And there, the black splotches where the Soviet defenders huddled and fought back as the Germans unleashed a storm of steel on them.

Four Yak fighters floated above a formation of Sturmoviks. Roza and Stitches's pairs bracketed the ground attack planes at separate levels two hundred metres apart. They were too low and exposed for Roza's liking, something driven home by the columns of smoke that obscured her vision. But this was the way the Sturmoviks worked, and if the fighters were to do their jobs, they couldn't stray too far away.

The Air Army was putting so much pressure on Red, he was foregoing the usual training regime and throwing new pilots into the fray. Even he and Cricket were flying missions. Squadron assignments had been completely thrown out the window in the name of expediency. Roza had flown with three different wingmen since Dema died. None of them were as good, but thankfully, none of them had been killed yet.

By rights, she should have been flying with some yellow-mouthed replacement. But on this mission, Stitches had managed to get Timur assigned to her wing. With three months at the front, he counted as a veteran.

She, Timur, Stitches, and Starik scanned every segment of the sky constantly. Dozens of aircraft were in the vicinity, many of them fighting each other, an extension of the cataclysm on the ground. It wasn't enough to simply spot silhouettes; they had to be smart enough to know what concerned them and what was someone else's fight. All this while not losing awareness of the fighting on the ground, which was close enough that bullets and shells, either stray or intentional, could catch them.

The Sturmovik commander made a course correction, turning to fly over a wooded patch of ground where troops were sparse. To their left, an enemy armoured formation came into view. The Sturmoviks would sweep back around and attack the tanks from their vulnerable rear quadrant. This was the critical time, thought Roza. Just hit them and get out. She was still eager for a fight, propped up on stimulants from Dr. Krupenya. She hoped the Sturmoviks would be done their mission and get out so she wouldn't have to worry about babysitting them.

And there they were. Vultures. "Stitches," she said, "six vultures. They look like fighters. Height one thousand, maybe one-two. Three o'clock, bearing southeast. Timur, get ready."

"Hold on," Stitches replied. He didn't elaborate, but she sensed it too: something was off about the enemy's behaviour. They weren't moving to intercept the Sturmoviks. Could they be adjusting tactics, or did they just not know what they were doing? The Luftwaffe was scraping for replacements too.

Then Roza saw another group of contacts. Stitches called them out, and she was upset she hadn't seen them earlier. The original group were flying too low and not as fast as interceptors should have been.

Stitches reported to Giraffe, "Six Fw 190s in Mikhail-Eight. Looks like they're in fighter-bomber configuration, with another two heavies in escort."

"Copy that, Osprey One-Zero. Can you intercept?"

Roza and Stitches didn't need to speak. They were each calculating options in their cockpits, all the while keeping watch over the Sturmoviks, relying on Timur and Starik to keep watch behind them.

The Sturmovik commander initiated descent into an attack run. Soon they'd be entering their circle of death, looping over the enemy tanks, firing rockets and dropping bombs in succession, all while their rear gunners swept the skies with an umbrella of bullets. Even the best

Luftwaffe pilots weren't going to tangle with that. The Fw 190s moved into position for their own attack on Red Army positions.

"Moving to intercept," Stitches said to Giraffe.

Roza said, "I'll hit the heavies, you stay with the Sturmoviks." What she didn't say was "I need this."

"Affirmative," he replied.

Roza trusted Stitches would handle his part. She waggled her wing and took Timur on a wide loop, gaining altitude. They followed a path that would disguise them against the swarm of other dots battling in the sky, as with the sun behind her she hoped to get an angle on the enemy fighter-bombers.

"Okay, Timur," she said, suppressing the annoyance at having to explain things in the open. Dema would have just followed by instinct, but with a new wingman she couldn't risk being unclear. "If we're right, that higher pair of heavies are escorts. See how quickly they're moving forward? They're going to try to sweep us away. The other six are lower and slower and loaded with bombs. We need to force those six out of formation and get them to jettison their bombs."

She left out saying that after jettisoning, those Fw 190s would be just like the other fighters and it would be eight against two. So they had to make their first pass count.

The two escorts circled slightly below them as the six fighter-bombers caught up. The Germans seemed aware they were being stalked. She could only hope the sun's glare would throw them off. The angle would never be better than it was now. She waggled her wing, then banked hard into a steep dive, an arrow streaking at the enemy formation.

The two escorting Fw 190s moved to intercept their path. It was a matter of nerves. She trusted that she'd timed it right, that she could get in her shots against the six more vulnerable heavies before the escorts could get to her. Were her instincts still good?

She and Timur rapidly closed in on their prey. Streaks of yellowish tracers already cut through the air from behind her; Timur had fired too early. She waited another fraction of a second. The Fw 190 in her view tried to evade, but he was a touch too slow. She pressed the triggers and her plane bucked with recoil, sending a stream of yellow fire cutting across the enemy's tail. Pieces of metal dropped away. She pulled hard to climb away, looking back to see the escorts trying to chase her with their tracers.

Tank-destroying munitions tumbled uselessly from beneath the fighter-bombers. But there was no time to exult—there were still six of them. At least their air strike had been thwarted. They would regroup and go on the attack, and join their two brethren.

She anticipated the nearest Fw 190 wanting to climb with power to get into an attack angle, so instead of chasing, she turned in the other direction, looping around tightly in her nimble Yak. The vulture came into view at just the right spot momentarily, and she fired.

Again, she went into evasion. Timur wasn't as good as Dema at keeping up, and she was frustrated but wanted to keep their integrity. So her course changes were less extreme, but still enough to evade the enemy. They wound around and around.

She glanced side to side, looking for her wingman. He had two heavies on his tail. Now orienting herself, she saw that Timur was below and just to her left. Instinctively, she threw herself into the line of fire.

Bullets tore through her fabric wings with a muted ripping sound. Timur dived and banked away, and now his pursuers locked on to her. She looked behind; two more enemy fighters bore down on her. She turned hard to evade them as streams of tracers cut across her path. Her plane jolted from the impacts. Flames licked outside the armoured glass of her cockpit.

The controls stiffened, making her feel as if she was wading through a morass. A glance back confirmed the four Fw 190s were staying close.

She knew she was on the fine line between brave and stupid. She fought the instinct to keep struggling with the controls and slid open the canopy to bail out.

When she jumped clear, the Fw 190s passed close by, and fear clutched her heart that the wash from the planes would tangle her parachute. She let herself drop down for as long as she dared, which might have been one second but felt like a minute. Then she pulled the cord. The chute yanked hard on her groin and underarms. She thought she'd be ripped apart. Despite the sun, the wind made her shiver as she drifted down, watching the Fw 190s turn. There he was. The Night Raven. She hadn't realized he'd been in the fight. None of the fighters she'd faced had flown with any particular skill. Maybe he'd been hiding and stalking her the whole time. Or maybe he wasn't that good. That possibility brought a smile to her face.

A pair of Fw 190s altered course toward her. She drew her pistol in a futile gesture. But they didn't fire, only made a wide circle around her. In the Night Raven's cockpit, the pilot's hand went up to his helmeted and goggled head. Was that a salute? That was almost worse than being shot at.

Down below, she saw a quieter part of the battlefield. She tried to yank at the cords to steer herself toward a grassy field close to some Soviet soldiers. Hitting the ground in a crouch, she attempted a roll. Pain flared in her leg and she ended up flopping forward. She flailed with the parachute for a while before finally unhitching herself.

Standing above the tall grass, she waved at the *makhras*. It took a while for them to notice. She shielded her eyes from the sun so she could confirm they were actually coming. Except the shape of the helmets didn't look right. And what had appeared khaki earlier was field grey. Germans.

She ran to a patch of brush for cover, holding her pistol. The sudden movement must have alarmed them. They levelled their rifles and fired, forcing her to hit the ground. There was nowhere else to run, and for a moment she laughed at the idea of meeting her death on the ground.

Then the dirt and scrub in front of the soldiers erupted as a Yak roared overhead, spitting cannon and machine-gun fire at the enemy infantrymen. The Yak circled as the Germans disappeared into the tall grass. The fighter landed, rolling up close to the bushes where she was hiding. It had a yellow bort number, 17. Stitches.

He slid the canopy open and she scrambled in and squeezed herself awkwardly onto his lap.

"You know, I always had a dream I'd take a girl up in a plane with her sitting on my lap. Somehow, I imagined it would be more romantic."

"Shut up and get the hell out of here!"

He duly throttled up. From this angle she couldn't see the German troops anymore, but over the wind she thought she could hear bullets whizzing past them.

"What were you thinking?" she said as they climbed. She scanned the skies, but the formerly busy sector was now clear of other planes.

"That I was rescuing you," he said.

"I don't need rescuing!" She exhaled. "What about Timur? What about the Sturmoviks? Those are your priorities."

He raised an eyebrow. "The Sturmoviks did their job and the heavies didn't want to tangle with their circle of death. They've already left the area. We're all on thirty-three. Starik and Timur are leading them back. Now stop talking and let me catch up."

Neither of them was comfortable with the silence. Stitches said, "Anyway, you're too valuable to lose."

In that moment, she really wished she wasn't.

CHAPTER 32: SPIRAL

Aelya snapped awake. She stared at the underside of her fighter's wing. Her crew scurried around, ignoring her presence. It still wasn't ready yet. She checked her watch. The exhausting days bled into one another, to the point that she'd forgotten how long it had been since the battle began. Even so, her body clock reliably got her up for every briefing.

She rolled out from the shade, attacked immediately by the relentless sun. She squinted as her eyes adjusted, entertaining the thought that this was a reality where she hadn't lost one of her pilots. But no, it was real: Spam had disappeared while they were escorting a group of Peshkas back from a bombing run. Up till then, it had been routine, easy almost, with barely a sighting of the enemy. They'd been so close to returning unscathed. Then suddenly, after checking in at a navigation waypoint close to the front line, Spam, the last pilot in their formation, had simply vanished.

These things happen, she told herself. Just move on.

She slogged through the muggy air that hovered over the airfield. Every day, it grew more rank with the stench of fuel, chemicals, sweat, vomit, and human waste. Though she wouldn't ever miss the winter of Stalingrad, it was better than this.

The action in the command post was hidden under camouflage netting. As she passed through a flap, she hoped to be greeted by good news, that some infantry unit had called in about picking up Spam. But instead she encountered an eerie quiet.

There was none of the constant motion from the staff that she'd come to expect during battle. Frost listened on the phone, stone-faced and rubbing his forehead. Cricket leaned over a map table, his shoulders slumped. Legend stood behind him, looking uncertain.

The radio operator had the speaker tuned to Luftwaffe radio, turned up to an unusually high volume. The enemy was speaking in shaky Russian, with the same clipped, guttural barking she associated with German. "Your leaders are lying to you. We've destroyed as many aircraft today as we did the first day of the war. This time, you won't have a year to recover. And your most famous pilots are dead. Medvedev, White 67. Tomenko, Red 21 . . ."

That was Red's real name and bort number. She tuned out the rest of the names.

"Turn it down," Cricket ordered the radio operator. "He's just repeating himself now."

Stitches entered, squeezing past Aelya. "Frost, I need the latest coordinates for—"

Frost, the receiver still glued to his face, put a finger to his lips.

"Is it true?" Aelya asked Cricket in a low voice. He acted as if he hadn't heard her.

Frost hung up the phone, hands shaking as he did. "Ground troops confirmed seeing the crash. The plane markings matched. And there was a body." Frost crossed his arms, still not looking anyone in the eye. "Fortunate, as far as these things go, to have been shot down over friendly territory."

Aelya felt as if ground had given way beneath her. She held on to a tent post. Red had seemed indestructible. He'd been through so much: Spain, Finland, and now this war. He was so tough, he would probably come back from the dead to haunt the enemy. But of course that was idiocy. He was mortal, like everyone else.

Frost, as regimental navigator, was now in charge. Stitches, who had been in quiet conversation with Legend, nudged the new commander on the arm. "Tractor's squadron is on its way back. Do my orders stand?"

Frost was slow to emerge from his daze. "What was that?"

"We're supposed to fly cover over a ground sector. What I'm asking is, do you still want us to do that? Or do you want us to hit those bastards where they live?"

Aelya looked at Stitches, trying to get his attention without interrupting. What was he talking about? Frost had a similar confused expression on his face, but Cricket's lips curled into a grim smile.

"Let's hit Orel West, while the Green Hearts are taking off or landing," said Stitches.

"Yes," agreed Cricket, "it's time to strike back hard against the enemy, before the shock of this loss overtakes the regiment."

Frost didn't respond. That was all the confirmation Stitches needed. As he stepped out, Aelya tried to catch up with him. She had to talk as he ran.

"Shouldn't we take some time to plan this out? I think we need cooler heads. Orel West could be a hornet's nest."

Stitches stopped. "I'm sick of the Green Hearts getting the better of us, day after day. It's time to show them what the VVS is made of."

"You're trying to prove a point. You should be thinking about the good of this regiment. That's what Red would have done."

"I *am* thinking of the good of the regiment. I've seen this before, when our previous commander was killed last summer. If we don't do something now, everyone will fall into a spiral, and things will get worse and more of us will die. We need to kill some Germans. Now."

His eyes were wide and his breath heaving. Aelya had never seen Stitches so off-kilter, at least not since Petrushka had been injured. By now, they were close to the shelters where the planes were stowed. Their raised voices had drawn out the rest of Stitches's squadron.

Stitches looked at Petrushka and Roza. "They killed Red." He let that sink in. "We're going to hit them back on the ground. At Orel West."

"I'm in," Petrushka said. "But I need a ride. My engine got shot up on the last sortie."

Stitches put a hand on his old friend's shoulder. "Sorry Petrushka, you'll have to wait." He looked at Aelya. "We'll do this smart, attack in waves, so I'll need you to lead the next flight. I'm hoping this isn't going to be a one-time thing."

Aelya frowned. This was exactly the sort of response Red would have hated. He'd been livid when he was ordered to hunt down the Night Raven instead of focusing on their normal operations.

"Stitches, wait," she pleaded. "If we're going to hit their airfield, it should be a proper strike with Sturmoviks, not just a flight of four taking shots. This is mad."

"You have to be a little mad in this line of work. It's why we're all here."

Roza tapped her on the shoulder. "If you're so concerned, why don't you help us? Timur had to make a belly landing near the front lines. He's still not back yet, so we're short a pilot."

Aelya nodded before even thinking it through.

"I'll be your number one," Roza said.

They had fought so often over this stretch of terrain, Aelya knew the path to Orel intimately. Many dots headed the other way. The sky was full of targets. But they were single-minded about hitting the Green Hearts where they lived.

Despite the thirst for revenge, Stitches kept his wits about him and ordered them to take a circuitous route to the north of the airfield, to strike from an unexpected direction. As they made their turn back south, Aelya spotted contacts heading on a similar path.

"Looks like Stukas. They're in no hurry. I think they're waiting to assemble with their escorts."

"Leave them," said Roza. "Let's keep going. If we haven't been spotted, we can hit the Green Hearts on the ground and cause more damage."

"You're talking about dereliction of duty," said Aelya. "We can't pass this up. Bombers are always our priority, remember?"

There was a silence over the radio. Finally, Stitches relented. "You're right. We'll hit the Stukas first, then see what happens."

Flexing her fingers on the controls, Aelya mentally practised following Roza's moves. She remembered what it had been like when they'd flown together the previous year. Roza always pushed the envelope.

Aelya followed her into a dive. The Stukas had spotted them and tried to cover each other with an umbrella of fire from their tail gunners. Roza and Aelya altered course, using their superior manoeuvrability to get beneath the Stukas. The enemy saw what was happening and tried to evade. Lightly armoured, the slow German dive bombers stood little chance.

Roza and Aelya, and then Stitches and Starik, savaged them in successive passes. By the time the Stukas jettisoned their bombs and retreated, each of the pilots had accounted for at least one kill. Aelya even chuckled as they climbed away, the act of following Roza liberating her from other thoughts.

Starik swore. "Boss." That was what he called Stitches. "The escorts are here and they're angry."

"This is big," said Stitches. "I'm looking at about ten heavies, coming in from bearing one-nine-zero, height, maybe one-five-zero-zero."

While destroying the Stukas, they'd lost so much altitude and speed, the enemy fighters arriving on the scene had all the advantage now.

Where the hell do they keep coming from? Aelya thought. Didn't the Soviets greatly outnumber the Germans now? That had certainly been the case in the late stages of Stalingrad.

Stitches ordered a regroup. He and Starik had already been climbing after their last run against the Stukas. Roza and Aelya were in the danger zone, having expended height and speed on the last attack run, so it was up to Stitches and Starik to keep the enemy off their tails.

The Fw 190s turned to attack Stitches's pair. Roza climbed and Aelya followed.

Aelya spotted something else. "Vulture! Coming out of the sun!" The warning came just in time, and they barely broke away from the path of enemy cannon tracers.

"That's got to be the Night Raven," Roza said of the latest German fighter, accompanied by his wingman. "Let's stick to him."

Whether or not it was the Night Raven, the German pilot had a deft hand. Even his wingman had difficulty staying in support. As Roza and Aelya tried to anticipate his twists and turns, Starik spoke over the radio. "I've got maybe six on my tail. I can't shake them."

"Split low," said Stitches. "I'll try to double back."

While Starik might think there were six enemy fighters following him, it was more likely that six of them were taking turns diving at him, trying to get him into their sights. Even if Stitches didn't have his own fighters to deal with, the most he could do to help would be to disrupt one or two attacks.

"Let's break off, Lily," Aelya called out. "We need to assist."

"He can handle himself. I've almost got the son of a bitch," said Roza.

Aelya knew that Stitches should disengage completely. They needed to count themselves lucky and keep Starik from harm. There was nothing further to be gained by seeking revenge.

But Stitches only said, "Go get him, Lily."

"Keep up, Mars!" Roza screamed. Even at full throttle and prop pitch, Aelya's plane moved sluggishly. She realized she may have taken hits from a Stuka's machine gun. Still, Roza kept twisting and darting, jousting with the enemy. An Fw 190's shadow passed in front of Aelya. She managed to get a shot at the wingman trailing behind it. Her cannon's recoil didn't help the feel of the plane; she could only glance briefly at her target and thought she saw smoke.

Soon, the Fw 190s used their power to pull away and Roza swore in frustration. They didn't have the stomach for a dogfight.

Neither did Aelya. "Osprey Leader," she called as the two sides pulled apart, "shall we thirty-three?"

Stitches swore. Aelya looked all around her, but she already knew to expect only two other Yaks. Starik had been shot down. There was no hope of staying in the area. The Fw 190s still menaced them, and this close to their base more heavies were probably taking off to finish them while they were isolated, many kilometres from the support of other units.

"I can't see a parachute," Stitches said.

"Come on, Stitches," Aelya practically shouted over her transmitter. "We're isolated. Let's move."

"All right, Giraffe, this is Osprey One-Zero, requesting a thirty-three."

CHAPTER 33: BREAKING POINT

They'd been up since long before sunrise. The crickets still chirped, louder and more persistent than the distant gunfire of a battle that had been raging ceaselessly for over two weeks.

Roza sat on the patchy grass next to Stitches; they leaned on each other as much for physical as emotional support. The rest of the regiment sat around them in a similar daze as the command staff conferred quietly, consulting maps by half-shuttered oil lamps. Down to eighteen pilots, just over half strength, the regiment all fit within the camouflage tent. Beyond the shelter, the sky was dark with clouds obscuring the moonlight.

After days of flying and fighting from sun-up to sundown, even Roza allowed herself that guilty wish fighter pilots held in their hearts: that flights would be cancelled due to weather.

That seemed unrealistic at the moment. Rumour had it that General Rudenko, the 16th Air Army's commander, had been threatened with execution by Stalin himself for not aggressively preventing the Luftwaffe from hammering the Red Army in this sector. Rudenko in turn passed on the threat to his subordinates, including General Platonov. Platonov had given Frost a hiding so fiery and loud that he could barely hold on to the telephone receiver.

For the past hour, Frost huddled with his brain trust, scratching out landscapes in the dirt and issuing briefings to the pilots, only to have calls come in scrapping all the previous plans. The German attack seemed to

either be in its last throes or on the verge of a breakout. Cricket, Troyanov, and Baby, now bumped up to regimental navigator, waved their
hands, pointing to the map table and pacing awkwardly like characters in
a slapstick silent comedy. Roza laughed quietly and it somehow felt ap-
propriate.

The pain that plagued her leg was intense and she slid her hand over
to grip Stitches's, trying to meet his eyes. He stared at the map Baby had
drawn in the dirt. Occasionally, she exchanged looks with Aelya, who sat
with Lucky. How fortunate that those two still seemed to have retained
their youthful appearance. In the civilian world, they'd probably be considered cadaverous, but compared to everyone else here, they appeared
positively glowing with health. Honeybee tried to hide her deathly com-
plexion by slathering on makeup, something she could get away with now
that Red wasn't around to object.

The phone rang and Frost answered. He recoiled at the loud barking
from the other end. The toll of the battle had made him haggard.
Whereas a touch of silver at the temples had once given him a distinguished look, it now made him appear elderly. As he took the abuse on
the phone, his body appeared to shrink from it.

"But Comrade General—" More unintelligible shouting over the
line. "We've already done that." More shouting. "Yes, I understand. We'll
make it happen." He hung up the phone gently and said under his breath,
"Somehow."

Frost gestured to Baby. "Cancel the last orders. We need to draw up
a new plan."

A groan passed through the pilots. Petrushka got up.

"Stay where you are," Baby ordered. "You're all still on alert."

Petrushka smirked, as if it was a joke. He and Baby were frequent
drinking companions. But there was little room for friends in Baby's new
position. Slowly, Petrushka returned to the dirt, which showed an impres-
sion of where he'd been sitting.

And so they waited. And waited.

Dawn broke through but brought a thick haze with it. Another call. The clerk handed the receiver to an apprehensive Frost. This time it was quick, and without shouting on the other end. When he hung up, the acting commander waved his hands to address everyone. "We're standing down for the day."

Every pilot's simultaneous sigh of relief seemed to expel, for a moment, the oppressive mugginess that had tormented them all morning.

Cricket stepped into the middle of the group. "I would suggest, with the comrade commander's accession"—a barely perceptible shrug from Frost—"that no pilots be given duties until supper is called in the canteen."

The basic functions of Roza's brain celebrated the chance to rest, even as the back of her mind registered that a day, even a week, wouldn't be enough to build them up to proper combat effectiveness.

Wordlessly, the pilots left the tent, their steps shiftless, little motivation steering them in any direction. They barely acknowledged each other on the way out. Once again, Roza leaned against Stitches, and he against her.

They cleared the camouflage shelter in the growing light of dawn. Dr. Krupenya met them outside with a platoon of canteen waitresses at her back, each with a ladle and a heavy metal canister.

"I just heard there'll be no flying today," the doctor said. "This is the perfect time to take in some nutrients and regain weight. You're all wasting away."

They lined up diligently, driven by muscle memory. Petrushka got his bowl of porridge, then declared, "Ladies first," allowing Sirin to go ahead of him. The men parted way for Honeybee, Aelya, and Roza. As Roza got her bowl, she saw Petrushka whisper something to Stitches, and he got a scowling rebuke from his former wingman.

"What was that about?" Roza asked as Petrushka stepped away.

After a pause, Stitches replied, "He doesn't have full confidence in our new set of leaders."

"Well, complaining about it sure helps," she said dryly.

"He thinks I need to get involved."

"He's right. Everyone here looks up to you."

"I don't think I can handle it. It's tough enough dealing with one squadron, let alone three. I can't even sort out the tribute to Red that Frost asked me to organize."

She stroked his arm. "As long as whatever you say is from the heart, it'll be right." What kind of a funeral would it be without a body anyway? The *makhras* who'd found Red had already buried him beside the wreck of his fighter.

A jeep hurtled alongside the runway, kicking up a cloud of dust. Roza turned to shield her porridge from the dirt-choked air. Idiot, she thought. The motor pool was where they sent technicians too incompetent to do other jobs. A few of the pilots coughed and spluttered, and she expected them to give the driver a tongue-lashing; the silence that followed was surprising. She looked at the jeep. Colonel Dmitriev glared at her from the back seat.

They made her stand outside the command tent, like a schoolgirl awaiting reprimand. Before Dmitriev had finished his first sentence, his big block of a driver guided her to the jeep and out of earshot.

The other pilots hustled away to the club or their quarters after Frost made it clear he didn't want a spectacle. She sat in the back, her feet up in the space between the front seats. She wouldn't show anyone what was worrying her. Had she jeopardized everything she'd been working toward?

The conversation between the regimental staff and Dmitriev was a short one. Stitches was there too, and she'd expected him to at least stand up for her. But he showed none of the passionate posturing he had when defending Ulanova.

Frost, Stitches, and Dmitriev filed out of the command tent. Frost put a hand up to stop the other two, then approached the jeep on his own. Roza got out and stood to attention. While Frost didn't have the same aura of authority Red had, he'd always struck Roza as kind and generous. She wanted to show him respect in front of Dmitriev.

"Am I in trouble, Comrade Commander?" she asked.

Frost worked up a slight smile. "Far from it. Your recognition as a Hero of the Soviet Union has been confirmed. We haven't gotten the paperwork yet, but I'll ask Legend to make arrangements for your travel to Moscow for the ceremony."

He held his hand out, but she didn't take it. "Really, in the middle of a battle? It looks like the sky is already clearing up. We could be flying tomorrow."

"Not you. You're standing down."

"So you're making operational decisions based on the say so of a glorified circus barker from SovInformBuro?" She pointed at Dmitriev, who smirked slightly. "Let's see what General Platonov has to say about it."

"This *is* an operational decision. Colonel Dmitriev just came from seeing Platonov. If our division is associated with good propaganda, the Air Force will release more resources to us."

"So one of your best pilots is a small price to pay, then. You know they're not going to let me come back."

"I know. And maybe I think that's best for you too."

"No, you can't do this!" She swore at him.

Startled, Frost struggled to say, "You forget your place, Comrade Lieutenant. Stand down."

Tears trickled down her cheeks. What was she going to do? How could she go back to Moscow now? They all thought she'd done her duty. But she'd let her wingman die. She'd let the Night Raven get away. She couldn't be finished just like that.

A pair of hands grabbed her. "Listen to your commander," Stitches said softly. "It's time to go back to your family."

"And do what? Remind my mother to get to work on time? Tutor Zhora in math?"

"Yes." He held her hands. "Live."

Frost cleared his throat and disappeared into the command tent.

"How can you say that?" Roza asked Stitches. "I came back here for you."

"You know how I've always felt."

"Well that's perfect," she spat. "Great, you win." She hated him in that moment. Rage built within her.

"Is Captain Akhmatov causing a delay?" Dmitriev said from where he stood, still a respectful distance away.

"I'm trying to help you, Comrade Colonel," Stitches retorted, turning to Dmitriev. He turned back to Roza and quietly continued. "It's not about winning. Your time to fight is over. Sometimes, that's just the way it is."

She felt an impulse to strike out. Instead she raised her hands, then hugged him tightly. She whispered into his ear, "I can't leave you."

"I want you with me, but I couldn't be happier knowing you're safe. Your family can be whole again. If you came back for me, then you can leave for me. You of all people should understand. I need all of this to mean something."

"It's not my job to give meaning to your war."

"You're right . . . you're right." He sighed. "You know what your job is? It's to serve your country. That means going with that man"—he pointed at Dmitriev—"and giving the people a symbol that will mean more than any one of us can."

He stroked the hair on the back of her head. Tears flowed and she didn't care who was watching. He caressed her cheek and smiled. "And anyway, why are you so sure we need you? You're only our second-best pilot."

Roza slapped him on the arm but couldn't help smiling. She threw her arms around him and held on tightly, her tearful eyes buried in his chest, the gold star pressing against her cheek.

"After the war," she said.

"After the war."

CHAPTER 34: THE OPPRESSIVE HEAT

A thick, soupy miasma permeated the shade of the camouflage netting. It was the same stench that suffused the whole base. Reclining against an empty crate at the edge of the operations tent, Aelya was in danger of dozing off, blithely hoping her senses would sharpen when it came time to fly.

"Relax," Honeybee told the two new men, boys really, sitting on boxes to one side. "It's shaping up to be a boring day."

The static toe-to-toe ground fighting of the previous days had given way to a war of manoeuvre as the Germans fell back. The enemy had retreated even farther than their original lines at the start of the battle, fearful of being enveloped by the massive Soviet counterattack developing in the north. Operations spread wide across the terrain. As a result, the days when the sky was choked with aircraft seemed to have passed. Aelya had only encountered the enemy once on that morning's free hunt, a pair of Messers that might have been on reconnaissance and fled as soon as they'd been spotted.

Honeybee's words did little to soothe the yellow-mouths. They fidgeted, eyes darting up at her, then to the other pilots of the squadron, then back down. They hadn't had any chance to practise flying with the rest of the formation. Aelya was nervous having them on this mission, and she suspected the other veterans felt the same.

The tempo of operations remained blistering. Maximum effort was demanded, and Frost didn't have the stomach to push back.

"Everyone" did not include Roza, however. None of the pilots liked losing one of their best, but no one held it against her. They couldn't begrudge her a chance to be with her family. She'd been hustled away without even a chance to say goodbye. Aelya bore no resentment. Perhaps she had worked out her feelings the first time she'd thought Roza was leaving the regiment. Still, they all felt an undeniable sense of emptiness, as if they were always short a pilot.

Honeybee continued the briefing, addressing the new men. "This one's a free hunt. There's no one to protect and no one to intercept. It's up to me to determine what's a target of opportunity, and when I do, I want you to hang back up high. Watch and learn. You'll get your chance soon enough, and if you try to help you'll probably make things worse." She broke into a smile. "Besides, there's no use in dying now. You haven't saved anything for us to divvy up yet."

One of them paled, looking nauseous. The other tried to keep up a front of bravado.

This would be the first combat mission for the new pilots, whose names Aelya had studiously avoided learning. "Stay calm," she reassured them. "Like Honeybee said, watch and learn. We've made it this far—you can too."

As for the rest, Vino, Lucky, Sirin, Genius, and Timur remained. The weeks of ferocious fighting had been enough to turn the latter three into hardened veterans.

"Are you sure the sector assignments are right?" said Sirin, who had been officially transferred to this squadron, now Honeybee's at last.

"Most of you may be illiterate, but I'm not," said Honeybee.

Aelya couldn't tell if they were actually friends. Their business arrangement, like flying together, seemed more a necessity to them than anything else. Honeybee's schemes were as vital as oxygen to her. Sirin used them to carve out her own identity outside the shadow of her stepfather; the whispers of her connections to the NKVD were fading with every delivery of contraband she secured.

Sirin said, "It's not that I doubt your orders, but the zone of operations is pretty far from the main fighting."

"Those are the orders," their squadron commander said, not very convincingly. Like the others, Honeybee thirsted to get into the thick of the action, if only to pad her victory totals and their accompanying monetary bonuses.

"Well, that sounds about right," said Sirin, not looking satisfied. "Just another boring assignment for the 'girls' squadron.'"

"Just shut it, all right?" said Honeybee. "I've heard the chatter. Let's deal with it later."

Aelya had overhead Petrushka remark that Honeybee's squadron was the designated dumping ground for all the women and the new pilots. While she agreed this was more than a coincidence, she felt the need to defend them against the insult. "We aren't some club for outcasts. Vino and Lucky have been through Stalingrad. And you others who've been with us since the spring have shown you have what it takes. If we're being asked to train new guys, it's because they know we'll do it properly."

"Lovely words, Mars," said Honeybee. "You and Lucky, take the yellow-mouths and stay in high cover. My pair and Sirin's will hit the target first, whatever that might be."

The squadron got to their feet. Honeybee turned once more to the rookie pilots. "Cheer up. Once you've done this, you'll realize nothing else in your life will ever matter as much."

The engine roaring, Aelya had to bang hard on the side of her cockpit to get Katya's attention. She mimed a drinking motion, and after an unreasonably long back and forth, Katya finally fetched a metal cup with water.

Zina would have understood instinctively. Though she knew it was selfish, Aelya cursed her former crew chief for leaving her.

A sparkling green orb soared over the airfield. With the flare signalling they were cleared for takeoff, Giraffe station relayed their final instructions.

The squadron's free hunt involved making large, loping figure-eight flights over four different waypoints mapped out for them by Baby. All along the route, they flew past the black smoke of burning fuel, burning grass, and burning flesh that loomed day and night, as constant as the sun and stars. Plumes rose as if from a thousand chimneys of a vast city, concentrating in a solid cloud of darkness enveloping the sky to their southwest, where the battle was centred.

It was at the third waypoint that Aelya spotted a fast-moving cluster of dots. "Vultures. Possibly enemy fighters, squadron strength, maybe less. Ten o'clock, height one-five-zero-zero. Bearing, one-eight-zero."

Honeybee quickly ordered them higher and away, trying to get into a good position behind them.

"They're fighters all right," she said as they passed in the distance. "Something fishy about them being this far out of the combat zone. They may be a first wave of escorts. Mars, take Sirin and engage them. And 41 and 78, you're switching onto my flight. We'll stay high and look for the bombers."

Aelya acknowledged and ascended in a wide turn, followed by Lucky, Sirin, and Timur. She wanted to cut behind the path of the fighters, to put the sun behind them.

With greater height, she could now see there were six Fw 190s. Four of them peeled away and climbed toward them. Aelya gritted her teeth. They'd been spotted. These four were trying to match their altitude. She led her flight into a turn and the enemy turned with her, positioning themselves at the opposite side of an imaginary circle formed by their flight paths.

"Honeybee," she said over the radio, "engaging four heavies. Keep an eye on the other two."

"Copy that."

Aelya tried to break the enemy formation, ordering Sirin to climb even higher and bracket them.

"We have more vultures," said Honeybee. "They're moving slowly. I think their bombers are here. They must have been trying to sneak over a quiet sector. Boy, are they going to get a surprise."

She called in to Giraffe and moved to engage. "New guys, stay high and especially watch out for those two other fighters hanging around."

One of the new pilots replied, "I don't see them!"

Honeybee sighed. "Dammit. Okay, just watch our backs. I'll bet they'll try to come from the direction of the sun."

"Wait, are we sure those are German bombers?" said Genius, flying on Honeybee's wing. "I don't recognize the type."

"Well if they were ours, we'd recognize them. Stop thinking so much and let's kill them."

From the corner of her eye, Aelya just caught Honeybee and Genius diving to attack. Meanwhile, her four Yaks continued their dance, their German partners matching their moves, not provoking any action. She didn't like it and kept watching for an ambush from on high.

"We've got more vultures incoming," said Lucky. "Four o'clock high. I think it's the Night Raven!"

"Calm down," Aelya said. There was no way Lucky could tell from this distance who these four new silhouettes were. She started thinking that the Night Raven was akin to a fairy-tale monster, like Baba Yaga, and that his story was told mostly to scare the younger pilots. As a result, their own fevered imaginations were making the Night Raven bigger than he deserved to be. She wasn't happy that her wingman was falling for it and getting twitchy.

"Follow me." She led her four planes into a turn, then sharply descended into a split S, coming out in the opposite direction. The newcomers tried to alter their course to intercept, but they had too much speed and passed by, close enough for Aelya to see they were Fw 190s. Along with the original heavies Aelya had been tangling with, all eight German fighters changed course to try to catch her. Her heart hammering at her rib cage, Aelya used all the speed from her manoeuvre to gain the height advantage again.

One of the new pilots called out, "I've lost my wingman."

"Who is this?" said Aelya.

"Uh, Molchalin."

"Your number!"

"Seventy, uh, seventy—"

"Okay, I got it. Look high. Look toward the sun. Any enemy fighters?"

"No. Wait, I think I see them. Two of them."

"You've no business being in a dogfight. Power up and fly toward the sun, but gain as much height as you can."

Aelya said all this as she continued twisting and turning, trying to bring the enemy to battle. They weren't quite avoiding her, but they weren't fighting either. They were drawing her away.

She kept watching for Honeybee but had lost sight of her. "Honeybee," she called. "Honeybee—Sirin, break off. Try to get back up high and see what's going on with the bombers."

The radio crackled. "Hold your horses. I'm busy," Honeybee snapped in a familiar tone that reassured Aelya.

Aelya kept looking for and identifying dots in the sky around her. The eight Fw 190s seemed even more distant now. Were they withdrawing? Sweat made her fingers itch. She wasted precious seconds trying to figure out what was going on.

Finally, she saw a streak of yellowish tracers in the distance and was confident Honeybee was aiming at the bombers. A sudden flash of orange flared against scattered clouds and a trail of black smoke appeared. Then another flash of orange.

Someone swore over her radio. Then screamed. A woman's voice.

Aelya wanted to fly over and help, as if she could get out of her plane and pull Honeybee from her cockpit.

An inhuman screech blared out of Aelya's headphones, penetrating her skull.

She swallowed and ordered her flight to regroup. "New guy, climb with us. Can you see us?"

The agonized wailing over the radio shredded her ears and she wanted to rip her helmet off, but she needed to keep her comms open.

"Genius, what's your situation?" she asked. She couldn't hear anything above the screaming. She felt the contents of her stomach rise.

She looked around. Outside of the other four remaining Yaks, the sky had cleared. Finally, Honeybee's radio cut out.

Aelya swallowed back bile and took charge. "Giraffe, this is Sparrow Two-Zero, calling in a thirty-three for Sparrow Squadron."

She located a plume of smoke she thought might be Honeybee's wreck and called it in. There was nothing left to do but fly home.

CHAPTER 35: RUNNING

Aelya ran, but her feet couldn't gain traction. She flailed, her legs pumping through nothingness. Above and behind her, a beastly shadow loomed, its jaws crunching with the screech of grinding metal. Before it could swallow her into darkness, flames burst from its mouth, consuming her. Her eyes opened.

She wanted to rise to her feet, but the seat strap restrained her. She was in her cockpit. Her plane was motionless on the ground. Her heart beat fast, and at first she thought she heard it thumping. But someone was outside the canopy. Katya. Aelya slid it open.

"What happened there?" Katya asked. "You just kind of stopped."

Stitches jogged up the compacted dirt airstrip behind Katya.

"Get your plane off the runway," he said. "Tractor's flight needs to take off."

She let Katya guide her still-running Yak off the landing strip toward a camouflaged shelter, where her crew chief had set up a ladder and workbench.

When Aelya exited her aircraft, she was numb, trying to comprehend how she had fallen asleep in the cockpit. Sweat splashed as she removed her helmet. She wiped drool from the corner of her lips.

Katya set to work immediately, calling in the crew to swarm over the airplane and get it ready for its next sortie within the hour. She glanced at Aelya but said nothing.

Aelya stumbled out of the shelter, her legs weak, her pulse fast.

Stitches walked over to lend a hand. "You're trembling."

"I fell asleep in the cockpit," she said.

"I know. You almost took out Katya with your wing."

Aelya gasped.

"But you didn't," Stitches said, his smile unfailing. "You sort of rolled on for a bit, then stopped. You must have hit the brakes while you were asleep. I knew you were good, but I didn't know you could pilot the Yak with your eyes closed."

"Don't joke about it. It could have been a disaster." What a dereliction of duty, she thought. And from a newly minted squadron commander, no less.

"Come on, it's not so bad. I once fell asleep mid-flight, coming back from a rough patrol in the summer of '41."

"This wasn't after combat. There's no excuse. I just . . . blanked out." She straightened herself out and smoothed her field uniform.

"Hey, don't worry about it. This pace can kill anyone. And now it's just another story to tell." He clapped her on the shoulder in a way that felt neither condescending nor trite. "Listen, while I have you here, your squadron has more numbers than mine. I thought I could take someone off your hands. Make your transition to commander easier. How about Sirin?"

She nodded.

"Uh, that was supposed to be your cue to act all indignant and try to shift one of your yellow-mouths onto me."

"I'm sorry. Okay, take one of my yellow-mouths."

"You really are out of it."

She sighed. "Anyway, we're probably even now. I lost another man today."

Stitches stared at her. "I thought you didn't see the enemy."

"We didn't. I have no clue what happened. Our new guy just disappeared."

"It happens."

"It happens," she repeated. Just another loss. Another name crossed out from the roster. Like Honeybee.

Her breaths grew laboured. Her heart pounded, still not slowing since she'd woken. She bent over to retch, but nothing came out.

"I can't do this," she said, panting. "I can't do this."

He held her and kept her from falling. "Yes, you can."

"I can't even stay awake in the cockpit and they want me to be a squadron commander?"

"At least you're well rested."

She hit him on the chest. "Stop it! Stop joking!" she screamed. "You can't solve everything with a joke! Just like you can't just ignore a problem and hope it goes away. We're all dying, bit by bit. Everyone knows it and we can't do anything. So stop pretending everything's fine!"

She dropped down, sitting on the ground. She wanted to cry, but tears wouldn't come. Katya looked in her direction, but avoided eye contact. Stitches put his hand up to signal the crew chief to continue working on the plane. He went to a workbench to pour water into a metal cup and crouched next to Aelya.

As she drank, her rage dissipated. With that calm came recognition that Stitches was dealing with his own heartache after Roza's departure. "Are you going to be all right?" she asked.

He nodded. His eyes were drawn and only a little gleam of his usual brightness was visible. "It was for the best, really. Anyway, don't make a big fuss about it."

Zina ran into the shelter, out of breath. "I'm glad I found you," she told Aelya. "I have some good news. The *makhras* managed to rescue Honeybee. She's hurt badly, but alive. Not sure where they took her, but I imagine she'll be in the area field hospital once she's patched up."

Aelya was agitated, unsure how to feel. She'd rapidly made peace with Honeybee's death, and now she battled to keep her emotions bottled up. She hugged Zina, crushing a piece of paper her engineer was holding, and then Stitches and Katya joined in.

Zina pulled back and straightened out the paper.

Aelya glanced down at the sheet of mechanic assignments. As squadron commander, she needed to approve the roster. "I don't know. It looks fine. I trust you." She signed the sheet and gave it back to Zina.

The squadron engineer looked about to say something, then nodded. She shared a quiet word with Katya before leaving.

Stitches looked at Aelya.

"What?" she asked.

"Nothing."

"We barely care who we send into battle, so what difference does it make who gets what technician? And anyway—"

"Honeybee's not coming back."

Had she been thinking that? She'd relaxed when Zina told her the news, thinking she didn't need to be squadron commander anymore.

Stitches said, "You're right about who we send into battle. With the amount of training the new guys get, I wouldn't trust them to fly a crop-duster. Red never would have tolerated that."

"We need the numbers. Air Army HQ is putting way too much pressure on us. I don't know if even Red would have found a way out of it. But . . ."

They shared a look. Something had been welling up these past few days, an undercurrent all the experienced pilots felt. After surviving Stalingrad, they all thought they were invincible, no matter how irrational they knew that to be. Now they couldn't possibly believe they were going to live, and there was no one to pull them out of that downward spiral.

"This fighting," he said. "I think any leader would be overwhelmed."

She wanted to say something about Frost but couldn't find the words. She hoped he would understand what she was thinking.

He did. "Frost is a good man. When he was a squadron commander, his pilots loved him."

"Maybe he cares too much," she said.

Stitches sighed. "Yes, I think that's why Red had him bumped up to regimental navigator and away from commanding missions." He eyed her suspiciously. "What is this? Is Petrushka starting some sort of campaign?"

"Something has to change. We're at the breaking point."

"We're beyond that," he said. "But that's the job."

"I know. We all know it. But . . . maybe it would make a difference—make us do the job better—if there was someone we trusted. You know, speaking up for us."

Again, neither of them felt able to say things in the open about their commanders. But Aelya knew that Stitches, who had some sort of checkered past, didn't fully trust Cricket. The *zampolit*, for all his chumminess, was a Party man through and through. Baby had an eye on further promotion and had taken to parroting Air Army command on everything. And their chief of staff, Troyanov, was still a soggy piece of bread, way in over his head.

Stitches shook his head. "No, don't look at me. You need to find someone else. I've made terrible mistakes."

"We all have. It's part of the job."

"No, not like that." He squinted, his eyes welling up. "I was expecting Roza to give me absolution. I knew she wanted her family together again and I just wanted one good thing to come out of this war. I put those needs ahead of the squadron's. I thought, if I could just let her get that happiness, then maybe I'm not so bad."

"Bad?"

"You don't know what I've done. To my parents."

"You said you were an orphan."

"I might be. I don't know." He looked at her as if considering taking her into his confidence, but she knew he'd already made up his mind. "The black vans took them away. For being Tartars. And I turned my back on them. Pretended not to be who I was."

She tried to make sense of someone who would do that. Roza's father had been taken away and she'd had to change her name. Aelya couldn't imagine what they would have done to Stitches. What would she have done if she'd been in the same position?

"Stop it," she said. "The past is just that. You don't need to make up for it."

"But I tried to. I was selfish. I wanted to fix myself. You're putting your trust in the wrong person."

"We're putting our trust in a good person. No matter what you may think. The decisions you made, that you will make . . . they all need to be made. We trust you with that. Because we know you're a good man. You always were, and you don't need to prove it."

She locked eyes with him, remembering all they had experienced: the battles they'd survived by the skin of their teeth, the bitter winter that had broken the Nazi war machine, all those they'd loved and lost. They hadn't even known each other for a year, but it was as if between them they had lived several lifetimes.

"Thanks, Mars," he said. "You're always there to put me back together."

She smiled. "I seem to remember needing to slap a bit of sense into you at Stalingrad."

"I still have marks." He exaggerated rubbing his cheek, then flinched as if ready for another strike.

"It's all right," she laughed. "Keep joking, even when I scream at you. I need it."

He nodded. "I'll talk to Frost, try to be a voice of reason and see if we can switch things up somehow."

Stitches's crew chief, Nemchinov, whistled at him from across the runway.

"Looks like I'm up."

"Stitches, wait. Do you remember that time we ate snow covered in peach syrup?"

He nodded.

Aelya smiled. "Well, I got to experience at least one good thing out of this war. And that's thanks to you."

"You're a good friend, Mars. Don't you forget it."

CHAPTER 36: A TEST

The Yak's engine was still revving down when Aelya hopped out and shoved Katya's helping hand away. "It's no good," Aelya said. "It's totally unresponsive in the horizontal."

Katya kept her face calm as she paced the length of the plane while her crew readied it to be taken to the shelter. "If it was totally unresponsive, how did you even land?"

"You know what I mean," Aelya snapped. The roar of a Yak taking off drowned her out.

Even as a layer of fog threatened to descend over parts of the battlefield, the regiment had been scheduled to continue operations. But Stitches successfully pressed Frost to bargain with General Platonov and his superiors for a day of rest. Frost explained to them that the number of planes had not yet caught up to the number of pilots. In exchange for the break, however, the regiment promised to have a full complement of fighters ready by next morning. The mechanics went full speed on repairs without complaint, knowing this was needed to give the pilots a much-needed break.

By mid-afternoon, a few Yaks had been rebuilt and the pilots were making test flights. Aelya had finished her run. Stitches, KV, and another pilot were in the air. Cricket was due up soon, another move designed to bolster the regiment's camaraderie while its morale was frayed.

"Now I see it," said Katya, pointing at the Yak's tail fin. "The stabilizer's slightly bent."

"And you let me fly like that?" Aelya said.

Katya maintained her placid mask. "I checked it. It was fine pre-flight."

"Then how did it get that way?"

"Excessive loading, probably."

"Excessive loading," Aelya said, mimicking her. "It's a test. I wasn't flying it that hard."

Katya cocked an eyebrow.

Aelya said, "I had to see if it's good in a dive. Otherwise, how will I know it's ready for combat?" She groaned, then stripped off her parachute and threw it into the cockpit, storming from the runway.

She found Zina in the squadron's maintenance shop, an open air affair under camouflage netting. A half dozen technicians were stripping down a badly shot-up Yak while the squadron engineer barked instructions. Tools banged and a radio speaker chattered, but Zina still noticed her enter. "What is it?" she asked.

Aelya hesitated, looking at the wreck. The engine cowling was completely charred and riddled with bullet holes. "You've got your hands full."

"This?" Zina nodded at the plane. "It's done for. We're just cannibalizing it. Should be enough parts to patch up three planes. At least then we'll have working rides for everyone."

"I'll come back later."

"No, no, you can talk. My girls know what to do—they don't need me breathing down their necks." She held Aelya's arm and guided her out of the work area to a corner where a stack of crates afforded some privacy.

Aelya sighed. "It's not working out with Katya. Can you give me a new crew chief?"

Zina twisted her lips, mulling over how to respond. "I think you just need to get used to her working style. You need to be more direct with her."

"I do, and then she disagrees with me. There's no trust between us. I can't fly like that, I can't."

"She has very strong opinions. That's why she's good. I admit I'm biased, but I would never let your plane have less than the best possible care."

"The best possible care would be having you on my crew instead of running after your promotion." Even as the words came out, Aelya wanted to take them back.

Zina's eyes went wide, and Aelya saw the hurt in them. The engineer inhaled deeply. "Aelitochka, I thought this was supposed to be an off day. I've seen you more relaxed going into combat."

Aelya sat down on the dirt, her knees up, burying her head in her arms. Zina crouched beside her. She should have felt unburdened, even a little, to not have the responsibility of leading in combat, if just for a day. But an oppressive weight lingered over her.

She noticed Petrushka's voice over the radio. "I don't know, I suppose, 'Farewell'?"

"How about, 'I long for the day when we can be together like Pierre and Natasha'?" Legend responded.

"Who the hell are they?" Petrushka asked.

"They're from *War and Peace*."

Aelya looked up and asked Zina, "What's going on?"

"Petrushka's dictating a letter. He got one of those notes girls are sending to the front, and now he thinks he's in love."

"Doesn't he know everyone gets the same notes? It's part of a Komsomol program."

Zina sat down. "Let him have his dream."

"And why is Petrushka getting Legend to write it out? Isn't his flight supposed to be in readiness?"

"He's dictating it from the cockpit before they go up for a test flight. Writing letters off duty would take away time from drinking and gambling."

Aelya cracked a smile and leaned her head against her friend's. "I'm sorry. I should never have said what I did."

"It's all right. I know how much those extra stars can weigh you down." She tapped Aelya's shoulder boards, which had been freshly sewn with the insignia of a senior lieutenant. As a squadron commander, she might receive another star for captain.

"I said those things because I'm afraid," Aelya admitted. "I keep thinking unless every single thing is perfect, I'm going to die."

"There's no need to be worried about your plane. Katya is a fantastic chief." They exchanged a look. All this time, Aelya had been wary of Katya, remembering when she pulled out that pistol.

Zina asked, "You trust my judgment, don't you?"

Aelya nodded.

"Then trust her. You can't waver. I'm sorry, but that's your job. I don't want you to let any of your doubts see the light of day," said Zina. "This is about more than just comfort with your crew chief. You need to lead by example. If Katya loses your confidence, the other mechanics will stop trusting her, and each other."

A leap of faith, Aelya realized. Not just faith in Katya, but in herself. That's what it took to be a leader.

"I know it hasn't always been easy," Zina continued. "I wanted to keep working on your crew, I really did. When the war started, I knew I should do something meaningful. I know you did too. That's why we're here. I thought I was a failure when they didn't select me as a pilot. I've had a chance to make an impact as a technician. And now, as an engineer. It's like something that was always meant to be. Something good that can stay with me when all of this is over. Thanks to you."

Here was another person thinking of after the war. As she was for Roza, she should be happy for her. Aelya forced a smile. "It was something that was always within you."

"And whatever you need to be ready for, it's in you as well." Zina gave her an encouraging punch on the shoulder.

On the radio, Legend and Petrushka were still going on about the letter. Legend said, "I certainly think a little warmth and personality in your letter would go a long way. At least, that's what my parents tell me."

Stitches's voice crackled over the speaker as he made his test flight. "Oh come on, how hard can it be? Just crib a little bit from Pushkin, a little bit from Mayakovsky. Worked for me in school."

More voices came over the line, cut with laughter. Aelya chuckled and waved for Zina to continue her work. Finally, she felt a bit of that release the other pilots were exhibiting on this day off. It soothed her to listen to their banter, even though it violated all dictates of radio discipline. It was as if they were waiting for a tram, shooting the breeze. It reminded her of the noises of city traffic. Life.

"Whoops, almost lost me prematurely there," called Stitches.

Was that a joke?

Petrushka called out, "Stitches, was that you?"

"It's nothing."

Aelya stood and walked around the maintenance shop, peering at the cloudy sky. She tried to identify each pilot by their flying mannerisms. There was KV. She wasn't as familiar with Cricket's style, but it was smooth compared to the third one, a new pilot. There was one other silhouette, apparently struggling with power.

"Hey, you all might be interested in this update," Legend said. "We've got a report from the 466th. They think they've shot down the Night Raven."

"Dammit, Lily's going to hate that when I tell her," Stitches said.

"Boo," said Petrushka.

"Are you jeering Lily's selfishness, or the 466th for getting him," Stitches asked.

"Can it be both?"

Could it be? Aelya wondered. The Night Raven was really gone? Another shadow that hung over them was gone. And now Stone, not to mention Dema and perhaps a hundred others, had been avenged.

"Who was it who got him?" Petrushka asked.

"One of their free hunters. Lugovoy," said Legend.

"No," said Petrushka.

"He's Little Sasha, isn't he?" asked KV.

"What are you talking about? He's Big Sasha," said Petrushka.

"Petrushka's right," said Legend.

"More important question . . ." said Petrushka, "Why are the 466th getting free hunter assignments?"

Amid the clamour that followed, one lone message pricked Aelya's ears. "Just got to—" The radio reception was bad.

"Stitches," KV called out.

There was a muffled explosion. An anguished cry over the radio.

Aelya couldn't move. Zina ran out to check, and when she looked back, the expression on her face meant everything. The control tower called out to each pilot in turn to check in.

"Osprey One-Zero . . . Osprey One-One . . . Osprey One-Two . . ."

The line crackled. "This is Cricket. Sorry, I mean Osprey One-One, reporting." He was composing himself.

"Osprey One-Three reporting in." The new pilot.

Finally, the radio crackled once more. "Osprey One-Two here." KV's voice. Flat. Dead. "Osprey One-Zero is down."

Stitches.

CHAPTER 37: SURVIVORS

The sun was back with a vengeance. Unsheltered, Aelya's plane roasted on the field. A ladder pressed against the cockpit, ready for her to climb. She couldn't. Paralysis gripped her.

Katya handed over the checklist for her to sign. She made herself move the pen, even with a thousand thoughts rebelling in her head. She'd gone out of her way to switch to a fighter that Zina's team had repaired. Zina's work was under investigation because of the accident. She tried to block out other thoughts, to focus on how she needed to show confidence in Zina, and in Katya. The inquiry would surely exonerate Zina, and she trusted her. But fear kept creeping through the barriers Aelya had raised.

Ever since her first combat, when a German bullet had pierced her windshield, she'd lived with the possibility of death. She would recite to herself at dawn that she might die that day. As much as she thought that was at peace with that, she knew now she had been lying to herself. There was no peace. Because she truly knew now she was going to die. Because Stitches had died.

She convulsed, hyperventilating, and had to bend over to catch her breath. Finally, Katya asked, "Are you all right?"

A shadow crossed her view.

"Comrade Commander, it's time," Lucky said. He held his pistol by the barrel, a bullet in his other hand.

Aelya straightened up, tugged on her parachute harness as if she'd just been checking it. She took the pistol and the bullet. She chambered a round, extracted the magazine, and inserted the bullet, then slapped the magazine back in.

"Are you ready?" Lucky asked as he reholstered his weapon.

She could breathe now. The grass around them was a vivid green in the sun, swaying gently in the breeze. If this day was to be her last, at least it was beautiful.

The officers' club of Rogachevsk airfield barely qualified as a club, and certainly not as a building. A handful of tables and chairs sat amid a cluster of trees, shielded from the sun by the ubiquitous camouflage netting.

Aelya dragged herself in with her squadron. She had time before her next sortie and she needed to be with fellow pilots.

There was no boisterous joking, no singing. The gramophone lay on a rock in the corner, playing an accordion waltz. Dominoes clacked at one table, without the usual boastful commentary. Newspapers ruffled.

Lucky dispensed tea from a samovar. Frost had wisely taken away the extra vodka and homebrew from the club. They couldn't be trusted with it, not now. Roza, Honeybee, and especially Red had been the lifeblood of the regiment. With Stitches gone as well, it felt as though they couldn't even call themselves a regiment anymore.

Aelya thought about her first kiss, when she'd fallen after leaping out of the cockpit, after she and Stitches had made an emergency landing in their two-seat trainer. For a while, she'd thought she loved him. The intensity of his loss showed it was about more than love; she'd lost a part of herself. The pangs hammered at her chest.

She took a place next to Lucky, leaning against the stack of crates that served as a bar. "I hate those slow missions," she said.

"I have absolutely no problem with them."

"There's too much time to think afterwards. At least after an engagement, we get wired, constantly replaying it in our heads until the next sortie. Everything they send us on is too quiet, too safe. I hate it."

Lucky had nothing to say. She turned to watch Petrushka. He sat on a log stump, away from the dominoes that normally absorbed him. She wanted to say something to him, but what? She rose and found another stump and sat next to him. He didn't look at her. She continued to sit, hoping that just by being there they could share their hurts and lift each other up somehow.

Petrushka drew a flask from his pocket and took a swig from it. "There's no one left from '41. Just me," he said. "Everyone else was smart enough to get promoted. No one's going to make it past two years."

"Speak for yourself," Tractor called from the domino table. In his thirties, he was the old man of the regiment. "I've been doing this since '36." Tractor might have been in the Air Force a while, but he'd been teaching at an academy for most of the war when the regiment picked him up in Astrakhan.

Petrushka should have had a quip. She wanted to slap him. He usually had a response for everything. Make a joke, she thought. Say something! He'd once joked about his cousins eating each other in besieged Leningrad. How could he now have nothing to say?

The radio crackled. "Third Squadron, report to operations."

Petrushka stood. He and five other pilots put down their dominoes, their newspapers, and their drinks, and leaped into action.

Aelya sat, willing her eyes not to blink. Because every time she closed them, she saw Stitches's face.

"With respect, Comrade Commander, our squadron is not being used to its best capabilities." Aelya was following Frost around the command post as he signed orders and read reports that clerks handed to him.

"I think you're doing an excellent job," Frost said. "Not every mission has to involve combat."

"But none of them? Why do we keep flying patrols over empty sectors?"

Legend handed a report to Frost, eyeing Aelya with some concern.

"The battle is moving fast, across a wide front," Frost said as he skimmed over the report. "You can't always be where the action is."

"But what about escort missions or interceptions? Why are we only getting half the sorties the other squadrons are?"

Frost groaned as he finished the report, slapping it down on table. "They lost six tanks?"

"Yes, Comrade Commander," Legend said. "Observers think the culprits were Henschels."

The Henschel was the strange-looking German bomber that Honeybee had encountered. It flew low and slow, like the Sturmovik, but carried a bulky 37 mm cannon beneath its fuselage.

"Why do they keep getting through?" Aelya asked as she turned the problem over in her head.

Frost shook his head. "Let's leave that discussion. Your people aren't ready yet."

"What's that supposed to mean?" she said.

"Your squadron's adjusting to you as their leader."

"So is Petrushka's."

He wouldn't say anything.

She pressed on. "Did you know people are calling us the 'girls' squadron'?"

"I would have thought you'd be proud. You've shown how fully capable you are as fighter pilots."

Aelya's eyes narrowed. "Have we?"

"Do you want me to find a suicide mission for you? Are you in such a hurry to die?" Frost said.

Aelya winced, remembering that Stitches once said the same thing. She composed herself. "All this chivalry belongs to an earlier age."

"I can't have you young women dying because I put too much on you. I can't have that on my conscience."

"You need to send us into the same danger as everyone else. Can't you see how much we're needed?"

Frost started to say something to Aelya but stopped. He turned to Legend, who'd been switching his gaze between them. Leaning in, they whispered a few words to each other, then Frost dismissed the adjutant with a fatherly pat on the shoulder. He said to Aelya, "I've received an update about Gorbataya. She's been moved to the field hospital at Kostino. Since you and Dolidze were close to her, I'd understand it if you two went to pay her a visit. Bronfman can take over breaking in your new pilots this afternoon."

Aelya wanted to challenge him, to ask him if it was an order. But she knew she shouldn't speak for Sirin. And she desperately wanted a chance to speak with Honeybee, to connect with someone who could remind her that the regiment could still live.

The dread hit her when she saw the field hospital. It had been with Aelya ever since she got onto the back of the truck. She wondered what her friend would look like. Would her body be broken? She couldn't form an image and didn't want to, for fear of what she'd see. Sirin hopped off the truck with her, her motions stiff; perhaps she was riven by the same thoughts. The truck they'd hitched on rumbled away. She and Sirin gulped down air simultaneously and entered.

Once a workshop of some kind, the hospital had a weathered, broken-down appearance that screamed of dilapidation and decay. It held little hope for the bodies inside. Dust floated in their faces. Mould grew on the walls. The windows were mostly destroyed, some of them with shards of broken glass still hanging in their frames. A constant chorus of hacking, coughing, moaning, and the occasional scream assaulted their ears. The smell was vile.

"Honeybee will get transferred soon," Aelya said to reassure herself. After all, this was an evacuation hospital; every patient here was only temporary.

They gingerly made their way around the beds and the wounded, some of them just lying on blankets on the floorboards. Perhaps Honeybee wasn't here and they'd missed her. Did that mean she'd died? Aelya felt a twinge of relief and angrily suppressed it.

She grabbed a passing nurse. "We're looking for Senior Lieutenant Gorbataya."

All she got was a shrug.

Sirin tapped her on the shoulder and pointed to a doorway, through which they could see yet more rows of moaning patients, all covered in bandages, some soaked red. Here a missing leg. There, a face wrapped up, looking as if it was missing something as well.

Aelya steeled herself and crossed the threshold. Past the nurses criss-crossing between the beds, she caught a flash of platinum blonde hair and her heart stuck in her throat.

A patient lay like a prone ghost, wrapped up in white. And next to her, on the edge of the bed, sat Roza.

CHAPTER 38: BURNED

Aelya was barely prepared for Honeybee. She couldn't do this too, couldn't see her. But she forced herself forward.

Roza held open a copy of *Red Star* and was reading aloud that the Allies had finally launched an attack in Italy. Honeybee's eyes were closed, the rest of her face hidden under bandages, her once luxuriant hair matted with blood. Her arms, folded on her chest, were red and raw from burns.

Upon noticing Aelya and Sirin, Roza leaped to her feet. Before Aelya could get any words out, Roza had wrapped her and Sirin in a wide hug.

"Fancy seeing you here," said Sirin as she slipped free.

"I've missed you so much," Roza said.

"Everyone misses you too."

Aelya could sense the dreadful question coming from Roza and turned to look at Honeybee. "How is she?" She and Sirin knelt at the bedside.

Aelya was relieved when Roza focused on their injured comrade. "She hasn't been able to talk. From what I can see, she seems to have good moments and bad, but at least she's not getting worse. It's hell trying to get hold of a doctor, though."

"I can't believe you've been perched here reading to her like some Komsomol volunteer," said Aelya. "That's so sweet of you."

"It's only because she's on so many painkillers, she doesn't know what's going on. That way she'll never know I was nice to her."

Aelya couldn't help smiling as her eyes welled up with tears. "How did you even end up here?"

Roza grew animated. "That's the best part. Dmitriev drove me to division headquarters to fly me back to Moscow, but Platonov stole his Li-2 to go to a conference, so we were stranded."

Sirin's brow furrowed as she pointed to Honeybee's right arm. "I don't like how swollen this is. Has anyone looked at it?" She leaned in to sniff, then wrinkled her nose in disgust.

Aelya cast her eyes around at the misery. The moaning and coughing. The dust drifting through the room, sticking to congealed patches of blood on half-rotted wood planks. "We have to get her out of here."

A short Red Army lieutenant approached the bed, dragging his right foot. Neatly trimmed ginger hair framed a rosy, clean-shaven face. Definitely not a *frontovik*. He had a wet cloth in his hand, which he placed on Honeybee's swollen arm.

"It's the best I could do, Kulik," he said, then looked at Aelya and Sirin. "Oh, hello. Judging by your uniforms, you must be from Sparrow Squadron." He introduced himself as Lieutenant Rabinovich, a writer for *Red Star*.

Sirin held up the newspaper. "Did you write something in this?"

Rabinovich smiled broadly as he opened the paper and pointed at an article recounting a *makhra's* reunion with family that hid among partisans for two years.

The journalist gestured at the pilots. "It's perfect you're here. Now I can expand my story. I wanted to write about how our fighting men and women come to grips with their wounded colleagues."

Sirin narrowed her eyes. "They'll never let you publish that."

Aelya asked Roza, "How did he find you?"

"Actually, Comrade Rabinovich was the one who got me here in the first place. I didn't feel like hanging around at division headquarters for a couple of days waiting with Dmitriev for a ride. I was at the SovInform-

Buro office and Rabinovich was there. We got to talking about his story idea, and I thought I might as well go on a trip. Next thing I know, I hear a woman pilot is laid up here."

"Is Dmitriev around?" Aelya said.

"He's outside. He can't stand the sight of blood." Roza crouched to put her arms around her two comrades. "I don't believe in fate. But if I did, I'd have to think it had some hand in bringing us together."

"A happy reunion," said Rabinovich.

"So tell me what I've missed," said Roza. "How's Stitches?"

Roza knew from their looks.

Sirin put a hand on Rabinovich and guided him away.

Aelya couldn't speak, so Roza did it for her. "He's dead."

She always knew this was coming. But each day, somehow she'd convince herself it wouldn't happen. She'd asked for updates on the regiment at division headquarters, and then when she heard they were standing down for a day, she even allowed herself to be encouraged.

Now that the words had been spoken, everything poured of out Aelya, but Roza didn't hear much, only a few words here and there that she picked up. Enough to know it was an accident, and not from enemy fire. She tried to convince herself it was better that way. But somewhere deep down, she felt it was worse.

Her mind was already moving, cycling through images and sensations. Lying next to him, her fingers tracing a line down his arm, tickled by his coarse hair. She imagined that body, so warm when next to hers, now broken, alone.

She sat on the bed, flipping the copy of *Red Star* over in her hands, scanning the black ink letters, not reading anything. Aelya crouched next to her, gently stroking her shoulder. It was pathetic and Roza hated it.

With Red, with Dema, with Stone, and with all the others she'd known, she could get back into the air and fight. But this time it was different, and she knew why but tried to suppress it. She just needed to do something.

"I want to see him," she said. "I want to go to his grave."

Aelya held her hand, looking dubious. "Roza—"

Sirin had returned and patted her shoulders.

Rabinovich said, "I'm so sorry to hear about your friend."

Aelya lashed out, saying, "This is not for your story."

Chastened, he took a step back but kept observing them.

"I need to go back," said Roza. "At least to say goodbye to the others."

Aelya grimaced. "I'm not sure—"

"You're worried about Dmitriev? Come on! That doesn't even matter at this point."

"It's not that. Not really. It's just . . . you sound like you want to fight again."

Honeybee moaned. Her prone form rolled onto its side and Aelya gently tried to guide her onto her back. "It's all right," Aelya said, stroking Honeybee's forehead. "We're all here. It's Mars. With Lily and Sirin."

"Even if she could hear you," said Roza, "she's too loaded with painkillers."

Honeybee's body convulsed, to the point that she arched upward and Roza and Aelya were compelled to push her back down.

"We can't leave her like this," said Sirin.

Aelya stood. "I just had a thought. What about Dmitriev?"

Roza groaned.

Aelya continued, "No, what I mean is, he's waiting for an Li-2 to Moscow, right? He can arrange for Honeybee to be transported with him. Then she could be taken to a better place. How about the First Moscow Medical Institute?"

"Dmitriev will never go for that," said Roza.

Aelya looked at Sirin. "It's a good thing one of our friends can be quite persuasive."

When it seemed safe to let go of Honeybee, Aelya gathered the other two pilots to whisper a plan. Roza warily eyed Rabinovich, who seemed to want to record everything in his mind for some future story, but Aelya signalled for him to join them. She had a part for him to play, and he agreed to it.

They left Honeybee as comfortable as they could, and then all four of them exited the hospital to find Dmitriev. At the side of Kostino's main thoroughfare, he smoked and chatted with a blue-capped NKVD captain. When he saw the women approaching, his face soured.

Roza narrowed her focus, as if going into combat. It revived her. "What's the matter, Comrade Colonel?" she said. "You have all your remaining sparrows here, available for a good morale-boosting story. Comrade Rabinovich is ready to oblige as well."

"That's part of your old life, Kulik."

Aelya stepped in front of Roza. "Comrade Kulik's not done here yet. She never got a chance to say goodbye to that life. And now Captain Akhmatov is dead."

Dmitriev's face softened. "That's sad to hear. He was always very helpful."

"What I propose," Aelya said, "is for Comrade Kulik to return to our unit, just for a day or two, in order to say a proper goodbye. Rabinovich will come with us. He's already thought of an angle for his story. The burdens of sacrifice. Of course, we don't expect you to wait around at the front all this time. You can return to Moscow, and you can bring our wounded comrade with you. She needs to be transferred to the very best care. First Moscow. That would make a great story about advances in Soviet medicine."

Dmitriev cocked an eyebrow. "More delays, Kulik? And I don't have time to babysit an unconscious patient."

"That's exactly what you're going to do," Sirin said, pointing a finger in his face.

"Who the hell do you think you are?"

"Senior Lieutenant Sofia Davitovichna Dolidze, at your service."

"Davit Dolidze is your father?" the NKVD man said quietly, his lips trembling.

"Oh, that's right. Have you worked with him?"

The blue cap leaned in to whisper to Dmitriev. They conferred for a moment.

"All right." Dmitriev pointed at Roza. "But you had better come right back to Moscow as soon as Rabinovich has his story."

Roza shrugged. "What else am I going to do? Steal a fighter and attack the enemy?"

Aelya elbowed her, shaking her head slightly. Roza continued to smile.

Sirin pulled Dmitriev aside, steering him toward the hospital. "Let's take a look at your patient. You're going to ensure she gets to the medical institute comfortably. My father will be looking in on her for me."

Roza couldn't believe that was true but was impressed by the bluff. She was so grateful Sirin had stood up for her. She wanted to give her a big hug but couldn't risk breaking the spell of intimidation Sirin had cast.

Roza and Aelya followed them into the hospital. Rabinovich tagged along, dragging his infirm foot. They said their goodbyes to Honeybee. Roza kept it quick; anything more would have been painful. A pair of orderlies brought a stretcher over. Dmitriev gave her one more stern warning about coming back to Moscow to rejoin her family. With that, she, Sirin, and Rabinovich followed Aelya out the back of the hospital.

Aelya pointed to several ZiS trucks already overflowing with passengers and cargo. "One of those is bound to drive by Rogachevsk."

As she approached the trucks, Rabinovich tapped Roza on the shoulder. "I'd better go get our suitcases."

Sirin said, "Let me help you."

The journalist waved her away. "I might have been rejected for frontline duty, but I think I can handle a pair of suitcases. Just make sure you find a truck."

Aelya signalled success to Roza and Sirin. The three of them squeezed into a cargo bed alongside a dozen others, forced to scrunch their legs against several crates. The truck started up almost immediately.

"We need to tell him to wait," said Sirin.

Roza shook her head. "No, I don't want a reporter making a spectacle. Let's go."

Aelya stared at her but said nothing.

The truck rolled slowly out of Kostino, forcing its way through throngs of civilians, soldiers, and other vehicles. Soon, the bustle of activity in the town gave way to the sounds of battle in the countryside. The setting sun glowed on the horizon, and Roza felt a weight lift. The first star twinkled up high.

The last letter she'd received from her father told her to look up at the night sky. He assured her that wherever he was, he would look up and she should know that the stars were just the same for them both. Just as beautiful.

The stars seemed constant as though they would be just the same after the war. But that wasn't true. Roza knew from her astronomy classes that new stars were born and stars died all the time. The stars lied to her, like everything else.

CHAPTER 39: FATHER OF THE REGIMENT

Roza flipped a pair of dominoes between her fingers at a table in the club. With her other hand, she held a glassful of vodka. The place was empty except for the attending sergeant. He ignored her as he packed up the samovar, the cups, the newspapers, and the packs of cards that had made a reappearance despite their ban.

Aelya stumbled in, eyes bloodshot. "I thought you'd be in here," she said, pulling a log stump up to Roza's table.

"It's late," said Roza. "Shouldn't you be getting some rest?"

"I'm too wired. A hundred grams isn't enough." Aelya signalled to the sergeant, who pulled a bottle of vodka hidden in a crate and poured her a glass. "Being a squadron commander has to have some privileges besides staying up past curfew to attend meetings."

The two pilots raised their glasses and downed their drinks. Roza grew more numb and light-headed. "So," she said, "was it a tough day?"

"Not really. We only fly combat half the time. The other half is practice."

"How's the new guy liking our Yaks?" Roza asked.

A pilot who called himself Pepper had been in the truck they'd taken back from the hospital. Only halfway through the journey did he realize he was headed to the wrong airfield. Regardless, he was so happy was to be discharged and back at the front, he immediately agreed to Aelya's recruitment pitch, despite not having flown a Yak in over a year.

"He says he likes it better than the Lavochkin," said Aelya. "I think his combat experience is worth it, even if he's unused to the plane. He took our three-on-ones quite well."

"So that was your squadron I saw practising in the afternoon. Why do you fly three against one?"

"We always train in pairs, as if circumstances will be perfect. But we need to know what to do when we lose our wingmen. So that means flying alone, or joining another pair."

Roza laughed. "I don't think about stuff like that. I guess that's why you're a squadron commander."

Aelya shrugged. "I have no idea if it actually works. But sometimes, you just have to trust that you're doing the right thing." She sighed. "Stitches taught me that."

Roza stared at her empty glass. "That was a beautiful picture of him." The image of his face made her feel such a strong connection to him, she had felt her heart stop when she saw it lying over his grave. Aelya clasped her hand, and Roza broke down. "I really loved Stitches."

"I know that," Aelya said. "All he did, all he wanted, was for you to find happiness. He told me that."

"He always thought love would get us through the war."

Aelya was silent.

"What gets you through this war?" Roza said.

Aelya paused before saying, "It's like you said. Each other. Comrades."

Roza remembered saying that to Aelya when she was at her lowest at Stalingrad. A weight pressed down on her as she thought about it. Ever since she'd returned, she knew what needed to happen. "Don't make me leave again," she said.

"You can stay for a while. We still need to wait for that *Red Star* reporter." Aelya laughed nervously.

"You want me to just hang around, like some ghoul, reminding everyone of death?"

Aelya shook her head. "It's not like—"

"You're short on pilots. Take me into your squadron."

"What? No, you're not thinking straight."

"My mind has never been more clear."

Aelya sighed, looking away. "I'm in enough trouble as it is."

Roza knew that she had her. She just needed to give one more push. "Is that going to stop you?"

"What are you talking about?"

Roza wagged her finger. "You could have stopped me at any point. Sent me back home. You wanted me back here."

"That was for you. I thought you needed . . . I don't know, peace."

Roza laughed sharply. "Have you noticed we're in a war? There's no peace, not even at home. In fact, what is my home? This place is the closest I'll get. Help me get back into action. Talk to Frost."

"No, I can't. It's not right."

"You don't think I could help?"

"I'm not abetting some death wish."

"I have no intention of killing myself. I here to kill Nazis." Roza took her hand, looking at her intensely. "Your responsibility isn't protecting any one of us. It's to your whole squadron. To give them the best chance to do their job. And their best chance is having their best pilot flying."

Aelya shook her head. "What about your family?"

"*This* family needs me." Roza slammed the table. Her mother and her brother, that was part of "after the war." She couldn't think about it. The fact was, she was afraid to.

"I'm not going to let you throw away everything you've wanted," said Aelya.

Roza sighed, sitting up. "That's your choice. You're squadron commander."

"By accident."

"No. Red believed in you. That you do what needs to be done. I know that means something to you."

A jeep rolled up. It was Legend. He gave Roza a curt nod. "It's time for the planning session."

Roza said, "Go do your job, Comrade Commander."

The atmosphere was thick and heated within the command tent. Nevertheless, Frost was pale and shivering. He'd obviously been on the phone with General Platonov again. "Platonov just threatened to have me shot," he said flatly.

Aelya swallowed, but the other squadron commanders barely registered a reaction. This was only Aelya's third senior command meeting and perhaps these sort of threats were regular occurrences. Or perhaps everyone was just tired. It had been dark enough that Legend needed headlights to bring her here. The adjutant stood dutifully behind their commander, eyes bleary and red. Baby stifled a yawn. Sitting on crates made Tractor and Petrushka hunch over, looking decrepit.

She wanted nothing more than to go back to her quarters and collapse, but this was the job. Stitches had put up with it. So had Honeybee. Her heart ached that they weren't here anymore.

Baby slapped Frost hard on the back. "You can do it, Comrade Commander. We Russians always find a way."

Frost was Tajik but didn't correct his deputy. His shoulders slumped. "Damn that Platonov. If he thinks it's so easy to stop these Henschels, let's hear some of his bright ideas."

"It's not his fault," Cricket said with an earnest, conciliatory tone. "I heard General Rudenko threatened to shoot him if we keep losing tanks at this rate."

Aelya struggled to avoid rolling her eyes, not only at Cricket's optimism, but also at the hand-wringing over this new German bomber. "Come on," Aelya said, loud enough to perk up Tractor and Petrushka, who were flanking her on the crates. "The Henschel's not so bad. It's all about timing."

Baby had his hands in mid-gesture, surely about to condescend to her, when Petrushka said, "Of course she doesn't mind the Henschel. That big gun hanging down doesn't make her feel small and inadequate about her equipment."

Tractor snorted, nearly spilling the tea he was holding.

"Speak for yourself," said Baby.

Petrushka's eyes brightened and he pointed his finger. "Actually—"

Frost cleared his throat, eyeing Aelya. Petrushka bit back whatever savage retort he'd had ready. As much as Aelya didn't want to hear another crude comment, the fact that Frost wanted the others to put on a false face of civility in front of her was more upsetting. She was out of place among these men. How could she really be a squadron commander?

Tractor banged on his crate. "Of course they're killing our tanks. Fritz always loads the Henschels up with escorts. Where are all these fighters coming from? I tell you, if Air Army wants us to stop them, they need to send us actual help. An extra regiment with seasoned pilots, not just yellow-mouthed replacements. And maybe stop giving us ten different objectives every day so we spread ourselves thin."

Petrushka added his voice to the chorus. "I'm trying to pick our moments, but even so, we take little hits here and there. It's death by a thousand cuts. I lost another pilot today."

Frost looked exasperated. "We know we're not getting help anytime soon. Give me real solutions. If we don't stop the tanks from bleeding, we're all . . ." he was about to make a vague gesture with his hand but stopped.

Aelya opened her mouth to speak, but Baby butted in. "What we need to do is cover the tanks around the clock."

No, that was a terrible idea. Aelya dreaded a confrontation with Baby, but Tractor saved her the trouble.

"That's madness," said Tractor, scratching three days' worth of grey whiskers on his cheek. "We'd be spread too thin. They'd murder us."

Though she was trembling, Aelya felt moved to speak. "So we wait." Petrushka smirked, thinking she'd made a joke, but she pressed on. "The Henschels don't strike from the front. They cross our lines and hit our tanks from behind. So we wait in readiness for the observers to call it in, then we strike, in force, with numbers."

"I'm not having the whole regiment in readiness. Platonov would cut my head off," said Frost.

"You could have one squadron in the air."

"I don't have enough to spare."

"You would if you didn't give us all the garbage missions," Aelya mumbled.

"As I was saying, you've lost your squadron leader, and I think you need time to integrate as a new leader. Actually, I was considering giving Cricket command."

Baby nodded. Petrushka and Tractor looked annoyed but kept quiet.

Aelya glanced at Cricket and shook her head. "No. No, I'm sorry, and I don't want to offend our comrade *zampolit*, but he hasn't been flying regular missions. He doesn't know my squadron the way I do. I fly with them every day. Five or six sorties a day. I'm ready for this. *We're* ready for this."

"This isn't about what you want," Frost said. "Red would have put the regiment's needs above all else."

"Are you? If you did too, you'd reinstate Roza Kulik."

Frost stood and threw his hands up. "I am *not* disobeying a direct order. It's bad enough she came back. If word gets out to Platonov—"

"I don't give a damn about Platonov, and you shouldn't either," Aelya shouted. "This regiment is dying. You know what it's like out there. Red would have done something about it. He would have wanted his best pilots doing their jobs."

"Do you really want to do this, Senior Lieutenant?" said Frost, glaring at her.

Cricket held his hands up in a conciliatory gesture. "I suggest we take a break and let things cool off. How about some more tea?"

Frost groaned and stepped to a corner of the tent separated by camouflage netting—his makeshift private office. Baby stood to light a cigarette. Legend handed Aelya tea in a glass with a metal cup holder.

Cricket crouched by Petrushka and Tractor, leaning in conspiratorially. At first, she thought they were sharing a dirty joke. She hovered behind them, annoyed at being excluded, even if the joke was disgusting. But she caught a few words from Petrushka: "Do you think it could work?"

Tractor turned to watch Aelya over his shoulder. He'd been at the same school as Sirin and respected his fellow instructor. But she was an exception, and he'd never hidden his disdain for other women pilots.

Feeling unwelcome, Aelya approached the corner alcove. Peering behind the netting, she saw Frost kneeling on a small rectangular piece of carpet laid on the dirt. He noticed her and turned to sit cross-legged, grunting a greeting, then muttered to himself. She sat next to him.

Frost sighed. "Spam always knew the verses. I don't even know the right times to pray." He composed himself. She noticed now how terribly

Frost had aged. His hair was no longer just silver at the sides but going entirely grey.

"Are you religious?" he asked her. "I mean, obviously it's not something I'm against." She'd noticed over the course of this war that more and more soldiers were being granted a chance to worship more openly. It had been frowned on in the past, and she wondered if its acceptance was only fleeting. Surely the way Kalmyks had fallen under suspicion so easily didn't bode well for continued religious tolerance.

"I've never thought much about it," she said honestly. Her parents were dedicated socialists and believed that religion belonged to the old world of the czars. "I think it's enough to believe in the present world and try to make it a better place."

"And what about after that? Beyond life?"

She resisted the temptation to shrug. She really didn't know what to say, except to recite some form of what she'd been told in school. She knew that death was ever present in this war, but she couldn't think much of its implications beyond that. If after death people were truly judged by their deeds, what difference did that make when such cruelty and animosity was allowed to happen in life? She answered plainly, "It's the memories of our deeds and how we affect the people around us—those are the only things that will live on."

Frost rubbed his temple, his eyebrows furrowing, as if the answer to this question was bothering him immensely. Aelya seriously wondered if he was starting to crack under the pressure of command. It seemed unfair to judge him when this role had been thrust upon him against his will, but that was part of the sacrifice demanded of him.

An idea germinating in Aelya's head came to fruition. She wasn't sure it was good, but if Roza wanted in on the fight this was the only way.

"I have a plan to deal with the Henschels, but it will need Roza Kulik."

"I can't risk the White Lily, not with the political directorate breathing down my neck."

"Forget those orders. You need to think about sacrificing for the greater good."

"Isn't that what I do every day?"

"What's one more risk, then?" She sighed. "I don't think you always had such a problem with women leading a squadron. You respected Auntie, didn't you?"

"Of course."

"Remember that time I helped Auntie get back across our lines after her engine was hit? After all that, she died a month and a half later anyway. I thought everything I'd done had been a waste. Then I had to sell her out. I signed off on a fable blaming her for someone else's mistake. Red made me do it. All to save the regiment. I thought I could never live with myself, but now I realize I'd do it all over again for the good of the regiment. Not because I want to, but because that's the responsibility of a leader. I was lucky there was someone to order me to do it."

"Red would know what to do."

"He's dead. You're our leader now. Lead!"

He straightened up and nodded. "Tell me about your plan."

CHAPTER 40: THE TRAP

Aelya gripped the control stick tightly, her breath straining to make its way through her lungs. The die was cast. No more hard decisions now. Just act. Accept the risks.

With the sun barely peeking over the horizon, the fight below only made itself known by the smoke and flames that reached out toward their six fighters. Aelya imagined she could sniff the fumes over the tang of fuel that permeated her cockpit. She imagined hearing the explosions above the sound of her own engine.

She and Lucky, Vino and Timur, and Sirin and Pepper moved crisply in pairs staggered by height. They swept in a large figure-eight loop, alternately exchanging height for speed and vice versa. Aelya had plotted out the two areas in their operational zone where combat was the fiercest and timed their route so they'd reach each at maximum speed, ready to hit the enemy.

It wasn't just a matter of looking for contacts in the sky; she needed to discern which of the dozens of silhouettes were the ones she was looking for.

A report from Giraffe broke through the low-level chatter in Aelya's headphones. A large group of fighters inbound. In a way, the ferocity of the battle on the ground simplified matters. The entire Soviet counteroffensive hung in the balance. Just like the VVS, the Luftwaffe was throwing everything they had into striking their enemies on the ground.

Whether these were fighter-bombers or escorts looking to clear the sky, she knew exactly where they were headed.

Lucky was the first to spot them: eight Fw 190s. "Judging by their speed, these are escorts," he said.

She could hear the edge in his voice, keen for battle. She smiled as she recollected his transformation from hapless yellow-mouth to veteran wingman over the past six months.

"All right, Sparrow Squadron," she declared, "we're going in two waves. Sirin, you're with me. Vino, stay in cover. You know there'll be more out there." Despite the lack of clouds, the enemy could still hide using the sun, battlefield smoke, and general confusion.

Aelya banked hard into a dive, Lucky following her. She was fortunate; at this angle, she could approach the heavies from behind, slightly left of centre. The vultures had no doubt expected to see Yaks coming from the front, trying to intercept them, not knowing Aelya's group was already in the air waiting.

The distance closed rapidly. An Fw 190 turned violently, spotting the danger, but Aelya was already close enough to make out the green heart and pressed the triggers. She twitched her plane to avoid debris.

Sirin dived after her with Pepper. Within seconds, she said over the radio, "Another vulture down."

Aelya took her four attacking fighters on a climbing turn to regroup. She could see the six remaining Fw 190s powering upward to try to regain the initiative. As Vino's pair rejoined her, both groups of adversaries circled each other, alternating height and speed, looking for an advantage.

Pepper said that he'd taken damage on his wing and had to disengage. So much for the new guy.

Aelya bit her tongue, then replied, "Vino and Timur, you're going in as coverage for Sirin."

"On your six!" Lucky shouted.

Aelya glanced back, instinctively breaking into a turn and hoping she'd chosen the right direction. A diving Fw 190 had the angle on her. Lucky moved himself into the line of fire.

For a fraction of a second, Aelya tensed in anticipation of a terrible mistake. But then, as she was hoping for—as she expected—her pursuer caught fire and spun out of control. The other Fw 190s in this new group broke off their pursuit.

A green-brown camouflaged Yak with a large white flower painted on its fuselage took the place of her pursuer and performed a showy victory roll.

"You cut it close," Aelya said to Roza.

"No, you cut it close. I was right on time."

Roza took her plane back into a climb, her new wingman, Genius, trailing behind her. He was Aelya's choice. None of the remaining pilots truly had the skill to keep up with Roza, but Genius's calm, cerebral demeanour, like Dema's fatalism, would allow him to read Roza's intentions in the moment without panicking. At least, that's what Aelya hoped.

Roza and Genius climbed away. "I'll chase after these new vultures," she said. "Looks like you've got your hands full with the first crew."

The original six Fw 190s Aelya had hit were spurred into action, sharpening their turns and trying to close. The arrival of reinforcements must have emboldened them. Even more might be coming. Aelya looked around and saw other dots gathering, menacing. Her small corner of the battlefield grew crowded. The whole sky was pierced with metal and fire.

"Just watch your back, Lily."

As she and her group of five Yaks manoeuvred against the six Fw 190s, they were being drawn farther away from the battle on the ground. That's the whole point, she thought. Let the Luftwaffe think we're leaving the *makhras* undefended.

For days, they'd been trying to intercept the tank-killing Henschels by flying straight toward the front lines, only to be met by waves of German fighters clearing the area and never catching sight of the bombers. But it had occurred to Aelya that the Henschels liked to strike Soviet tanks from the rear. And so she'd convinced Frost that her squadron could not only hold the enemy fighters, but also draw others into the fray. Then, while the Henschels tried to quietly cross the lines and double back, the two remaining squadrons would scramble and hit them undefended. At least, that was the plan. If she was wrong . . .

She led her flight straight toward the enemy. For a second, it looked as though they would collide, but the Germans turned suddenly. Again the two formations circled each other. In the second she allowed herself to scan the rest of the sky, yellow and bluish tracers criss-crossed as shadowy forms closed on each other in the distance. Roza and Genius were in the thick of it. Flames burst from one of the shadows, then another. New shadows appeared above them.

"Lily, watch out—I see new vultures up high."

Aelya ordered her five fighters to break off and intercept these new fighters. She was trying to copy the Night Raven's tactics: block for their ace. Not the most efficient tactic for protecting the front lines, but that wasn't Aelya's job today. Hers was to draw attention, with the White Lily as the prime attraction.

The silhouettes chasing Roza grew as Aelya closed. Some of them peeled away to attack her. Behind her, other Fw 190s had moved to the chase. Aelya was in danger of getting caught in a pincer.

"Mars, Genius is hit. I'm sending him home. Do you copy?" More static. Roza couldn't tell if there was something wrong with her radio or Aelya's. It didn't matter. Genius would have to take care of himself; she had problems of her own.

Roza spotted danger when one Fw 190 looped back while she tried to chase down two others. She rolled and turned. The Fw 190 flew across her view. At a lower altitude but with more speed, she used the Yak's turning ability to bring the enemy into her sights, but then had to break off as two more heavies made an appearance.

By her reckoning, it was one against five. They were splitting up to attack her in turns. She tipped her plane forward and turned hard, then hard again. But again she couldn't line up an enemy fighter without being threatened by another one, dodging a tracer stream by metres. She was barely surviving. She needed to change things up.

She turned, dropped her power, and kept one wing low.

Come and get me, Roza thought. She searched the sky, desperately hoping to identify the right dots in time. There. Two of them, diving toward her fast.

She had to time this just right. Far from being the wounded prey she pretended to be, she went full throttle and pulled hard on the stick. The enemy would be expecting her to turn in the direction she'd been tilting her plane, thinking it was damaged, so she went hard the other way. A look over her shoulder confirmed how close the stream of tracers had come. She looped around as the Fw 190s pulled out of their dive and began to climb. She could just line up the trailing plane.

A quick pulse of fire from her cannon and machine gun sheared the tail off her target. The other heavies turned hard, losing formation. She dropped in behind another fighter and he swerved in panic before she could fire. The others were scrambling too. It was an old-fashioned dogfight. Roza smiled at the thought that she'd pushed the Germans into reckless tactics. In these close quarters, they couldn't use their superior engine power to their advantage. Tracers ripped the air ahead and behind her. Roza responded with her own. Silhouettes of fighters flashed across her view in the blink of an eye.

She pulled up and rolled, hoping to correctly time another dive at the enemy. There he was. She checked behind her and recognized a new threat only a heartbeat before a stream of tracers cut across her path and into her engine. Her plane rocked with the hits.

She jerked her fighter hard to the left, to where this new pursuer should have been. But the damage to her Yak made her a touch too slow. She lofted upward in her seat, her whole lower body coming alive with burning pain. The profile of an Fw 190 passed by. Green heart. Black raven.

Dammit, she thought, as flames flared across her windshield.

She watched the Night Raven and his wingman pull away. Behind her, the other Fw 190s were regrouping. Roza only allowed herself the briefest moment to notice her injury. Wetness bleeding out somewhere close to her stomach. She glanced down, hoping the mess she saw was clothing, leather straps or her harness, not her innards.

Her engine was on fire. Ingrained training caused her to tip the plane forward, the onrushing air putting the flames out for the moment. She grew light-headed.

Levelling out, she winced, trying to look back. Another pair to evade. It was only a matter of time before she was caught. But they stayed back, hovering but not diving. In another corner of her eye, one last pair of Fw 190s moved in a high, wide curve.

Oh hell, she thought. They're saving me for the Night Raven.

"Keep up, Sirin," Aelya said. She looked back, happy at least that Vino and Timur were doing a good job of covering for Sirin.

Farther back, the two clusters of Fw 190s grew more distant, no longer chasing them. Aelya had climbed high, away from the battle zone, feigning a retreat. It gave her the space to look for Roza and Genius. It was difficult to pick out the right shapes as planes hid among the smoke and terrain below. Banking again, she thought she could make out one silhouette, surrounded by several others, that seemed to be circling, herding it.

"We're going back in. Sirin, with the other two, keep the vultures off our backs. I'm going to try to get through to Lily."

She banked again and dived, her engine whining at a high pitch, the frame vibrating violently. At least a half dozen Fw 190s were in her way. She altered course, watching for Lucky to match her movements. Sirin's three now took the lead and headed directly for the enemy. If Aelya could time it right, she could get past the screen of enemy fighters and to where she thought Roza was taking the fight.

In her peripheral vision, an Fw 190 pulled level with her, then turned away, chased by Sirin's tracer stream. She had gotten through.

She was close enough now to see that the lone silhouette hounded by the others was indeed Roza's Yak. It alternated hard dives and turns to escape as successive waves of Fw 190s closed in, never quite getting within killing range. Roza's manoeuvring was like an ox's tail swatting away at a swarm of flies. She wasn't flying well, a touch slow on her dives, a touch wide in her turns. Above it all, Aelya's combat sense drew her to a pair of shadows lurking above. These last two entered a dive now, aiming to meet Roza just as she came out of hers. This was different from the feigned attacks. They were finishing her off.

Roza was losing height. Her plane dropped with each successive attack from the enemy. She was running out of space. The sights and sounds of battle on the ground were much closer now. Enemy fire from below was a real possibility, but above all else, she had to watch for the enemy coming at her from high.

Finally, she could sense him, even before she looked. He was coming for her.

Aelya raced with a single-minded purpose. Dangerous. Check behind, she told herself. As she did, Lucky said, "Vultures on our tail!"

"Scissor back, Lucky. Keep them away."

A quick glance forward. There was no time for deviation. As the menacing silhouette of the Night Raven closed on Roza's ailing fighter, she knew she had only one shot at this.

She had to trust in her wingman. She couldn't look back anymore. Her brain only processed the situation ahead. She might be able to reach the Night Raven in time, force him off Roza's tail. And then what? He'd power away and escape. There was another path. A cruel calculus was forming in her mind: save the White Lily or kill the Night Raven.

Fiery needles of pain coursed through Roza as she strained to look behind her. It was almost over now. She'd always thought she'd take down the Night Raven. She just never thought she'd die in the process. The back of her mind rebelled with thoughts of a future that didn't exist. Stitches was dead. Deeper still lay another future, one in which her mother and brother would always have a chance. But it would have to be without her.

The Night Raven would anticipate another evasion, a hard turn in a futile attempt to escape. She pulled back, hit the flaps, and swerved as a line of tracers cut across her path. Then metal smashed into metal.

Roza's move surprised Aelya. It surprised the Night Raven too, and he jerked away, narrowly avoiding collision. The Yak and the Night Raven's wingman came together, then pushed apart, both missing a wing and spinning helplessly toward the ground.

Aelya didn't think about that. The Night Raven's evasion had lost him momentum. He sensed danger and instinctively went into the power climb Aelya knew was coming. She could see the black raven symbol clearly and fired. She kept the triggers pushed down as the distance closed and flaming debris passed her windshield. Only just before collision seemed inevitable did she pull away.

Now she afforded herself a glance back. The Night Raven's Fw 190 descended from view, trailing smoke as it dipped behind Aelya's fuselage. No sign of a parachute.

And what about Roza? With luck, she had bailed out.

"Vultures incoming, Mars!" said Lucky.

Her plane bucked forward just as she heard his warning, interrupted by staccato metallic thunks. Stupid, stupid. She'd been caught admiring her shot.

The control stick was wrenched from her grasp for a second. She glanced at a pair of Fw 190s breaking off. Behind them, more dots struggled in the distance, lost against the fires and smoke of the battle below, glowing a hue that turned the day into a prolonged sunset.

"Lucky, where are you?"

No response. Was he dead, or was it her radio?

A loud crack ripped over the noise of the engine and her fighter fell into a spin. Struggling with all her might, she thought only of keeping herself airborne.

But the plane wouldn't respond. It kept plunging and plunging.

CHAPTER 41: WAITING

Zina fiddled with the spark plug, forgetting why she'd even picked it up. She placed it back on a metal tray with the others, patting it gently as if trying to soothe it. She leaned over a clipboard on the table and put a check mark next to a number, not sure it was correct. Her gaze veered past the camouflage netting that covered the parts depot.

Outside, the technicians of Petrushka's squadron scrambled to ready their planes in the open, happy to risk exposure to enemy attack in exchange for a quick turnaround. The pilots sat near their planes, waiting mostly in silence. Whatever celebration they'd had over hammering the Luftwaffe in their last sortie had subsided.

Beyond that line of planes lay the runway. Katya was there at the end, one of those little dots among the grass, faithfully waiting for the sight over the horizon that would signal good news.

Zina turned her attention back to the inventory. Her squadron's parts had been raided in a frenzy as first Tractor's and now Petrushka's squadrons had landed and been ordered to return to the air as soon as possible, even as they waited for Aelya's squadron to return.

She knew from the sporadic radio reports that the action had been fierce. Pepper had returned earlier with his crippled ride. They'd heard that Genius crash-landed somewhere, and his mechanics hoped desperately to hear that the infantry had found him. But of the others, they'd heard nothing.

The chance of a terrible loss weighed down on Zina, as she knew it weighed on Katya. Whatever her disagreements with Aelya, Katya took her responsibility seriously. When she sent a pilot up in one of her planes, it was as if she was a mother sending her child to school.

Zina just wanted to be with Katya, but she knew she couldn't do that. She was squadron engineer and she was responsible for all the technicians. She had to suppress her feelings and not show any favouritism.

She picked up her clipboard and sighed. Then she gave in to temptation and took another look outside. She gazed longer than she'd told herself to. A dark speck crossed the sky.

She dropped the clipboard and ran so fast, she had to hold down her cap. Sweat soaked her overalls. More specks in the sky circled slowly, trying to line up with the runway, a strip of compressed turf so long, it seemed to disappear into infinity.

She neared a dozen technicians kneeling on the grass as if in prayer, holding their hands above their foreheads to shield their eyes from the sun's glare. There was Katya, staring urgently into the distance. She turned and locked gazes with Zina. Tension was chiselled on her face as her eyes searched Zina's, looking for reassurance. Zina wanted to grab her and hold her tightly. But she stopped and looked out in the same direction.

The dots over the horizon formed themselves into wider shadows. She almost leaped with excitement. One. Two. Three. Too few.

Zina wasn't like Aelya: she didn't have the knack of identifying pilots by their flying motions. But there was something painful about the way these planes flew. Two of them looked mechanically damaged. They all appeared hindered in some way, as if the planes themselves felt the loss of their comrades. Zina shut that thought out of her mind.

The first Yak skidded along the runway, the holes prominently visible, the tail section shredded. The mythical bird-like creature painted on its side would have suffered a fatal injury.

As Sirin's mechanic helped guide her off the runway, Zina and Katya trailed closely behind. The canopy opened. Sirin started to say something, but nothing came out of her mouth. She just numbly stood up as her crew handled the plane.

"What happened?" asked Zina, walking alongside the plane. "Who's still out there?"

"I don't know. We got so spread out. There were so many vultures. I have no idea. I only know Vino and Timur are behind me. I lost contact with the others."

Surely there were many explanations, Zina told herself. Their radios could be out. She shared a look with Sirin in which they tried to will their hopes into reality.

"How'd the other squadrons do?" asked Sirin.

"They shot down five or six bombers. No tanks lost."

Sirin nodded, then bent over the other side of her cockpit to vomit. Emptied, she leaned against the top of her windshield and buried her head in her arms.

Another plane landed. Zina read the number. Vino.

And then the last silhouette in the distance descended to the runway. Timur.

Zina squeezed Katya's arm. As Sirin, Vino, and Timur were helped out of their planes, she would need to organize the crews to get them turned around to go out for another sortie. But a distant buzz caught her attention.

One more dot, trailing smoke.

Zina knew it wasn't Aelya. Not with those tentative, wobbly man-oeuvres. Her mind fought against this idea; perhaps the controls were damaged or Aelya's normally smooth landing was otherwise disrupted. She didn't want to wish it was her over anyone else, but favouritism be damned. Aelya was the other Smolensk girl, her connection to the world before the war.

The bort number appeared as the plane slid around for taxiing. Lucky.

Lucky's mechanic bounded toward his plane. Zina stood transfixed as Lucky emerged from his cockpit. Katya and Liza, Roza's crew chief, stood with her. He looked at them all and shook his head.

CHAPTER 42: BEYOND

Pungently intoxicating grease fumes penetrated Aelya's nostrils. Grit collected between her fingers and scraped her bare knees as she crawled on the factory floor. Machinery clanged and whirred, vibrating her bones in a constant rhythm. Her father stood above, bathed in such bright light that she could barely see him beaming. He bent down to scoop her up.

The light grew all-encompassing. Her eyes fought to adjust. She turned away from its source, a brightly burning electric table lamp next to her bed. Reading aloud, her mother spoke of gardens carved from red rock and the history of Mars. She smiled and stroked Aelya's cheek before returning to the book. This was not how she normally thought of her mother. The warmth was alien to her. With rapt attention, Aelya rolled onto her side and leaned on her elbow. She ignored Vasya's shuffling in the bed behind her; her sister was trying to tie a scrap of fabric around her tattered doll, mumbling made-up words.

She looked at Vasya. They were walking side by side, along the footpath leading to the workers' dormitories of the aviation plant. Her teenaged older sister droned on. ". . . and then I thought, no, that sort of thing might work on Sonya, but not me. I turned my head at the last second, so his lips touched me right here." She pointed to a spot on her cheek, and leaned in. She grabbed Aelya, as if telling her the most important thing in the world. "Give a little but not too much—that's the way to catch them."

Aelya feigned gagging.

A lump caught in her throat. She shook with nerves, trying to stand at attention. Vasya was gone, and so were the familiar surroundings of the aviation plant. She was inside a classroom painted slate grey, staring at a dull, chalk-dusted blackboard almost indistinguishable from the walls. She lowered her eyes to the woman seated at the table. Marina Raskova, her idol, stared back at her.

Memories of her life. But these were memories of memories, thoughts that had passed in her final moments in the cockpit. They flooded back to her now. These were the impressions that stayed with her —not struggling with the control stick, looking through the canopy desperately at the green-brown earth rushing toward her.

Her eyes opened, and she convulsed with a scream. She was on her stomach. Breathing was difficult, and she tried to turn over, but an intense pain in her left shoulder made her yelp and stop.

A hand gently but firmly pushed her back onto the floor. "Be quiet. Don't draw attention to yourself," a man whispered.

There was something reassuring about him. Peasants spoke of saints and angels. Was this the afterlife Frost had been so concerned with?

Her eyes focused on a wall built of logs. Grit and dirt from the floor poked at her cheek. She squirmed. So hot. There were other voices. Moaning and screaming.

A man called out something indecipherable. Her new acquaintance placed a cloth that stank of sweat over her head, then rushed to attend to a call. She strained to face the other way, dropping the cloth to the floor.

She took in the contorted human shapes in the room around her. They writhed, bleeding, their scraps of uniforms barely visible through the red, brown, and black filth caked on them.

The thick humid odours of the overcrowded log cabin wafted over her and she convulsed, wanting to retch. The windows, sloppily boarded up, leaked sunlight but not air through the gaps. It hurt to breathe. No, she wasn't dead.

She tried to push herself up, but her shoulder throbbed, stinging, a wave of pain surging through her body. She flopped down and rolled onto her good shoulder.

The man returned. "I'm sorry we have no painkillers here. Try to think of anything else. But above all, you must survive." He leaned in to her ear. "Your Party cards are in still your boot."

Now she noticed his uniform. Field grey. German. The wounded men around her. All German.

The cabin door burst inward. Two Germans armed with submachine guns strode in. They jabbered at the doctor, who responded, almost kneeling toward them, waving his hand at the back wall where Aelya lay.

She wanted to speak, to cry out, but it caught in her throat. The worst had happened.

She was a prisoner.

The Warbird concludes in
WOUNDED FALCON

HISTORICAL BACKGROUND

A description of the historical events leading up to the German invasion of the Soviet Union can be found in the Historical Background section of SPARROW SQUADRON.

Operation Barbarossa

In the early hours of June 22, 1941, German forces crossed into Soviet territory, signalling the start of the largest invasion in history, codenamed Operation Barbarossa. The days that followed were disastrous for the Soviet Union. The invaders held numerous advantages, but many factors internal to the Soviet Union hindered its ability to resist. Years of terror from purges resulted in subordinates who wouldn't make any independent decisions without confirmation from higher up. The Soviet armed forces were only partway through a massive program of modernization, with much of the equipment on the front lines hopelessly outdated. In the field, many Soviet leaders still adhered to old tactics, whereas the Germans had learned from two years of continuous warfare.

Two advantages the Soviets did have were space and manpower. They proceeded to utilize vast amounts of both in exchange for time. The Germans used mobile armoured formations to surround entire armies, capturing and killing hundreds of thousands in a matter of weeks. The Red Army threw thousands of raw recruits into slaughter, some even without weapons. As the Germans advanced, they found the land inhospitable. Josef Stalin ruthlessly ordered a "scorched earth" policy, burning crops and destroying infrastructure, preventing their use by the enemy, but bringing untold misery to the civilian population.

Despite these efforts, it seemed to much of the world that the collapse of the Soviet Union was imminent. Yet there were already signs that this invasion might not play out like the lightning warfare in the West. Much of the Soviet populace were weary of Stalin's terror. But Adolph Hitler's troops committed widespread atrocities, including systematic murder and enslavement, turning many who might have welcomed the Germans against them. The Germans' rapid advance left thousands of Soviet soldiers unaccounted for behind their lines. These Soviet soldiers became partisans, guerrilla fighters who disrupted German supply lines, which were already overstretched across the vast lands of the Soviet Union. Whole Soviet industries moved eastward, saving them from capture and preserving the ability to rebuild the Soviet arsenal.

In the north, Finland joined the Germans to besiege Leningrad. In the south, the invaders captured Kiev and the agricultural fields of Ukraine. The big prize remained Moscow. Hitler's muddled command caused critical delays in the attack on the Soviet capital. Then autumn rains brought on the muddy season, called *rasputitsa*. The German advance ground to a halt in a sea of muck and mire.

The onset of cold weather in November froze the ground and allowed the attack to start again. During this time, Stalin remained in Moscow, held a military parade, and made a speech that galvanized resistance. Soviet intelligence confirmed Japan wouldn't join their German allies in this fight, so crucial reinforcements started arriving from Siberia. The Western Allies agreed to provide vital supplies.

The Germans came within 30 kilometres of Moscow. A determined Soviet counterattack and the bitter cold of winter threw them back in defeat. The lightning invasion had failed and both sides settled in for a long war.

The winter that followed was one of the coldest on record. Many German soldiers lacked winter clothing and suffered terribly. But the Soviets, themselves exhausted from resisting the initial invasion, couldn't push the enemy back. As summer weather came, the Germans saw an opportunity to renew the mobile warfare that had given them so much success earlier in the war.

Instead of Moscow, Hitler changed his objective to Soviet oil fields in the south, and to the city of Stalingrad (now Volgograd.) A vital shipment point on the Volga River, Stalingrad had the added allure for Hitler of being named after his arch-enemy, Stalin.

Using mobility and close coordination with air power, the Germans advanced rapidly once again, scoring a series of devastating victories. The late summer of 1942 marked the furthest reach of the German invasion in the Soviet Union as they approached at Stalingrad.

From August through November, thousands of German soldiers hurled themselves against the city's defences. They pushed the Red Army to within metres of the Volga River at some points. Yet the city held. Then on November 19, 1942, the Soviets launched a devastating counter-attack. They trapped an entire German Army, 300,000 troops, in and around the city. Cut off from supplies and suffering from the harshness of Russian winter, the Germans struggled on until surrendering on February 2, 1943. At that time, only 90,000 Germans remained to be taken prisoner.

The Soviet counterattack continued through the winter, driving west to the city of Kharkov. It was briefly liberated, but the Red Army had overextended itself and was soon pushed back in defeat. Spring rains then brought a halt and allowed both sides to lick their wounds. The front lines stabilized, leaving a glaring point of contention on the map: a 250 kilometre wide bulge centring on the city of Kursk. The stage was set for one of the largest battles of the war, and a last desperate stab at victory by the invaders.

FURTHER READING

I am indebted to far too many sources in my research to count. The list below is by no means complete and is intended to only offer a sampling of books that can help you learn more about the people, places, and events that appear in this novel.

On life in the Soviet Union: *Everyday Stalinism: Ordinary Life in Extraordinary Times: Soviet Russia in the 1930s* by Sheila Fitzpatrick

For a succinct summary of World War II: *The Second World War: A Short History* by R.A.C. Packer

On the war between Germany and the Soviet Union: *Hitler's War on Russia* by Charles D. Winchester

On the Battle of Kursk: *Armor and Blood: The Battle of Kursk: The Turning Point of World War II* by Dennis Showalter

On the Soviet Air Force during the war: *Red Phoenix Rising: The Soviet Air Force in World War II* by Ilya Grinberg and Von Hardesty

On women in the Soviet Air Force during the war: *Wings, Women and War: Soviet Airwomen in World War II Combat* by Reina Pennington

For first-hand accounts from Soviet women combat pilots: *Women in Air War: The Eastern Front of World War II* by Kazimiera Jean Cottam

AUTHOR'S NOTE

While the gap between RAVEN'S SHADOW and its predecessor was longer than I wanted, it did give me a chance to absorb some lessons from the first book.

I thought a lot about the difference between historical accuracy and being true to the spirit of the historical story that I wanted to tell. If SPARROW SQUADRON was balanced in favour of the former, this novel tilts more toward the latter, in service of what I hope is a better story. I don't intend any disservice to historical persons, but this novel is fiction and it is my story to tell. And if you're reading this, I hope the result has proven worthwhile.

Throughout the process of writing this book, I was very fortunate to have an amazing team to support me. My beta readers Charlotte Kieft, Pete Dulgar, and Mark Abraham helped me so much with their sharp observations and honest feedback. Caroline Kaiser's expert editing was a pillar of strength I could always count on. Daria Tikhomolova's artwork and cover (from an original design by Kit Foster) gave my words the visual backdrop that I hoped for.

Finally, and always, I have to thank Annabel, for bringing out the best in me.

ABOUT THE AUTHOR

DL Jung is an enthusiastic student of history and enjoys blogging about it, in addition to writing historical fiction. He also writes fantasy and horror fiction as Darius Jung.

Jung is married, with two children, and lives in Toronto, Canada. They are lucky enough to spend part of the time in New Zealand. Outside of writing, he has tried stints as an industrial engineer, a film and TV script supervisor, and a professional game show contestant. RAVEN'S SHADOW is his second novel.

You can follow the author on Twitter at @DariusJung or visit the author website www.dariusjung.com.

Independent authors are greatly dependent upon online reviews to promote their books. If you enjoyed this book, please consider supporting the author by leaving a review online.